D0794315

THROW THE DEVIL OFF THE TRAIN

**Center Point
Large Print**

Also by Stephen Bly and available from Center Point Large Print:

Creed of Old Montana
Cowboy for a Rainy Afternoon

**This Large Print Book carries the
Seal of Approval of N.A.V.H.**

THROW THE DEVIL OFF THE TRAIN

Stephen Bly

CENTER POINT LARGE PRINT
THORNDIKE, MAINE

This Center Point Large Print edition is
published in the year 2011 by arrangement
with the author.

The text of this Large Print edition is unabridged.
In other aspects, this book may vary
from the original edition.
Printed in the United States of America.
Set in 16-point Times New Roman type.

ISBN: 978-1-61173-024-1

Library of Congress Cataloging-in-Publication Data

Bly, Stephen A., 1944–
Throw the devil off the train / Stephen Bly. — 1st ed.
p. cm.
ISBN 978-1-61173-024-1 (lib. bdg. : alk. paper)
1. Large type books. I. Title.
PS3552.L93T47 2011
813'.54—dc22
                                             2011007252

in memory of
W. Scott Walston

loved & missed

Center Point Publishing

600 Brooks Road ● PO Box 1
Thorndike ME 04986-0001 USA

(207) 568-3717

US & Canada:
1 800 929-9108
www.centerpointlargeprint.com

CHAPTER ONE

"Is he dead?" The high-pitched voice whined.

"If he isn't," came a low rumble, "I could fix that."

"I ain't killin' no man over a saddle."

"And a gun. He's got one of them new Colt revolvers."

"I still ain't killing no man over a saddle and a gun."

"I bet he has a bag of gold on him." The lower voice had the power of a salesman on a slow day. "He's as dirty as a prospector."

"He ain't as dirty as us."

"Suppose he does have gold. Would it be alright to kill him then?"

The high-pitched bleat continued. "How much gold you reckon he has?"

"At least a couple twenty-dollar gold coins."

"Maybe you're right. For forty dollars, why cain't I just hit him over the head with this fence post?"

"If you don't knock him clean out, I'll have to shoot him."

"You got a gun?"

"I'll use his."

"Okay, but you do the shootin'. I ain't shot nobody since the war."

7

"Maybe he is dead. Shorty said he'd been laying there on his saddle without movin' since daybreak."

The whiner seemed hesitant. "If he's such easy pickin's, why didn't Shorty clean him out?"

"Maybe he did."

"He could be asleep."

"In the middle of the day? Who sleeps in the train yard in the middle of the day?"

"Old man Ticcado did. He was sound asleep right smack dab on the tracks."

"He was crazy."

"Why do you say that?"

"You have to be crazy to marry one woman when you was still married to another."

"Well, it didn't work out too bad."

"What? He got run over by a train."

"Yeah, but they sent half to one wife and half to the other."

"I say it's goin' to be simple. I'll reach for the revolver. If he raises up, you clobber him with the fence post."

"You got any whiskey? I could bust a skull better if I had me some whiskey."

"We'll have plenty of whiskey when we pick him clean. You ready?"

"I reckon."

"I'll just reach down here nice . . . and . . . slow," the low voice whispered, ". . . and . . . stop!" The last word was a shout.

8

"Stop? He ain't raised up."

"Don't hit him."

"Is he dead?"

"I don't think so. He's got one eye open and a saddle pistol shoved in my belly."

Race Hillyard opened his other eye. An unshaved man with matted hair and a tattered brown suit hovered over him. "Tell your pal to put down the post," Hillyard growled.

"Put down the post, Cuke. You heard him."

The little man with a big, black mustache jumped back, but held onto the broken piece of four-by-four.

Hillyard shoved the first man so hard, he tumbled to the dry dirt of the train yard. "Is there any reason why I shouldn't shoot you two? You were going to kill me."

The one called Cuke dropped the post. His bare toes wiggled through the holes in his boots. "Me and Willie thought maybe you was dead."

Hillyard backed up, but kept his gun pointed at the men. "It's alright to steal from a dead man?"

Willie struggled to his feet. "They don't complain much."

Cuke wiped his broad nose on the back of his tattered shirt sleeve. "Don't shoot us, mister. Times is tough. They run us out of our homes after the war and won't give us decent jobs out here."

9

"You two Rebs?" Hillyard asked.

Cuke threw his shoulders back. "We didn't rebel against nothin'. We are proud veterans of the Army of Northern Virginia."

Hillyard shoved his saddle gun back into his bedroll. "That's what I wanted to hear." He reached in his coat pocket and tossed the man a coin.

Cuke turned it over in his hand. "A silver dollar?"

"That's to buy dinner for both of you. I was on the losin' side of the war, too, boys."

"No foolin'?" Cuke scratched his head like a dog looking for a flea. "We didn't know that."

Hillyard's glance whipped around the train yard, as if he expected another ambush. "Would it have made a difference?"

Willie eased close enough to smell the garlic and whiskey on his breath. "To be honest, mister, probably not." He leaned against Race's shoulder. "These is tough times, alright. A man's got to do what's right for himself."

Hillyard felt his Colt being pulled slowly from his holster. His clenched right hand caught Willie under his narrow, pointed chin and lifted him off his feet. The gun blasted into the air, as the man slammed motionless to the dirt.

The Colt retrieved, he turned towards Cuke, who stumbled backwards through a cloud of black powder smoke.

"Get out of here," Hillyard roared.

"Eh . . . yes sir . . . I eh, didn't know Willie was goin' for your gun. I reckon you want your dollar back."

"No, keep it and get out of here."

"Thank you, sir. Us southerners need to take care of each other."

"I'm not doing it for you. Nor the South. I figure it's my Christian duty."

"Well, praise the Lord, brother." Cuke stopped in his retreat. "Say, if I had me a twenty-dollar loan, I could go west and start all over. Could you spare . . . ?"

Hillyard cocked the hammer of his revolver and aimed it at the man's head.

The man pushed up his hands. "No offense. I'm goin'." He paused. "I reckon you're a Baptist."

By the time Race Hillyard shouldered his saddle and hiked across the tracks, a crowd had formed on the platform next to the westbound train. A few boarded the train. The rest milled about saying farewells.

The distant gunshot sounded like a celebration fired in the air, but the man in her arms didn't need outside encouragement. Soft, unchapped lips pressed firmly with only a twitch of anxiety.

Catherine graded it a level three kiss, perhaps headed for a four.

She threw her arms around his neck and clutched tight. His whole face now felt warm and moist. The low moan bubbled up like lava from some buried source.

That's better. A definite four. I knew you could do it. But this is where I stop. I never go to a five in public. Especially in a crowded train station.

She released her grip to study the wide, brown eyes and intense face. *Women would murder to have such shapely earlobes. They seem wasted on a man. Hmmm . . . is that a smirk or a leer? This close, his nose does not look quite so long.*

Like reverse poles on a magnet, his lips jammed against hers again.

He's trying for a five, but he's way too aggressive. She felt her mouth mash back against her teeth. *Rose tonic water . . . men with silky soft mustaches always use rose tonic water. Why is that?*

"Move it." The tone jarred her as if from a dream when she was trying to stop falling off a cliff. "You two step over by the baggage and do anything that won't get you arrested. I've toted this saddle all the way from the stockyard and I'd like to board the train."

Catherine's eyes popped open. The growling speaker's sun-tanned face was caked with a tad less dirt than his broad-brimmed black felt hat.

Thick mustache, wide chin, hasn't shaved in

several days. He does not use rose tonic water.

She tilted her chin. "Please, I'm going away for a few weeks and I don't want him to forget me."

The tall man in the rumpled charcoal-gray suit and dingy white, tieless shirt tipped his hat. "Lady, nobody on this train platform is going to forget that kiss. Now, move aside."

Catherine suppressed a smile. "Must you be so rude?"

Mister, you think that was memorable? You have no idea what a level five kiss looks like. And I'm quite certain you will never find out.

The steam blast from the train caused her to stumble forward. Catherine clutched the hard, cold, rawhide saddle horn. The saddle crashed to the rough wooden deck of the station platform.

The man's face reddened, accenting his thick, black eyebrows. "Lady, you are a . . ."

"Just a moment!" The one in the crisp, three piece suit and unchapped lips stepped between them. "I say, are you insulting my fiancée?"

I like that. A little color does men good. Women rouge their cheeks, but men are limited to anger or embarrassment.

"Mister, you probably just got the best kiss Omaha has ever witnessed." He swooped down and hefted his saddle. "No one is insulting anyone. This saddle is heavy. I'm tired. I want to get on the train." He shoved his dusty wool suit

13

coat back to reveal a holstered revolver. "Get out of the way."

Is he threatening to use a firearm? I assumed this only happened in Mr. Buntline's torrid novels. This must be what Gretchen meant when she said to be on the lookout for western ruffians.

Catherine slipped her hand into Mr. Rose-Tonic-Water's arm. "It seems obvious this man's coarseness is equal to his insolence." When she raised her chin, she felt the hatpin strain that kept the turned-down brim of her Tuscan straw hat at a rakish tilt across her brunette bangs.

The man in the three-piece suit shuffled Catherine Draper to the side. His lanky arms still encircled her waist. "It is as if all manners and decency are left on the banks of the Missouri River," he huffed. "One more kiss?"

Catherine heard the conductor yell something. Several men shoved by them. "Everyone is watching," she offered.

His linen suit has an aroma of mothballs . . . but then, every odor in a train station seems repulsive.

"I certainly hope so," he murmured.

She noticed a tightness in his voice, an urgency in his arms. This time their lips mashed until she felt her cheeks bulge and her dusty brown lace-up shoes lift off the ground.

Where do men learn to kiss? Someone should

14

give them lessons. Unlike ladies, I suspect they do not spend hours in front of a mirror practicing.

She gasped for a breath. "Whoa."

He leaned close to her ear, his thin voice a soft whisper. "Thank you for allowing me to see you off. Will you wave to me from the window?"

"Of course."

Catherine enjoyed the swish of her navy blue and gray faille dress as she sauntered toward the train car. Several more impatient men boarded ahead of her. When she reached the steps, she tugged a linen handkerchief from under her light blue, button-trimmed chevron cuff. She turned to view his retreat to the platform and a circle of friends. She waited for the whole group to turn her way. Then she dabbed the corner of each eye and offered a shy wave.

Inside the coach a pentecost of languages and a menu of aromas greeted her. The sweet and the rancid blended without rhyme or recipe. Catherine hurried to the first pair of bench seats facing each other on the right side of the coach.

The man with the dirty felt hat occupied one window seat, his saddle the other. His long legs bridged the aisle between them. With his chin on chest, hat pulled over his eyes, she noticed a thick roll of black dirt . . . or a scar . . . on his neck, just above the yellowed collar of his white shirt.

She positioned her floral valise and matching

purse in front of her like a barrier of protection, then cleared her throat. "Excuse me, I need access to the open window."

He neither moved nor spoke. The black leather shafts of his square-toed boots disappeared into the gray legs of his worn, wool trousers.

He looks out of place in a suit . . . even without a tie.

Catherine raised her voice. "I said, do you mind moving?"

A tan-faced boy in the seat behind them, about one year or so old, let out a short scream. His mother picked a small red wooden block off the floor, wiped it on the sleeve of her multi-colored wool dress and handed it back to him.

Catherine stooped down and glanced out the open window at the group of men on the platform. "You can't possibly be asleep yet. I saw you flinch when the little boy cried out. I need to wave at someone through the window."

He didn't look up. His deep voice startled her, like it rolled out of a dark room thought to be empty. "You talking to me or my saddle?"

She brushed dust off her sleeve with the back side of her pale yellow glove. "Your saddle isn't blocking the aisle."

Somewhere at the back of the train, couplings collided as another car was added. The coach jolted forward. She braced her hands against his knees to keep from tumbling.

He sat straight up and shoved her back. "Good grief, lady, I'll move. You don't have to attack me."

I'm sure he has a mother somewhere wondering, "where did I go wrong?"

"I have no control over the coach. If you'd just scoot over, I'll send my greeting and then be gone."

His booted feet banged to the floor. "You going to kiss him again?"

She plopped down on the vacated seat next to the window. The dark brown leather felt warm and smooth, with a faint aroma of barn sweat. "Probably not."

Your hair is dirty and you need a cut. Phillip has his hair cut every four weeks.

"Do you object to kissing?"

The man leaned back and circled his thick fingers inside the buttoned collar of his shirt. "It's overrated."

"Oh, my, what words of wisdom." With her back to the obnoxious man, Catherine opened her purse, pulled out a small mirror, then adjusted the cluster of artificial buttercups, heath blossoms, and fern that perched on the knot of her ribboned hat.

"But then, I haven't had a lot of experience with kissing . . . like that."

She glanced at the mirror. His face peered over her shoulder. "Yes, I can see why." She stuck

17

her head out the open window. Even the heat and drifting steam felt fresher than the air inside. She sensed perspiration beading on her temples.

Above the noise of the crowd and the train, Catherine heard laughter from the men huddled at the far side of the platform. She waited for the one with the silky mustache to turn her way.

Out of sight, out of mind, no doubt. Ah, dear Phillip, you have never, ever forgotten me.

When she caught his attention, she put her gloved hand to the side of her mouth. "Goodbye, darling," she called out.

The man lumbered toward the coach, then waved back with the enthusiasm of an actor bringing down the curtain on the first act. "Take good care of yourself, sweetheart."

"Oh, yes." The train pitched forward. Catherine righted herself, then held her hand over her heart. "I'll write to you every day."

From down the line, someone hollered, "All aboard!"

He jogged a few feet from the window. "Tell your Aunt Demetria we will all be praying for her."

The train rolled forward. She pressed her gloved hand against her full, rose-colored lips and blew him a kiss. "Until I'm back in your arms, my love."

He slowed his trot and slid out of sight.

Catherine pulled inside the window as the train rattled out of the station. Brick walls and white-cased windows hurried east. She adjusted her hat and brushed down the wrinkles of the rounded end of the pale yellow sash. She tugged the valise to her lap and stared out the window.

I'm not sure why most of my life feels like it is lived at a distance, as if I'm watching it from across the street. I have no idea why I get so demonstrative in public. It's a good thing Phillip understands that.

"That's my seat, lady." The voice was insistent, devoid of kindness or grace.

She noticed a small hole in the elbow of his suit coat. *Single men should hire a woman to tell them what to wear.*

"I shall find another."

"When?" he growled.

She looked back at the hefty woman with two babies in the next seat. The lady shrugged.

Catherine stood. "Rest assured, I do not intend to sit with anyone so ill-mannered."

As he slid next to the window, the train slammed to a stop. Catherine tumbled towards him again. His rock hard arms prevented a collapse into his lap.

He shoved her back upright. "Lady, you are a chummy thing."

"That's insulting. You know it was unintentional." She peered through the crowd on the train car. "Have you seen our conductor? I must talk to him."

He leaned back, calloused hands behind his neck. "Are you going to report me for being grumpy?"

"I'm sure that reporting your rudeness would not change you in the least and prove futile to improving the comfort of this trip. I have a question concerning tickets."

The large lady in the next seat leaned forward. "The conductor came through before you boarded. I'm sure he'll return."

The man again stretched his legs across the side aisle and rested them near his saddle.

Catherine noticed the fence posts alongside the tracks. "Why aren't we moving?"

The lady with the sleeping infants suppressed a yawn. "Honey, they just roll us out of the station where they can make up a train. We could be here a while."

Catherine clutched her valise with one hand, her purse in the other, then pushed her way down the center aisle.

She passed the woman in a multi-colored wool dress perched with two black-haired infants so small they looked like ornaments attached to her arms. The next four bench seats were filled with dirty men who wore knee high leather boots. One had a mining pan over his face as he leaned back, that amplified his restless snores. All the men seemed as tired as infantry after a lengthy battle. She had seen that look before . . . way too many times.

A gray-haired lady with skin more olive than Catherine's sat in the next to last row. Beside her, a pale man in a linen suit stared straight ahead and curled his thick black mustache. His sickly face looked so thin he seemed skeletal. She peeked over the back platform to the next coach then retraced her path.

The other side of the train car held a blanketed man with long, ink black, wild hair handcuffed to a small man wearing a bowler and a badge. The long-haired man leered at Catherine, revealing two missing upper front teeth. He pointed to his knee, as if offering her a chair.

She scooted past him and several other men. Six girls in matching bonnets and gingham dresses were crammed in seats, three to a row. Catherine guessed them to be in the fourteen to seventeen year age group. They sat straight-backed with expressionless faces.

Too close in age to be sisters. Perhaps a class on a trip, but not a very happy one.

A full-bearded hulk of a man sprawled next to a short-legged dog who resembled a gray watermelon with legs. Two bushy-haired men in grimey duckings inspected her as if selecting meat in a butcher shop. In front of them, a hardware drummer thumped on his catalog to point out some treasure to a placid, white-haired old-timer. That brought her back to the front of the car. Four angry men wearing guns on their hips bellowed conflicting rules of a card game as one in the corner shuffled a deck.

Catherine scooted back into the side aisle and frowned at the man with the hat pulled over his eyes. "This is the only open seating until the conductor comes. Would you mind moving your saddle so I may sit by the window?"

"My saddle likes the view."

"Isn't that nice." She plopped her valise down next to the saddle. "But, I might point out, I paid for a seat and . . ."

"So did my saddle." His chapped lips moved, but she could not see his eyes.

I read that western men treated women with courtesy and dignity. He must not read. "What did you say?"

"Lady, I bought one ticket for me and one for my saddle. That seat is paid for. He's sitting in it. And I'm tired."

Catherine rubbed the back of her long neck. "Why on earth didn't you check your saddle with the baggage car?"

"I did that once and they lost him. He spent the whole winter in a train depot in Elko, Nevada. The emotional scars run deep. He still has nightmares over it. So now, any time we travel together, I buy him a ticket."

This is as futile as trying to reason with a carpet-bagging judge.

"Wouldn't your saddle enjoy the safety and comfort of the trip more by sitting next to you?"

"Nah, he and I don't get along that well."

Catherine crimped her arms across her chest. "That's incongruous."

"Yeah, that's what I try to tell him, but have you noticed that saddles are a stubborn breed? They never listen to reason."

One of the angry men behind her muttered something about "no guns or knives." She didn't look back, but tapped the reclining man's shoulder. "You aren't going to move your saddle for me?"

"Lady, there are two empty seats. You can sit next to the saddle or next to me. Your choice."

Catherine gazed down the aisle of the coach again. The six young ladies with gingham bonnets stared at her as if waiting for a cue. This time when the train jolted forward, she staggered back and managed to turn around and drop into the rear seat next to the saddle. She hugged the valise and purse.

Wait until I tell Phillip about this. He will be outraged.

"Not a good choice," he mumbled from under his hat.

"You think I should sit by you?"

"I don't think you'll like your back to the door. Every time someone comes in from the Pullman car, you will crank your neck around to see who it is."

"You're worried about my neck?" She noticed a button missing from his white shirt down near his belt buckle.

I'm sure sweat and grime holds a shirt fastened long after the buttons wear off.

"And other things."

Catherine brushed her bangs back. "Which other things?"

He pointed his finger as if lecturing children about the dangers of playing in the street. "When that door opens up, a gust of wind and dust will blow your skirt up in the air. For most ladies, that causes some consternation."

"That's ridiculous."

"Depends on the woman."

"Why is it you are so intent to have me sit next to you?"

He sat up so quick, she jerked back towards the coach door. "Lady, I'm praying that you are a short liner and will be getting off at the first stop."

Oh, my, he has such drawn blue eyes. I don't think he's slept in days. The fruits of a reprobate and restless life, no doubt.

She tugged off the glove of her right hand. "I am very content to sit right here. As I told you, it will only be until the conductor comes through. I intend to move up to a Pullman compartment."

"Whatever." He yanked off his hat and ran his fingers through matted, dirty hair. "It's going to be a long trip. Eight days will seem like a month." He jammed his hat back on, leaned forward, elbows on knees, face resting in his hands. "I plan to sleep through most of it."

She squinted out the window as a freight car rolled by on the track next to them. "It's only four days to San Francisco."

"Have you ever taken this trip before?"

"No."

"I have. It will take at least eight days. Only express trains make it in four-and-a-half days. This is not an express, and even then, it seldom happens." He turned to the hefty woman with huge amber eyes who listened behind him. "Isn't that right, lady?"

When she leaned forward, the folds of her neck rolled out like waves. "He's right, honey. It took me fourteen days last January. We were stuck in the snow three days and three nights with nothing but buffalo robes and peach brandy."

Catherine yanked the glove off her left hand and examined her slender fingers. "It's not winter now. I'm sure we'll make it in four or five days."

Oh, Phillip, you are right. My left hand will

look so much more appealing with a beautiful gold wedding ring.

"I am in rather a hurry because I have someone waiting for me," she continued.

"Your sick aunt?" he asked.

Catherine fussed with the gamp of pale yellow faille at her waist. "Who?"

The man tugged his hat down to his chest and scowled at her. "You told Mr. Passion that you were going to visit a sick aunt."

Catherine threw her shoulders back. "I said no such thing."

He leaned back to the large lady. "That's what she said, right?"

The perfectly round face winked at Catherine. "She most certainly did not. The man at the station called out, 'Tell your Aunt Demetria we'll be praying for her.' "

"Doesn't that presume she is going to visit a sick aunt?"

"There are other reasons for prayer," the lady replied.

The man slumped back down in the seat. "So, you are saying your Aunt Demetria isn't sick?"

Catherine ran her tongue across her lips and tasted the bitter coach dust. "I'm saying I don't have an Aunt Demetria."

The woman waved a fleshy hand. "I have an Aunt Delutha. She's rather obese. I always feel petite around her."

"If you don't have an Aunt Demetria, why did Mr. Sweetlips say that?"

"I have no idea in the world," Catherine shrugged.

I have to admit he has nice-looking teeth. But then, so did my first pony.

"That makes no sense." The man rubbed his cheek as if nursing a toothache. "You must have hinted about an aunt or something of the sort."

"It makes sense to me," the big woman broke in. "After all, my Farley thinks I'm taking the children to a Temperance Convention in California. Isn't that a laugh?" She slapped the man's shoulder.

He flinched. "I've had more meaningful conversations talking to my saddle."

Catherine dropped her wool valise on the floor and faced the window seat. "Mr. Walker, I trust you are enjoying the scenery."

Without lifting his hat, the man muttered, "My name's not Walker."

"I'm not talking to you. I'm talking to your saddle. On the back of the cantle is the name, 'D. E. Walker, Visalia, California.' "

"That's the name of the saddle company."

She kept her eyes on the saddle horn. "Does he always treat you with such disrespect? I just don't know how you put up with it. What? He does what to you? Oh, my, how horrid."

"Lady, you're crazy." He sounded croaky, like water gurgling down an empty pipe.

"Strange you should say that. Mr. Walker claims the same about you. He told me the only time he's had any peace and quiet was when he leaped off the train in Elko. He spent the entire winter peacefully lounging about the train station next to a pot-bellied stove."

The big lady chuckled. "I like the way you think, honey. You remind me of Pepper Paige. I was with her in a horrible blizzard at April's place when she talked to her mirror all night long."

"You're both crazy," the man sputtered.

Catherine leaned toward the lady. "You know, when a person thinks everyone else in the world is mad . . ."

"Says something about him, doesn't it?" She stuck out a fleshy hand. "Honey, my name is Francine Garrity."

"I'm Catherine Draper."

"Of the Memphis Drapers?"

"No."

"New Orleans?"

"No."

"Well, where are you from?" the big lady pressed.

"East."

Francine bit her lips and nodded. "Yeah, sweetie, me too."

"East?" the man growled, then slumped lower in the bench seat. "A mysterious woman of unknown ancestry? It's like I'm trapped in the script of a boring melodrama."

Catherine whirled around to the saddle. "Mr. Walker, is he always this incoherent? Usually more so? He must live alone most of the time. No, I cannot fathom what horrors you experienced stuck with him in a cabin in the Rockies all winter. You poor dear."

She reached over and patted the leather fenders.

The words leapt out like a sprung mousetrap. "Keep your hands off my saddle."

"Oh, my, what nasty jealousy." Catherine laced her fingers together in her lap. "Mr. Walker, I suggest you might need to talk to an attorney about this abuse."

"Lady . . ."

Francine jammed a finger into his shoulder. "Her name is Catherine Draper."

"Yeah, I know. Not the Memphis or New Orleans Drapers. Miss Draper . . . it is Miss Draper, isn't it?"

"Why do you ask?"

His voice rose with each word. "So I will quit calling you 'lady' and not get poked."

"You may call me Catherine."

"Okay . . . Catherine, will you please stop talking to my saddle?"

"You are the one who anthropomorphized it."

"That's a big word for a . . ."

"For a woman? Yes, college has a tendency to do that."

"He did what?" Francine boomed. "Is it something sinful?"

Catherine ran her finger across the engraved letters, D. E. Walker. "He made it human and talked to it like it was a person."

"So, you went to college?" When he rubbed his eyes, dirt rolled up in the crevices.

"I graduated from college in Boston."

"Oh, well, if you are educated, I suppose it's alright." His voice tightened with sarcasm. "Go ahead. Talk to my saddle. You two can discuss Schleiermacher and his growing influence on German higher criticism. Just keep it down. I'm still short on sleep. And whatever you do, don't get him talking politics. He voted for Sam Tilden."

"Where did you ever learn of Schleiermacher?"

"It's the kind of thing they teach in Seminary."

"You went to a theological college?"

"I didn't say that. Look, I really am worn-out. Talk to someone else."

She reached over and stroked the saddle, then whispered, "Sweetheart, perhaps when King Grumpy is asleep, you and I can step out on the platform and catch some fresh air." Catherine leaned closer. "What's that? At the next stop you want us to sneak off the train and run away to some little cabin and spend the winter together? Now that is a very tempting offer."

"You are nuts, Catherine. Absolutely nuts." He stared out at the Omaha train yard. "Perhaps I should just toss you out the window."

"Mr. Walker, I don't know why you travel with him. What? You don't even like sitting next to the window? It makes you dizzy? He does it on purpose to torment you? Oh, you poor, poor dear. Listen, I have an idea. . . ."

"Forget it," he barked.

"Mr. Walker, why don't you sit over here by the door, where you can relax, and I'll sit in that cramped corner next to the window."

"Don't touch my saddle!"

"Nonsense, I will not have you torment poor Mr. Walker." She stood up. "Honey, you just scoot over here and . . ."

The man drew his gun, but didn't cock the hammer. He held it low. One of the angry men playing poker stomped over to them. "Lady, do you need some assistance?"

Catherine sat back down by the door. "Would one of you handsome gentlemen please shoot this man dead?"

He glanced over at the drawn revolver, now cocked. "Are you joking?"

She frowned. "Yes, unfortunately, I am." She turned toward the window. "I'm sorry, Mr.

Walker, we tried. Mr. Tyrant uses a gun to bully defenseless women and inanimate objects."

Francine rocked a sleeping baby in the crook of her left arm. "Catherine, I mean this as no chagrin, but how tall are you? I admired how you towered over the man across the aisle."

Catherine's shoulders slumped. "I like to say I'm five-foot-eleven-and-a-half."

"Are you really six-feet?" Francine gasped.

"With any kind of heel on my shoes, I am. I try to not think about it."

"If I had my druthers, I'd rather be tall than big-boned. That's my trouble, you know . . . big bones." Francine poked the man. "Mister, I believe Catherine is taller than you."

"I'm six-feet-two-inches."

Francine grinned and Catherine noticed perfect straight white teeth.

"Stand up and let me compare."

"Lady, I'm not going to stand up."

Catherine jammed his knee. "Her name is Francine."

"Francine, I'm not playing this game."

"Of course you are." Francine jabbed him in the ribs.

He reached for his revolver.

"Oh, that's fine," Catherine fumed. "You are going to draw your gun on a lady with two young children. There is a very strange person on this train, and it's you, Mr. Whatever-your-name-is."

Francine rolled her big amber eyes. "I always say, a man who won't give his name is hiding something. Perhaps he's Black Bart? Or Dirty Dan? Or Raymond the Ripper."

The man waved his arms. "Catherine . . . Francine . . . I will make a deal with you. I will tell you my name and even stand up and show you my height. But then you cannot talk for a solid hour while I get some rest. Is that a deal?"

Catherine patted the saddle. "Does that include Mr. D. E. Walker?"

"Especially him."

"I reserve the right to talk to the conductor about my move to a Pullman compartment when he comes through," Catherine insisted.

"You may talk to the conductor."

Francine glanced at her sleeping children. "If Preston and Nancy wake up, I will need to talk to my children."

"Of course."

"Can we hum?" Catherine added. "I do love to hum."

"Oh, me too," Francine said. "My whole family are good hummers. Can't whistle worth a fig, but very good hummers."

"Forget it," he groused.

Francine slapped her big hand on his shoulder so hard, both children woke up. "Stand up, mister. You got a deal."

The man pulled off his dirty beaver-felt hat

and tossed it over the saddle horn. "I've been in gunfights more peaceful than this."

"Stand up straight, you two . . . back to back," Francine commanded. "Don't slump."

Catherine felt the back of their shoulders touch. The semi-bustle on her dress kept anything else from touching.

"He's right, honey. I'd say he's at least two inches taller."

Catherine scooted in on the bench seat next to the saddle. He plopped back down next to the window, shoved his legs across the aisle, and pulled his hat down.

"I believe you promised us two things," Francine said.

"Race Hillyard," he replied.

"Race?" Catherine questioned. "What kind of name is Race?"

"It's better than Herb."

"What does that mean?"

"It's a long story that I don't intend on telling you."

Francine rocked the youngsters back and forth. "Say, you wouldn't be one of the Hilliards from St. Joseph, would you?"

"Not Hillyards of St. Joseph, St. Louis, or St. Paul. Ladies, you are looking at the last of a proud family of Hillyards from Ash Fork, Texas. Now, I believe I have earned my peace and quiet."

I shouldn't have worn a dress with a bustle of any sort. If I had a drawing room, I'd change dresses . . . that is, if I had another dress. Well, I do have that dress. I'm not sure I want to wear it yet.

The train rolled back on the main track and picked up speed. Train yards and one-room, unpainted houses paraded by the window.

Whole families crowd in those tiny shacks. I trust they are happy.

She mused about that a bit, then snatched a glimpse back inside the coach. The man with the full black beard and watermelon-shaped dog slumped with his chin on his chest in deep sleep. The six young ladies behind him now giggled and visited as if at a tea party. Her gaze returned to the window.

A happy family. I wonder if they all understand the riches of that? It's taken me twenty-nine years to discover the value. Phillip always made me happy. That's what I remember most. Laughing. Racing to the river. Trying to count all the stars in the sky. I don't believe I have ever seen Phillip angry. Always such an incurable dreamer with a miracle waiting around every corner.

One of the card players yelled "rotten luck" and then stepped out on the platform to smoke a cigar. Catherine closed her eyes and tried to imagine Phillip. Then a blast of wind from the open door raised her skirt. She shoved her ankle-length navy and gray dress back down as her face turned warm.

"Well, I swear," Francine said. "I could see your . . . eh, never mind."

Catherine scooted across the aisle and plopped down next to Race Hillyard. "As for you, quit smirking at me."

He pulled his hat off his eyes. "I'm not smirking."

"I wasn't talking to you." Catherine brushed down the front of her dress. "I was conversing with Mr. Walker."

CHAPTER TWO

Catherine hugged her chest. She tried to take a deep breath but her dress felt tight. She pressed against her heart as she watched the square-shouldered man in the impeccable three-piece suit saunter toward the train platform.

Relax, Catherine. Just another minute or two. Oh, Phillip, I had no idea you grew so tall. You stood shorter than me when you left, as did all the boys. But now . . . sun-tanned face . . . strong arms . . . confident swagger. Brown eyes that tease and tempt. Why, oh why didn't I come out here and marry you sooner? Think of all the days we've missed being together . . . not to mention all the nights.

Her face warmed with that thought. She entwined her gloved fingers and squeezed her hands tight. When the approaching man tugged off his hat, thick, wavy dark hair drooped across his forehead.

I can't believe you've waited all these years for me. The women of California will be insanely jealous. But some things are just meant to be. "My spirit hath rejoiced in God my Saviour. For he hath regarded the low estate of his handmaiden: for, behold, from henceforth all generations shall call me blessed." Forgive me,

Lord, but I feel as honored as Mary right now. Everything in the past is melting away. The hurts and the pains and the sorrows will soon be gone. This is why I was put on earth.

The tall man stopped in front of the train platform to chat with several men. The topic caused a burst of laughter and chatter.

Phillip, don't stall . . . come over here. I want . . . well, I want us together, that's what I want. What is he talking about to those men?

Catherine leaned forward and strained to hear.

"George might like them more plump, but I say she's about as perfect a sight of womanly comeliness as I ever cast my eyes on."

"The lips are what attracted me . . . full, yet slightly pouting. Can you imagine what a kiss would be like? Worth a winter's wages."

A deep hoot seemed to escape from a dungeon somewhere. "I think Luke has fallen in love."

"For the third time this month."

Voices overlapped as Catherine tried to distinguish the words.

"Come on, boys, look at her." The voice was younger, higher-pitched, excited. "Those eyebrows give her away. I say you can tell a lot about a woman by a study of her eyebrows."

"And I say there are more important things to look at. Just a tad more plumpness in places wouldn't hurt."

"More plumpness"? I beg your pardon. I have to work every day of my life to make sure "more plumpness" does not overtake me. Phillip, don't let them talk about me like that.

The rattle and joust of the railroad car lifted her chin off her chest, but she didn't open her eyes.

Oh, posh. The train. I am still on the train. Dear sweet Phillip, here I am dreaming of you again. I haven't seen you in seventeen years, yet I think about you while I'm awake and dream about you in my sleep. How I wish this train ride was over. I know what you would say. You'd remind me that you came West in a wagon and it took almost four months. That's progress, but I do wish you had held me in those strong arms before I woke up. Were those men really talking about me?

"An up-turned nose like that is seldom seen in a girl over twelve."

I do not have an up-turned nose. It's small . . . rather dainty for a tall woman. I suppose it might seem up-turned when I have a fit of pride, but . . .

"You have to admit that's beautiful hair."

"Yep, we all agree."

You'd be even more impressed if you could see it combed down . . . wait . . . what?

Catherine heard a collective sigh from the men in the seat across the aisle.

The angry card players? I'm not dreaming this part. They're talking about me. The nerve. Don't they realize how vulgar and ill-mannered it is to speak like that? I should open my eyes and give them my potent Catherine glare. Some say my glower would melt stones.

"Luke, suppose you did get to talk to her. What would you say?" one with a bass voice chided.

Catherine kept her eyes closed tight.

"I'd say, 'excuse me, ma'am, do you have any plans for this afternoon?' And she'd say, 'Why, no sir, I don't.' Then I'd say, 'Why don't we go find a parson and get married?' "

This is really going too far.

"You decide all of that at one glance?"

"One glance? I've been studying her for quite a while."

This is mortifying. If I had a blanket, I'd pull it over my head.

"We could tell you weren't contemplatin' your cards." The words hammered down like a judge's verdict.

In the back of the car, a dog barked. Catherine thought of the watermelon-shaped canine.

I should have brought a dog with me. A large one with sharp teeth.

"I say she looks like a queen. She could be royalty, you know."

"Or she could be a floor scrubber."

"Look at those graceful hands. Are those cleaning lady hands?"

"I'll grant you that one, but you can't marry her, so let's play poker."

Yes, by all means, play your card game or I must say something to end this silly conversation. Why doesn't Race Hillyard speak up? And why in the world do I expect him to care about my honor? He's probably enjoying this conversation.

The rustle of shuffled cards ceased. "Where did we go wrong? I thought we educated Luke better than that."

"Maybe we should dunk him in the stock tank next time we stop. Just to cool him down."

Yes, that's a wonderful idea.

"Here, Adam . . . Eve wants you to have an apple. These are pretty good."

The crunch of a crisp bite made Catherine lick her lips.

"Let's get back to the game."

"It doesn't hurt for a man to get his blood racin' a little."

At the speed your blood races, you'll circle the earth in minutes.

"Luke, put away the French postcards. It's your turn to deal."

French postcards?

Catherine opened her left eye to peek at the four men in the opposite aisle. The crate they used for a card table now boasted a half-dozen red apples. The youngest of the four with a curly blond beard shoved a handful of postcards into his vest pocket.

They were ogling risqué French postcards? How awkward. How vain of me. How could I have imagined they discussed me? What if I had scolded them? I don't want to think about that. I will never assume any man is talking about me again. I am too tall, slump-shouldered, and have the figure of a picket in a fence. That's what Mr. Curtis Tweed told me when I was fifteen. I should have believed him. Oh, I do hope dear Phillip isn't disappointed when he sees me after all these years. I tried to explain what I look like now.

Catherine opened both eyes, brushed down the cuffs of her dress and stared at the saddle. "Well, Mr. Walker, I took a short nap. I trust you got some rest."

She glanced at Race. His face hid under his hat. "Does Mr. Hillyard always snore like this? Sometime worse? And he talks in his sleep? He describes unknown women? Oh, dear. What a distraction."

She felt a tap on her shoulder. "Is he asleep?" The soft, sweet voice belonged to Francine.

Catherine turned to the massive woman behind her. "I believe so. He is so drawn-looking."

Francine rocked wide-eyed toddlers in each

arm. "That's the way all the men looked when they came home from the war. Fatigued and wore out. It didn't matter their age, or which side of the battle they fought. Every man seemed drained."

Catherine rubbed her temples and closed her eyes again. She envisioned rows and rows of weary men in tattered uniforms. "The whole country was exhausted."

"You're right, honey." Francine licked her lips as if applying rouge with her tongue. "If you don't mind me asking, where did you spend the war?"

Catherine leaned back and stretched her arms. "My sister and I attended a girls' school near Boston for the entire conflict."

"No foolin'? You surprise me. I guessed that was a Virginia lilt to your voice. I never figured you for a Yankee."

Catherine shot a glance at the men across the aisle. Angry expressions replaced the earlier chides. None of them looked at her. "Good guess. I suppose even several years of teaching school in New England doesn't hide my dialect. I'm a southern girl from Virginia. Our parents sent my sister and me to my aunt's in New England. Daddy thought that safer for us. He really didn't think the war would amount to much, or last as long as it did."

"Sisters can be a pleasure or a pain, or both.

I've got a sister a few years younger than me. She lives out in Canon City, Colorado." Francine tucked the sleeping toddlers into blankets on the seat next to her. "Is your sis older or younger?"

"She's younger . . . by six minutes." Catherine felt her heart throb faster when she thought of her and Catelynn's last conversation.

Francine clapped her hands. "Twins?"

"Yes. Identical in looks . . ." An image of tall ten-year-olds with white Easter dresses and waist-length brown hair flashed through her mind. "But quite different in everything else."

"I always wondered what it would be like to have an identical twin. Can you imagine two of me?" Francine held up her massive hands. "Shoot, I'm big enough to make two of me right now. Where does your sis live?"

"Catelynn's been in New York a few years. She's an actress."

"Now, ain't that something? A very tall actress, no doubt."

"Yes, it does limit her roles."

Francine examined her fingernails as if looking for a clue to a mystery. "How did she get in the acting business? Did she have to study a lot?"

"She took classes, but she's always been rather expressive and emotional."

"I thought about being a ballet dancer," Francine announced.

Catherine clamped her mouth tight.

"When I was younger. Say, are your folks still in Virginia?"

Catherine rubbed the corners of her eyes. "No . . . killed in the war . . . Daddy at the warehouse when the Army of Virginia set fire to it . . . Mamma at home, in a Union artillery bombardment. Our rural area became a stage for three major battles. It was devastating."

Francine placed a soft, warm hand on Catherine's cheek. "Oh, honey, I'm so sorry to have brought up sad memories. My brother, Tiny, was killed at Vicksburg. And Daddy died on Missionary Ridge. That's where we lost the war, you know."

Catherine patted Francine's hand. "Sometimes it seems like we lost more than a war."

"I know what you mean, sweetie." Francine pulled a linen handkerchief from her sleeve and wiped off her little boy's chin. "You have any kin left in Virginia?"

"Just a few cousins. I'm not even sure. Most lost their homes and had to move. I have no idea where they live now."

Francine's eyes glazed into a vacant stare.

Catherine admired clumps of tall sunflowers along the railroad tracks.

After a long pause, Francine said, "I spent most of the war driving an ambulance. I've always been good with a team of mules and the boys needed to fight. So I drove the wagon and helped with the stretchers."

"That must have been grueling . . . and depressing."

"I still have nightmares," Francine admitted. "We only had room for so many in the wagon. The doctors ordered us to pick up just those that looked like they could survive with medical attention. That meant we had to leave many a dying man crying for help out on the battlefield."

"Oh, Francine . . . how awful."

"The docs helped us deal with it. Told us to consider if we weren't there, no one would survive. Couldn't save everyone."

"But what horrible memories."

Francine, you have beautiful hair and such a sweet face . . . if you were slim, the angry poker players would whisper about you.

"Sometimes they drive me melancholy." Francine curled the tuff of blonde hair that drooped next to her jade green earrings. "Say, what part of northern Virginia were you from? Up near the Maryland border by any chance?"

"Yes, our place was near Blackwater Crossing." Catherine stared at the back of her ringless fingers.

"You didn't know her, did you?"

"Who?"

"That Goodwin woman."

The shock of hearing that name stiffened

Catherine's back and straightened her slumping shoulders. "Goodwin woman?"

"Yes, the southern lady that got cheated out of her estate by some unscrupulous Yankee attorney. She pulled out a pistol and shot him dead on the spot. I think she was from up that way."

"Shot him dead?"

"Pumped six shots into his black heart, so I hear." Francine leaned closer. Catherine smelled peppermint. "She's a hero in my book. All of us Mississippi gals wish we had the nerve to do the same."

"I think you have the story a little wrong."

"You know her?"

"Eh . . . we grew up in the same town." Catherine rubbed the back of her neck and felt a roll of dirt. "Her attorney hailed from Richmond, not the North. After years of having the case tied up in the reconstruction courts, she discovered her lawyer took a bribe and released her family property to be used as a Union cemetery. She lost her temper, plucked a Colt .44 revolver with a snubby little three-and-one-half-inch barrel off his desk . . . just to threaten him. He panicked and grabbed her arm. When the gun tumbled to the floor, it discharged. The bullet entered and exited his left calf and lodged in a wood carving of Christopher Columbus. Just a minor wound for the lawyer.

But he pressed attempted murder charges against her, to force her to flee the county and never come back."

"No, that's not the way it happened," Francine corrected. "That's the Yankee version, honey. They don't want to admit that a southern lady is spunky enough to shoot the rascal dead. I heard about it from Leonie Mapson. Her cousin's husband's brother used to buy drill bits from Mr. Goodwin himself. So you know it's got to be true. If I ever meet that Goodwin woman, I'd like to give her a big hug. She let them know we might have lost the war, but we will not be trampled down by thieves and swindlers."

Catherine slumped in the seat and tried not to notice Race Hillyard's legs propped up on the bench seat next to his saddle. The box houses of Omaha gave way to cornfields, dairies and neatly groomed gardens as the train rattled west.

Catherine pondered Francine's account.

That is why I had to move to California. The war changed things forever. I need to start over. How do fabrications like that get started? I suppose it's what they want to hear. Lord, I can't believe I'm crammed into a stuffy coach car and the lady behind me mentions that incident.

A smile eased across her face.

At least I have my Phillip. My precious, loyal Phillip waits for me. You have no idea, my sweet, what it means to have your security to run to.

48

Paradise Springs sounds more and more like heaven on earth.

Dust fogged through several open windows, but a cider aroma wafted over the car.

She turned back to Francine. "Don't those apples look grand?"

"They bought them off the conductor when he came through."

"I missed him?" Catherine scowled. "I need to talk about upgrading my ticket."

"He'll be back." The black-haired little girl giggled as she was shoved over Catherine's shoulder. "Honey, hold Nancy for me. I need to take Preston to the privy to clean him up."

The squirming, barefoot girl in the flour sack pale green dress bounced in Catherine's lap. "How old is she?"

Francine stood and overfilled the aisle. "She's almost three but small for her age. Takes after my Farley. He's only five-foot-four-inches. Don't let her get down and run around."

Catherine peered into the girl's wide brown eyes and swept back the thick black hair draped down to her shoulders. "Hi, Nancy. My name is Catherine."

"I'm hungry."

"We'll be stopping for a meal break in a while. The brochure said that we stop for tasty meals every four hours and I think Nancy is a very nice name."

Nancy curled her lips and wailed. "I'm hungry."

The four men across the center aisle shouted about a fifth king in the deck. The one with short, curly blond hair sticking out from under his hat threw his cards on the crate, then yanked out his revolver. The hum and chatter in the train car tapered to silence.

"I say we take our ante back and find a new deck," he shouted.

The mustached man in the gray suit jumped up. "Luke, are you calling me a cheat?"

Nancy burst out bawling.

Catherine hugged the baby, stood, and stepped into the aisle. She waved a finger at the men. "Sit down both of you right now. And put that gun away. You should be ashamed of yourself, scaring this precious little one. You're an insult to your mother's hard work raising you."

Both men plopped back down in their seats. Guns returned to holsters.

A stocky man with almost no neck and a conductor's hat scurried up the aisle. His face reddened as he pointed at the blond man. "There is no brandishing of weapons on my train. That's clearly stated on the rules chart posted near the door when you boarded. You will be let off at the next station. I do not tolerate infractions."

"You kickin' me off the train?" the blond snapped.

Catherine slipped her free hand into the

conductor's arm and held it firm, but not tight. "Excuse me, sir, I think I can explain this situation." She let the Virginia lilt dominate.

"Who are you?"

"I'm Catherine Draper and I'm . . ."

"Are you with them?"

"Oh, no. I'm sitting over there by that . . . eh, saddle . . . which is something I want to talk to you about in a minute. But, you see, when Luke offered me . . ."

"Who's Luke?"

"Why the blond-headed one with the cute dimples." She squeezed the conductor's arm. "When he offered an apple to me and Nancy . . ."

"Who's Nancy?"

"Why, this is Nancy. Isn't she a cutie? Would you like to hold her?"

"No, I would not."

"I'm hungry," Nancy whined.

"As I was saying, dear Luke offered us an apple and I stepped over to fetch it. Then I noticed his Colt revolver. Well, my father, bless his departed soul, sold guns in his hardware store before the war, and as a young girl, I knew each one quite well. Samuel Colt once had supper at our house. But since I'd never seen that model . . . out of curiosity, I asked him to show it to me."

The conductor raised his eyebrows. "And he pulled it out to show you?"

"Yes," Catherine scrunched her nose. "Isn't he a dear?"

The conductor turned to Luke. "Is that true?"

"Sir, I come from the South. We feel it our obligation to defend a woman's honor. I trust you are not calling Catherine and the baby liars?"

The conductor rubbed his temples. "I believe that same attitude cost you a war. But I'll accept her word. It would be to your advantage to shove those guns in your satchels and leave them there until you exit the train. The next such incident, we will stop the train immediately and you will be booted off, no matter the location."

Luke stood up and pulled off his hat. "Don't forget to take an apple for yourself and one for the baby, Catherine."

"Thank you, Luke." She tapped the conductor on the shoulder. "Could we talk about my ticket upgrade now?"

He shook his head. "I need to finish my round first."

Catherine sat down, wiped the apple on her sleeve, then took a big bite. The sweet juices cooled her tongue and throat and washed away the acrid taste of railway dust. Nancy just licked on hers.

Francine returned with a sleeping Preston on her shoulder. "Was my Nancy good?"

Catherine hugged the little girl. "Oh, yes. She's a darling."

"Once you get her warmed up, she'll talk your head off. Takes after me." When Francine laughed, every part of her jiggled. "Where did you get the apples?"

Race Hillyard sat up and stretched his arms. "She sweet-talked the poker players out of them."

"I did nothing improper. Luke seemed delighted to give them to me."

"Which one is Luke?" Francine asked.

"The one with the cute dimples," Race growled.

"Oh, the blond." Francine reached over the seat to retrieve Nancy. She held the little girl above her head, then lowered her down slow. "I reckon it's big sister's turn for the privy. You hold Preston." She shoved the baby boy into Race's lap.

"But, I can't . . ."

"Sure you can. Catherine is busy eating that apple. Besides, you want to be a daddy some day, don't you?"

"Not today," he muttered.

Francine plowed down the center aisle. When she eased out of sight, the conductor marched up to Catherine. "You wanted to talk to me?"

"I want a Pullman compartment. I understand it's twenty dollars more." Catherine laid her hand on the dark blue wool surge sleeve of his jacket. "I'd like to purchase that now."

He stole a quick look at her hand. "Lady, the

time to buy that was at the station before you boarded."

"Yes, I know." She lowered her voice. "I didn't have the funds for it then."

"Speak up."

She cleared her throat. "I said, I didn't have the funds at the time I was in the station."

He pulled off his gold-framed glasses and rubbed the bridge of his nose. "But you do now?"

Catherine eased her shoulders back and refused to let them slump. "Yes, something rather unexpected came up. I'm sure someone as important as you can sell me a ticket even now."

"Yes, I have the authority to sell you the ticket. But a dozen other people, albeit not nearly as handsome and friendly as you, have asked me the same thing. The truth is, we don't have any more compartments available up there."

"But when I boarded in Omaha there were several extras."

"All taken now." A couple of the prospectors scooted through the aisle. The conductor squeezed over and leaned against her shoulder. "Of course, someone might get off and vacate one."

She didn't pull back. "You remind me of Captain Edmonton of Reeves Point. Were you a captain in the war?"

That drawl would impress the fussiest ladies in Richmond.

"I was a private who spent my entire time as a

prisoner of war guard in Chicago. And we still have no compartments in the Pullman cars."

"Could I have the next available one?"

"I told you, I've got a dozen others that asked."

She clutched onto his arm tighter. "Are you married?"

"Yes, I am. Just what are you suggesting?"

"Then you'll understand my dilemma. I'm meeting my fiancé in Sacramento. He wants to go straight from the train station to be married. I so want to arrive refreshed and relaxed. I want to look my best. Do you remember your wedding day?"

"It's all a blur, but I do remember my wedding night."

"Precisely my point. I knew you'd understand. Isn't there any way I could, you know . . ."

He leaned down to her ear. "Be next in line? Yes, there is but you won't like it."

Catherine pulled back towards Race Hillyard. "What do you mean?"

The conductor stood straight, then shrugged. "If you pay me the twenty dollars now, I will sell you a Pullman compartment ticket. The next available one will be yours. If one doesn't open up, you forfeit the twenty dollars because the ticket expires when we reach Sacramento."

Her gaze rested on the empty seat next to the saddle. "That doesn't seem fair, to pay for something I might not receive."

He shoved his glasses further back on his nose. "I figured you wouldn't like it."

She sighed. "Okay, I'll take that chance. My name is Catherine Draper. Please put me on the list. I'll get the money."

"Don't do it." The words snapped like a beaver trap.

Race Hillyard grappled with Preston as if he were a hot river rock.

"What business is it of yours?"

"You won't get a Pullman until the last miles of the trip. That's not worth twenty dollars."

She turned back to the conductor. "Is that true?"

"No way of knowing, but it doesn't matter to me. I have to continue my rounds. What do you want to do?"

"It's a dumb way to spend your money," Race added. "Your wonderful Phillip will be more impressed if you arrive rumpled and rich."

"Mr. Hillyard, I will choose how to spend my money." She dug in her valise. "My Phillip owns a prosperous grocery store and in no way needs my money." She handed the gold coins to the conductor. He wrote her name down and gave her a ticket. He tipped his hat, then moved on through the car.

When she reached over to retrieve Preston, the eight-month-old whimpered.

"Oh dear, Preston likes you better."

An almost-grin creased his deep-tanned, stubbled face. "Dogs and children aren't very choosy."

Mr. Hillyard, with a shave and a smile, you could almost pass for a pleasant chap. Why must you be so contrary?

As if he handled live explosives, he maneuvered Preston into Catherine's lap. "And I still say it was not a wise use of your funds."

The toddler's brown-eyed stare made her smile. The grin dropped when she turned to Hillyard. "Which is no business of yours. It would be worth twenty dollars to not have to sit here."

"You don't like babies?"

She patted Preston's soft, pink cheeks. "I love babies and can't wait to have several of my own."

"You and Mr. Phillip Perfect?"

"His name is Phillip Draper."

"I thought your name was Draper."

"It will be."

Race Hillyard stared at her with such intensity, Catherine turned her head. For a moment, the only sounds were the clack of the train cars on the steel rails and the blended murmur of fifty people talking at once. She took a deep breath. "Are you through gawking at me?"

"I was just figurin' out a few things." The voice was firm, confident, with no emotion.

"I doubt that." She felt her throat tighten. "We haven't known each other two hours yet."

57

"It's been three-and-a-half hours."

Mr. Hillyard, why do I feel I have to justify my every action to you? You are the last person on earth I need to impress.

"And just what have you learned about me in that short time?"

"Your name is not Catherine Draper."

"Yes, I admitted that."

"I believe it is Catherine Goodwin."

She spun toward him. Her mouth turned dry. "Why do you say that?"

"Because you whipped around and glared at me just now. Not only that, but when you told Francine your version of what happened to the Virginia lawyer, you described a lot of details. You knew the gun, the caliber and the length of barrel, which no woman would know or care to remember."

"You would be surprised how much I know about guns."

"That might be, but you also know where the bullet entered and where it exited, and what it struck after it pierced the lawyer's leg. I say only 'that Goodwin woman' would know such things."

Catherine rubbed her eyes with cold, sticky fingers. She bit her lip and kept focused on Preston. "Yes, it is true, but I would prefer you did not repeat it."

"I am not the type to do that."

"Thank you, Mr. Hillyard. The gun did hit the floor by accident and discharged. If I had intended to shoot him, I would have killed him, not grazed him in the back of his leg."

"I believe you."

"Thank you, again."

Preston whimpered. She held him to her shoulder and rocked back and forth.

I can't believe I've been on this train such a short time and already confessed one of my darkest secrets to the most irritating person here. I traveled all the way from Boston to Council Bluff being completely ignored and now this.

She watched as a lady in a burgundy silk dress entered the car, arm in arm with a man wearing a crisp, fog-gray suit. They laughed as they paraded down the aisle.

When Hillyard's hand gripped her elbow, she flinched. "One question."

"I trust it will be a pleasant one."

"No, I suppose it isn't. I'll ask some other time."

"You might as well get it out now. This feels like beat-up-Catherine day."

"I'd like to know why you feel compelled to use a sensuous voice and soft touch to get men to do your bidding?"

Her whole body stiffened. "I do what?"

"You use the charms of your gender to manipulate men."

"Mr. Hillyard, you do not know me well enough to talk to me that way."

He shrugged. "But the truth is you try to arouse men to your charms and then ask them to do something they would not normally do. Like a charmer, you say soft words in order to get the snake to dance. I noticed you had them dancin' in the aisle a while ago. I'm sorry if this makes you mad."

"You are not sorry. You said some very hurtful things on purpose. I can't imagine you treat all women this way. You are angry at me, and yet my actions are none of your concern. I think it is cruel, heartless, evil for you to inflict your misguided ire at me. Others may have treated you poorly, but I haven't. So just get mad at someone else, Mr. Hillyard. I will not put up with this."

His face flushed as he pulled back. They stared out the window at rolling, untilled farmland. His voice was so low it sounded as if he were thinking out loud. "You know nothing about me. Absolutely nothing."

"That response told me an awful lot." Catherine felt the courage to be aggressive. "Now that we have equally offended each other, just what makes you think I am sensuously manipulative?"

"You seduced poor Luke into giving you two apples."

"I most certainly did not seduce him."

"You threw yourself at him like bait."

60

"But I reeled it back in."

"Then you threw it away to the conductor, to get him to take your money."

"I did no such thing."

"Then why is it you couldn't talk to him without touching his arm?"

Catherine glared at him. "This is insulting."

"I'll tell you what is insulting . . . that you are the type of woman who would sell hugs, kisses, and fondle some stranger at the depot for twenty dollars."

Catherine stood up, Preston tucked against her shoulder. "I don't have to listen to this."

"Sit down. There is no place to go. You are upset because it's true. You are engaged to some luckless fellow named Phillip Draper in California. You didn't have enough money for a Pullman car when you left the depot in Omaha, but you had it by the time you boarded."

She rocked back and forth. "If you are trying to make me cry, you will not succeed."

"Do you even know that fellow at the depot's name?"

"None of this is your business, Mr. Hillyard."

"I'm just cautioning you not to toss your affections around so easy. I believe under all the charades, you are a decent lady. Save your fondness for Phillip."

"I assure you, Phillip will receive everything I have to give."

"That might be . . . but what you have to give will be used."

Catherine fought back the tears. "You have no idea the pain and suffering I've experienced in the past ten years. You have no clue of the sorrow, the grief, the lies, the deceit and the losses that I have been subjected to. Until you know the crushing burdens I had to bear, you have no right to judge me like that. You seem consumed with an evil cruelty and I pity your black, stone-dead soul. If I were not holding little Preston, I would slap you."

Race Hillyard slumped back in the seat. He leaned forward, his chin on his chest. When he sat up, he raised his open hand in the air, then slapped it hard against his own face. The sound echoed through the car. Everyone stared their way.

Catherine plopped down next to him. "What did you do that for?"

"Because I deserved it and your hands were occupied."

"You want to tell me why you're such a bitter man?"

He rubbed his forehead and released a deep sigh. "No, not yet."

Francine tromped down the aisle carrying a smiling, apple-eating Nancy. "Whoa, I heard that slap. I don't suppose you two are playing patty-cake? What on earth did I miss?"

"The uncivil war," Catherine replied.

CHAPTER THREE

"I most certainly am not going to sleep with you." Catherine sensed a hush in the train car.

"That's not what I said." His voice was so low the rattle of the tracks muffled the words.

Catherine bit her lip and refused to glance around. "You asked me to share a bed."

Race Hillyard tugged off his bullet belt and holster and looped it over the horn of the saddle perched on the seat in front of him. "I asked you if you would like to share the expenses of a sleeping board and pillows that turn these seats into a . . . eh, raised pallet."

With the babies scrunched on the seat, heads in her lap, Francine leaned forward. "He's right, honey. Those of you with seats facing each other can get a board, blankets and pillows to make sleep a little more comfortable."

Catherine entwined her gloved fingers. "He said, share a bed. . . ."

Race pulled his pistol from the holster and shoved it into his belt. "Look, it's a dollar extra apiece for the board and pillows. If you don't have the funds. . . ."

"What makes you think I don't have the funds?"

"You bought the fifteen-cent supper at that siding café, instead of the full meal for two-bits.

I assume you are watching pennies now that you spent all your kiss money on a Pullman upgrade that you haven't got."

"I haven't got it yet." Catherine unpinned her Tuscan straw hat and perched it on her floral valise. "Besides, I wasn't very hungry."

"The pot-roast was tough, anyway," Francine reported. "But the corn was sure sweet and juicy."

"I'll take the inside." He pointed at his saddle. "We'll put Mr. Walker between us. You take the aisle. I'll sleep on top of the blanket, fully dressed, as I'm sure you will."

"How do you know how I'll sleep?"

"We're in a train car with fifty other people, including four half-drunk drovers across the aisle. You will not be wearing a French negligee."

"My Farley gave me one of those one time." Francine studied a small cracker as if it were a rare jewel. "But it just didn't fit right, you know what I mean? So he framed it and hung it on a wall over our bed. Says it gives him inspiration." She popped the cracker into her mouth.

Catherine gazed at the empty seat across from her. "I am not sleeping in your bed even if we have fifty dirty, grimy witnesses."

"It's a shame to let those facing seats go to waste," Francine said.

"If you and the children would like to share

the sleeping arrangements with Mr. Hillyard, I'm sure Mr. Walker and I will be quite comfortable in your seat."

"Certainly." Francine reached down into her dull green purse. "Here's a dollar for my half of the rig."

Hillyard refused the coin. "Let's just forget it. Some things don't work out."

Catherine's shoulders arched. "Do you mean, you'll gladly share your bunk with a single lady, but refuse to do so with a married woman with children?"

Hillyard slumped down in the seat next to the window. "Something like that."

She refused to glance at her shaded, mirror-like reflection in the window. "So you did have something in mind besides sleep?"

He didn't bother looking up. "Forget the whole thing. I'm too tired for this. I thought it was an act of kindness. That's my mistake."

The train slowed as it curved to the right. She glanced out at the black, starless night. "You've slept most all afternoon."

"I have a lot of catchin' up to do." Hillyard yawned and stretched his long arms straight up. "I reckon I can continue to do that sittin' next to you, providin' you and Mr. Walker keep the conversation down."

Francine's thick, calloused hand gripped Catherine's narrow shoulder. "It's a shame to let one of them sleepin' seats go unused. Preston and Nancy sleep much more sound when they can stretch all the way out."

Catherine turned towards Race with arched eyebrows.

He sat straight up. "I suppose since Miss Draper and I will be sitting up all night harpin' at each other, it won't matter which seat we occupy. We'll trade with you, just for the night."

Catherine picked up her hat and pulled her valise to her lap. "And I'm sure Mr. Walker won't mind sleeping on the floor under the board."

"Well, I would have never imagined. What a pleasant surprise." Francine pressed her full cheeks. "We appreciate your generosity."

Hillyard stood and shoved on his dirty hat. "You gals get things moved around. I'll go fetch the conductor for that sleeping rig."

Francine hefted Preston. "I suppose you'll want me to pay the whole two dollars . . . since me and the babes will be using it?"

One small lamp cast a golden glow in the train car. Sounds filtered to an occasional cough or snore. Most windows were shade-covered and the few that weren't framed a black prairie night. A couple of partially open windows provided slight air movement that wafted dust, sweat and sweet perfume.

Race Hillyard scrunched down in the window

seat, his coat rolled up as a pillow, his hat pulled over his eyes.

Catherine leaned her head sideways on the leather seat, her face just inches from his ear. "That was nice of you to allow Francine the use of the sleeping seat."

"I didn't figure I had much choice."

"It is a logical decision. I must apologize for snapping at you the way I did."

"You sayin' that you didn't mean it?"

"After pondering, I realize that I would not have accepted those arrangements, no matter who offered them."

"Even if it were your beloved Phillip?"

"Not unless we were married. No matter how platonic the situation, my soul would have been in torment all night. But I was very wrong to question your motives. I don't know you well enough for that. I'm afraid I assumed you are a lecher like others I've known."

"Catherine, you are a very attractive lady." He opened one eye and peeked out from under his hat brim. "And I don't claim all my impulses are Puritanical. But truly, at the moment I offered to share the sleeping board, I was not contemplatin' ungodly thoughts."

"I believe you, Mr. Hillyard. I'm afraid we've got off to a rather adversarial beginning."

"All I want is a quiet, peaceful trip west."

"That's something we agree upon. Do you

think our conversing will disturb others?"

"I don't think anyone on this train gives a hoot what we whisper about. Isn't that right, Francine?"

Catherine peered over the seat to spy the large woman curled on her side, back against the train car. Preston and Nancy slept under her protective, fleshy arm. All three had mouths open, eyes closed. "I believe you are right. So, I have a question for you, Race Hillyard."

"Is it personal?"

"Yes, but not accusatory."

He unfastened the neck button on his dirty, white shirt. "I'm not real good with talkin' about personal things."

"But you know quite a bit about me."

"I know your Phillip waits in California to marry you. And that you shot a no-account lawyer in Virginia."

"And you know I lost my parents in the war and have an identical twin sister in New York."

"And the point is?"

"I know very little about you. Except that you've spent a lot of time outdoors . . . are more well-read than you look . . . and you haven't slept well for a while."

"That is the important part."

"I also know that you are ready to use your gun to get your way . . . about like I use my smile and soft voice."

Touché, Mr. Hillyard.

She opened her eyes. He was looking at her.

"You're right. Different weapons, same motive. Okay, ask me that personal question, but I don't promise to answer."

"Where have you been that made you so worn-out? And where . . ."

"You can't bluff me, Wyatt Earp, I'm going to kill you!" The drover shouted his threat from the aisle of the car, waving his cocked revolver in front of him.

Catherine clutched Race and tried to shove herself toward the train window. "Is he drunk?"

With dusty black hat hanging from a stampede string behind his back, the wild-eyed man stalked the aisle. "Come out, Earp . . . you cain't hide any longer!"

Hillyard shoved Catherine in the window seat, and scooted to the aisle, his Colt clutched in his right hand, lying in his lap.

Though most were awake now in the car, the passengers crouched back, trying to avoid the circling muzzle of the cocked revolver. One of the other drovers leapt to the aisle. "Put down the gun, Cantu. It's just another bad dream."

Cantu marched straight at his pal. The revolver weaved over the heads of the passengers. "I ain't listen' to you, Virgil. You ain't no better than your no-account brother!"

"I'm not Virgil Earp. I'm your pal, Gates. You

know me. Now, put down the gun and let's get some sleep."

"Draw, Wyatt, and I'll kill ya. I'll swear I will. And then I'll kill that yella skunk brother of yours."

Catherine's fingers clutched tight in front of her chin.

Lord, this can't be happening.

Another of the drovers stood. "Cantu, it's okay. Your old mutt, Tippy, is alive. Earp didn't shoot him."

Cantu pointed his .45 at the new target. "Where is he? Where's my dog? I don't see him. Tippy! Here, boy!"

"He's at the bunkhouse. Waitin' for you. Come on, put the gun down."

"I ain't putting this gun down until I deal with Earp."

Catherine leaned over to Hillyard. "Shall I pull the emergency brake cord?"

He shook his head, but didn't take his eyes off the man with the gun.

"Let's sit down and talk about a plan, Cantu." Gates inched closer to the gunman. "You don't want to go off half-cocked. . . ."

The blast ripped a hole in the wooden floor-board of the train car. The report vibrated through the entire car like a cannon blast on the Fourth of July. Catherine clamped her hands over her ears and coughed, as black powder smoke filled

70

the train car. When she blinked her eyes, Race Hillyard stood in the aisle, his gun pointed at Cantu.

"Put the gun down, cowboy. Don't give me a good reason for killin' you," Hillyard grumbled.

"Who in blazes are you?"

"I'm Wyatt Earp and I hope you know Jesus, because you are only seconds away from hell."

"You're Earp?"

"And you're dead."

"But we both have drawn guns. I could kill you."

"Cantu, did you ever get so drunk and sleepy that you could miss a target at twelve feet? Did you?"

"Well . . ." Cantu staggered back a step. "Maybe."

"I never have and this bullet is aimed straight at your heart. Did you ever hear of Earp missin' what he aimed at?"

"He's right, Cantu," Gates offered. "Earp don't miss. Holster your gun."

"How do I know you're Wyatt Earp?"

"How do you know I'm not?" Hillyard tramped down the aisle. "Give me the gun, Cantu . . . it's the only way you'll live to see mornin'."

"I'll shoot you."

"You won't shoot me. You're the type that won't do it, unless you can shoot me in the back on some dark, empty alley." Hillyard continued toward the cowering gunman, his wide blue eyes turning to Atlantic ocean green.

"Stay back, I'll do it." His shout hovered between anger and abject fear.

"Hand me the gun. It's your only choice."

"You killed my dog in Bozeman."

"I've never been to Bozeman. Give me the gun. I'm tired of this talk. I need the sleep. If I have to shoot you and toss you out the window to get some sleep, I will."

"I give you the gun, you'll shoot me," he hollered.

"I promise I won't. Did you ever hear of Wyatt Earp not keeping his word? If I wanted you dead, I would have shot you already."

The revolver dangled from Cantu's index finger, but he didn't release it.

Hillyard grabbed the man's arm, yanked it down with one motion and slammed the barrel of his own revolver into Cantu's forehead.

The gunman crumpled to the aisle.

The passengers broke out into applause as Gates scooted up the aisle. "Mister, you didn't have to cold cock him."

"I've seen the trick with the dangled revolver before. Beside, both Cantu and me need some sleep tonight."

Gates dragged his pal back up the aisle. "I still say you didn't need to bust his skull."

"No, I could of just shot him. I reckon I'm just an old softie."

Hillyard had just settled back down next to Catherine when a sleepy-eyed conductor shuffled into the car. "Was there a gunshot in here?"

"Accidental discharge." Hillyard nodded to the unconscious drover across the aisle. "Everything has been taken care of."

"I reckon you're goin' to stop the train and toss us off?" Gates shrugged.

The conductor peered out at the black night. "Not a good place to stop. We're in the middle of Big Springs Canyon." He glanced over at the unconscious Cantu. "What happened to his head?"

"He accidently bumped it into the barrel of my revolver," Race admitted.

"Lots of accidents in this car."

"It's not boring, that's for sure."

Gates wrapped a bandana around Cantu's head. "Maybe you ought to stop the train and let us get him to a doc."

"We're forty miles from a town."

"We've got our horses in the cattle car."

"I'm not delaying the rest of the passengers because of a drunk cowboy. In the morning, I'll need a full report of what took place."

The gunsmoke filtered out of the car as Hillyard scrunched back in the window seat. The rumble of the westward bound train seemed to settle everyone down.

Then Catherine leaned closer. "Not boring?" She pulled her fingers from their prayer-like grasp. "I was scared witless."

"I reckon I was just too tired to worry. Kinda dumb, I suppose."

"It looked brave to me. Was the man sleep-walking?"

"Or drunk. Or both. Some men do strange things in their sleep. We had a neighbor who walked in his sleep and kept setting his outhouse on fire."

"Oh, dear, what happened to him?" She noticed his eyes faded back to the sky blue color.

"You don't want to know." He shoved his revolver back in his belt and closed his eyes. "Something strange about this deal, though. I'm too sleepy to figure it out. But, they surely seemed like they wanted to get off the train in a hurry. They acted disappointed that the conductor didn't stop and toss them off."

Catherine watched his eyes blink close and his leathered, dirty face relax. She tried to listen to the muffled conversation across the aisle as she re-set the combs that held her brown hair high on the back of her head. When she finally nudged Hillyard's shoulder, his right hand reached for the belted revolver. The light in the car was so dim, she wasn't sure if he opened his eyes or not.

"Race, there is no way I can go to sleep with

the sound of that gunfire in my ears and the smell of black powder still wafting in this car. Don't forget you were about to tell me who you are and why you are so tired."

He rubbed his calloused fingers across his thin lips. "I'm from Texas."

"Somehow, I'm not surprised."

"Jackson Springs area. My father was a surveyor's assistant when the Allen brothers platted the city of Houston. During the days of the Texas Republic, he and an uncle moved fifteen miles south and built a small armament factory."

"I should imagine it was a good business."

"By the time the war hit, it was very prosperous. So much so, my older brother Robert attended a Baptist Theological Seminary. I was only seventeen, but read for the law with Judge Webb. Of course, once Texas seceded we wanted to join the army and save the Confederacy. President Davis had other plans."

"My father was a friend of Mr. Davis'." She reached over to swat a fly off his chin, but hesitated and pulled her gloved hand back.

"Mine had never met him. But Dad's reputation at the armament plant got around and he was asked by President Davis in 1862 to move to Macon, Georgia and help operate the big armory there." Eyes closed, Race swatted an inch in front of his chin, caught the fly and threw it to the floor. "Dad insisted he needed his sons to help run the place. Davis disagreed. So, there was a compromise. Robert went with Dad. I got drafted into the army. Mother stayed home by herself and held the place together, so to speak."

"What about your armory?"

"They boarded it up and all the workers went off to war. I followed orders down to Brownsville and spent the entire time aboard ship running the Yankee blockades with Captain King."

The train slowed down. Catherine peered out the window but blackness blanketed everything. "An army man in the Confederate Navy?"

"Officially, a corporal in the army, but I was a crack shot. They kept me in the crow's nest as a sniper. All I had to do in the war was sit up there in the salt air and shoot Yankees if a ship got too close."

The train stopped. "Did any get too close?"

"I was more successful than I care to remember. Shooting men hardens a conscience." He opened his eyes. "I reckon we pulled over to let another express pass through."

Catherine continued to stare out the window. "No sign of a town or stations, perhaps we stopped for the buffalo to cross."

"If buffalo tromped past, we'd hear them."

"All I hear is repulsive snoring. You're probably right. Just an express train." The cowboys across the aisle stirred a little, but when she glanced over, all seemed to be sleeping. Catherine lowered her voice. "I'm not sure they are happy with what you did to Cantu."

"That's what I think. Did it seem like an act to you?"

"You mean that whole scene of waving his gun and all?"

"Yeah, Wyatt Earp shot my dog. Seems like a scene out of a dime melodrama. That's got to be the stupidest line I've ever heard."

Catherine's eyes widened. "And shooting the floor?"

"He wasn't about to hit his pal . . . and he didn't want to hit a bystander."

"What would have happened had you not stopped him?"

"That's what I've been ponderin'."

The three cowboys crowded the aisle. Gates turned toward Race Hillyard. "As long as we're stopped, we're going to check our horses. We'll be back so don't cold cock Cantu again."

All three sauntered out of the train car and into the night. Race pulled his revolver from his belt and laid it on his knee.

"Do you think they went to look after the horses?" Catherine whispered.

"I'm not sure. Change seats with me."

She slid over to the window. "Do you think they'll be back?"

"Oh, yeah." Hillyard scooted across the aisle.

"Are you going to hit him again?"

"No." Race pulled Cantu's revolver. "Just neutralize him." He flipped the cylinder open and ejected the cartridges into his hand. He eased the gun back into the man's holster.

When he settled back into the seat, she leaned over. "You expecting a surprise?"

"I'm hopin' to get some sleep. But I intend to be ready for anything."

Catherine listened for the sound of another train, but heard only distant, muffled voices. She turned back to Hillyard. "So, what did you do after the war?"

He scrunched back down, his hand still wrapped around the walnut grip of his revolver. "I didn't make it back home for a few months. It took a while for the news of Lee's surrender to reach south Texas. And then lots of Confederate troops and families attempted to sneak into Mexico. I hung around to help them."

"You didn't want to stay in Mexico?"

"No," Hillyard rubbed his unshaven chin. "But maybe I should have. It took Dad and Robert a while to make it back to Jackson Springs, too. They had been in a Union prisoner-of-war camp in Chicago."

"I like Chicago."

"Not this part. Half the prisoners died there. When they arrived home, there was some turmoil with Mother. Seems she heard they both were killed when Sherman marched across Georgia. So, she took up with . . . well, anyway, two days after my father got home, Dad died of a heart attack."

"So very sad." Catherine brushed the corners of her eyes. "He was a victim of the war just as much as my father."

"I suppose so. I made it up for the funeral and six days later, Mother married Mr. Hironymous St. Claire from Louisiana."

"Oh, dear."

"He didn't like me and Robert . . . didn't like the Castle Street Armory . . . and didn't like Texas. So he took Mamma, Daddy's bank account, and most of their personal belongings to Virginia City, Montana."

The train lurched forward. Catherine studied Race's broad shoulders and set jaw. His beard looked only a day or two old. She wanted to reach over and hold her palm against his cheek, but laid her hand on his shoulder instead. "I know this has to be difficult to talk about. If you'd rather not, I fully understand."

"The words seem to be tumbling out tonight. That might not happen again." He peered out from under his hat. His blue eyes still looked tired, but much more peaceful. He closed them and let out a long, slow sigh that sounded like engine brakes a mile away. "Robert and I decided to open up the armory. We worked twenty-hour days and hired returning veterans who needed a job. The business began to take off. By the mid-1870s, we had made enough profit that some around the state claimed we provided the prime example of how to rebuild Texas after the war."

Her hand still rested on his shoulder. "So, you are a successful businessman?"

"Robert was the businessman. I partnered out in the shop making sure the equipment operated and the workers did a good job."

"I see a picture of two hardworking, successful young Texans. Any ladies in this scene?" She rubbed her fingers in a circular motion on his shoulder. The white cotton felt smooth and stiff and the muscles firm.

He reached over, plucked up her hand, and dropped it in her lap. "That's one of the parts I'm not going to talk about."

"You've revealed a lot in that action."

He turned to watch Cantu. "They've been gone a while."

"Are we changing the subject?"

"Yep."

The front door of the car flew open. A young girl with blonde braids and a flannel nightgown rushed into the aisle.

She sobbed so hard Hillyard reached out to catch her as she stumbled. "What's the matter, darlin'?"

"My daddy told me to run away and hide, but I don't know where I'm supposed to go."

"How about right here?" Race pulled her into the seat between him and Catherine.

"Honey, were you up in the Pullman cars?" Catherine asked.

"We have our own private car. Two men with masks broke in. They look like robbers, so my daddy said to run away and hide."

Race pulled out a red bandana and wiped her eyes. "Who is your daddy?"

"Judge Antone Clarke of San Francisco. My name is Amanda Sue and we're on our way home from Washington, D.C. where we had supper with the president."

"Why did your daddy tell you to run?"

"I think the mean men want to haul me off," she sobbed. "Can you hide me?"

"We can pretend she is our daughter if they come back looking for her," Catherine suggested.

"Not if Gates and the others are involved. They know us."

Catherine glanced over at the unconscious Cantu. "You think they are a part of it?"

"I told you somethin' strange is goin' on."

Amanda Sue tugged at his sleeve. "Quick, you've got to hide me."

"Darlin', under that sleeping lady and her children is a saddle. Scoot behind the saddle and hunker down against the train car. I promise I won't let anyone get you."

She scampered towards the seat. "They have guns."

He revealed his Colt. "So do I."

"But have you ever shot anyone? My daddy has a gun, too, but he's never shot anyone."

"Hide, honey." Catherine urged. "Mr. Hillyard has shot dozens of men."

Amanda Sue dove under the sleeping board that swayed with Francine's weight and crawled behind the saddle.

"Which door will they come in?" Catherine whispered.

"I'll watch the front one. You keep an eye at the back."

"Most everyone's dozed back to sleep. I think even that Francine slept through the gunfire. Race, what is this all about?"

Amanda Sue's voice filtered up like a soft violin note. "Are they gone yet?"

Hillyard leaned over. "Darlin', don't say another word until I call for you. Do you understand?"

"Yes, but I'm scared."

"Jesus will take care of you."

"Do you believe in Jesus?" the little voice questioned.

"Of course I do. Don't you?"

"Oh, yes . . . but I'm still very, very scared."

"Shhhh."

Catherine's lips were only an inch from his ear. "Do you think they are trying to kidnap her?"

"Sounds like that's what her daddy thinks."

"What will we do?"

"I'm workin' on a plan." Hillyard dropped to his knees in the aisle and reached back towards his saddle bags.

He held his finger over his lips. "Not yet, Amanda." When he returned to his seat, he held a second Colt. He unloaded his revolver and shoved the cartridges into the second one.

He handed the loaded one to Catherine. "Sit on this one."

"What?"

"Tuck it in the cushion and sit on it."

It felt hard and cold against her backside. "But your other gun is empty."

"Yeah, I hope this works. Keep watching the back door. The minute someone comes in with guns drawn, I want you to scream as loud as you can."

"Are you serious?"

"I want everyone in this car awake. Just pretend your Phillip is about to be run over by a trolley and you need to warn him to jump out of the way."

"Yes . . . I'll do it."

Phillip . . . dear Phillip . . . it's been hours

since I've thought of you. I wish you were here to protect me . . . but . . . well, perhaps Mr. Hillyard has more experience in this type of matter.

"Race, you won't let them take Amanda Sue, will you?"

"Of course not."

"Neither will I. I can shoot, you know."

"You can shoot lawyers, but that's like shooting rats. Can you shoot an ordinary kidnapper?"

Her lips curled into a slight smile. "This is no time for levity."

"It's the best time. Always be relaxed before you get into a gunfight."

"Now there is useful information."

"It's true. I remember one time . . ."

Catherine's scream pierced the train car like a streak of angry lightning that cracks the sky at the same moment the thunder rolls. Gates, Luke and the third cowboy burst in, guns drawn, through the back door.

Hillyard focused on the two men with short-barreled shotguns who shoved open the front door.

The short one with the thick black beard shouted, "Be quiet everyone. Ain't no reason for anyone to get shot. We're lookin' for a little girl who ran back this way. Where is she?"

Preston and Nancy wailed as Francine struggled to sit up. One glare from the two gunmen convinced her to lay back down and clutch the children.

"Grab his gun, Parker, he'll make trouble," Gates shouted from the back of the car."

Parker started down the aisle. "Which one?"

"The Texican with the Colt in the second row. He's the one that bashed Cantu and ruined your Big Springs Canyon set up."

Parker aimed the shotgun at Race. "Give me the gun."

Hillyard aimed the pistol at the man and cocked the hammer. "I don't think so."

Catherine squeezed her hands.

Race, you emptied the bullets out of that gun.

"This shotgun will tear you in two."

"And this .44 will scramble your brains. I'd say the hands are equal."

"Let's up the pot," Parker grumbled. He swerved the shotgun at Catherine's head. "Give me the gun, or this lady loses more than her fine looks."

Catherine clutched Hillyard's arm.

"You won't shoot a lady in front of all these witnesses."

"I'll not only shoot the lady, I'll shoot the witnesses."

"Give him the gun, mister," one of the miners shouted from the back of the car. "I seen what Parker Latiger done to a bank full of people

85

down in the Indian Nation. He ain't against shootin' women and children."

Hillyard eased the hammer down on the Colt and handed it to Latiger.

Catherine squirmed to make sure the other revolver was still beneath her.

"Cold cock him like he did Cantu," Gates called from the back of the car.

"Not until we find the girl. Look, folks, I don't need to shoot anyone. I'm just looking for the little blonde girl who ran back here. I've got business with her daddy and I have to take her to him."

"You mean you're goin' to kidnap her?" Catherine muttered.

Parker spun back toward her, but Hillyard stood and blocked his way. "Sit down, mister."

"Don't try to play games, Latiger. Everyone in the car knows you want to kidnap the girl, wherever she is."

The outlaw shoved the muzzle of the shotgun into Hillyard's midsection. He sat down.

Catherine clutched her gloved hands and tried to breathe out.

Is this real? It's like I'm caught in a bad dream.

"I'll ask once more, where is the little girl?"

Breathe in and out . . . relax. Race said not to tense up in a crisis. That's got to be the stupidest thing I've ever heard. If I was relaxed, it wouldn't be a crisis.

"Look around. Obviously, she is not here," Catherine offered.

"But you did see her? Do you mean a little girl ran in here and none of you fine citizens offered to help her?"

One of the teenage girls towards the back spoke in a soft voice. "She kept going right out the back."

Parker waved the shotgun towards the back. "Is that so. Who else saw her run through the car?"

The replies dominoed from one teenage girl to another until all six had spoken.

"I did . . ."

"Yes, that's true."

"She was in a hurry."

"Scampered right through to the next car."

"We all saw her."

Gates sauntered up next to the girls. "She didn't reach the back car, we already checked it out."

"I think I saw her get off the train."

"She ran out into the night."

"Among the trees."

"Yes, we all saw her."

"We called out to her."

"But she kept running."

Latiger motioned for the second man with a shotgun to approach the girls. "Isn't this interesting. Six young gals all have identical stories. And I don't believe a one of them. One is convincing, but six are a chorus of parrots, covering something up. Where is the little girl?"

The bearded man in front of the girls stood and when he did, the fat dog barked. "My word, leave my girls alone."

The barrel of the second man's shotgun crashed into his head. He dropped beside the yapping dog. The girls started to cry.

"Here's what I'm goin' to do. If you don't tell me where she is, Muley will crack the barrel of that shotgun into the first one's head. Then I'll keep askin' and Muley will keep bustin' heads until one of you tells me the truth."

The tall, gaunt man replied, "Can I keep me one these gals, Parker?"

"Only one?"

"I'd like two really. It's always handy to have a spare."

"We might just take the whole lot. Make sure their heads is the only thing you damage."

Catherine felt Race's hand slip back under her. She leaned forward as the handgun slipped out.

"Like I said," Latiger growled, "either you tell me where she is or . . ."

Hillyard jumped the outlaw. His left arm squeezed the man's neck, a cocked revolver rammed into his temple. "Drop the guns, boys, or the Parker Latiger gang ends right now."

"Where'd he . . . ?" Gates growled.

Catherine watched Hillyard shove the Colt

into Latiger's forehead so hard, the outlaw's shotgun crashed to the floor.

"All of you drop them," Hillyard ordered.

"We got you covered, mister, you can't stand against all of us."

"But he can't miss killin' me," Latiger whined. "Drop them, boys."

"Not so fast, Texican." Cantu staggered to his feet, waving his revolver at Race Hillyard's back. "I might have a headache, but I can pull this trigger."

"Looks like we got the drop," Gates called out. "Throw down."

Hillyard hollered over his shoulder. "Catherine, take away his gun and clobber him with your valise."

"My valise?"

"Pretend he's a Virginia lawyer."

She stomped across the aisle.

"Stay back, lady," Cantu challenged. "I'll shoot you. Before God and these witnesses, I'll shoot you."

"Yes, you will have to answer to God for your sins, but shooting me will not be one of them. Hand me the pistol."

"You're crazy. I'll shoot you."

She shouted back at Hillyard. "Is it alright if I clobber him first and then take the gun?"

"Suit yourself."

She raised the valise.

Cantu pulled the trigger.

Francine gasped.

Preston cried.

The older lady at the back cried out, "No!"

The gun clicked.

He pulled the trigger again. This time the click was followed by a crash of the heavy valise into the already wounded forehead.

Cantu crumpled to the floor.

"It misfired?" Francine squealed. "Honey, that was a miracle."

"Throw down those guns, boys," Hillyard echoed.

All four weapons clattered to the floor.

"You folks sitting nearby pick up the guns and train them on these fine gentlemen. If you get worried, just shoot them. It's justified homicide."

"What do you want me to do now?" Catherine called out.

"Take Amanda Sue to her father and tell the conductor to get this train moving." He turned to the others. "Boys, I want you off the train right now. If I see your face, I shoot Latiger. Once we get moving, I'll toss him off."

"Dead or alive?" Luke challenged.

"You'll have to wait to find that out. Take Cantu with you."

Catherine helped Amanda Sue crawl out from behind the saddle.

Latiger slumped. When Hillyard gripped him

90

tighter, the outlaw yanked a revolver from his belt and shoved it over his shoulder. "Mister, you are about to be shot by your own gun."

"I'm really tired of this game. Pull the trigger," Hillyard countered. "Get it over with."

Latiger squeezed off four clicks before Hillyard's gun crashed into his skull.

"Another misfire?" Francine exclaimed. "Jesus be praised."

CHAPTER FOUR

The train pitched forward.

When they gained a good speed, Catherine and Race dragged Latiger out to the platform between the cars and tossed him out into the Nebraska night.

Catherine clutched the cold iron railing. "Shouldn't we have held them for the authorities?"

Hillyard stared out at the black, formless landscape. "I just wanted them off the train before some bystanders got hurt. It sounds naïve and self-centered I reckon, but I didn't want to get bound up guarding prisoners, making reports to sheriffs and waiting around some prairie town for two months so I could testify in a trial. Not very noble, is it?"

The wind whipped her brown hair around her ears and she didn't bother brushing it back. "I know little about frontier justice."

He leaned back against the railing. "It's kind of like a bullet to the leg of a deceitful Virginia lawyer."

"That was an accident."

"Did you regret the pain you inflicted on him?"

"Not for a moment. I do see the comparison, although I'm not sure the Lord approves of either."

"You're probably right about that. Turnin' the other cheek has never been a strong point of mine. Are the judge and Amanda Sue alright?"

She wrapped her arms across her chest.

A shawl would be good right now. The emotions of the night must have something to do with these chills.

"The judge was tied up in his private car, but he's free now. Lots of hugging and tears. I left the girl there and hurried back. I thought you might need my help."

"I did need it earlier. You did great, Catherine. Were you scared when you disarmed Cantu?"

Another chill gripped her. She locked her jaw to keep from quivering. "I was so scared I had to act without thinking."

"That's what courage is all about. You allow your character to control the actions, not your brain."

The door to the front car opened and they stepped to the side of the platform as two men approached in the night shadows.

The conductor led the way. "Oh, here you are. Where's Latiger?"

Hillyard pulled off his wide-brimmed hat and rubbed his hair. "Someplace down the tracks. We tossed him off the train."

"Was he dead?" the conductor asked.

"Not when we dumped him. But he'll have a busted skull. I know I should have held him. I just wanted him and the others off the train before anyone got hurt."

The conductor pulled a small notebook and very short pencil out of his navy blue wool vest pocket. "What will I report to my superiors?"

Catherine clutched the conductor's arm. "Tell them that Latiger and the others threatened some of your passengers. They got angry and tossed them off the train before you could intervene and establish proper procedure."

"Well said," the man with the conductor stated. "You have a lawyer's mind."

"She has gotten close to lawyers from time to time," Hillyard said.

"Perhaps that will satisfy my superiors. I don't know why things like this happen on my train." The conductor turned to the man behind him. "This is Judge Clarke. He wanted to meet you."

The conductor scooted to the front of the train, leaving the stout man with a drooping gray mustache and black suit. "Amanda Sue told me all about how you hid her, disarmed the villains and saved her." The judge reached out his hand. "I cannot thank you enough. It is couples like you that make me proud to be a judge."

"Actually, we're not a . . ."

A swift kick in the shin silenced Hillyard.

"Is she your . . . eh, daughter?" Catherine asked.

The man stood tall. "Yes, and I'm not offended by the question. I married quite late in life. I assure you, her mother is considerably younger than I."

"Were they going to hold her for a ransom?" Hillyard asked.

The judge looped his thumps in his vest pockets. "And more. I believe it has to do with a man I sent to prison last year. We didn't get far enough along to hear the demands."

Catherine tried to study the judge's eyes, but couldn't read them in the dim shadows. "Perhaps you need more protection?"

"I was thinking the same thing." He rubbed his clean shaven chin. "Fortunately, an ex-Pinkerton man from New York is on board. He offered me his services for the remainder of the trip."

"Judge, if it were me," Hillyard added, "I'd sneak off this train at the next decent stop and switch to a different one. Someone knows you're here."

"That's a good idea. I'll talk it over with this Pinkerton fellow."

"Don't." Hillyard was gruff, blunt.

"You don't suspect . . ."

"Why not? You could at least send a telegram at the next stop and verify his credentials."

"You are a cautious man, Mr. . . . eh . . ."

"Race Hillyard."

"Hillyard. Where have I heard that name before? Is your family into timber?"

"No."

"Glass?"

"I'm afraid I'm the last of my family. All I want to do is get to California."

The judge reached for some gold coins in his vest pocket and stuck out his hand. "Think of these as a thank you from a very grateful father."

"There's nothing heroic about doin' the right thing, Judge. Keep the money to buy something special for Amanda Sue. She might have some nightmares over this."

"Amanda Sue is spoiled quite enough as it is. But she is already having daydreams about it."

"Oh, dear," Catherine added. "I trust they aren't too bad."

"She told me when she grows up she's going to marry a gunman, just like the Texican who saved her life."

Catherine laughed. "My . . . the nightmares are worse than I imagined."

The judge wiped sweat from his bushy, gray eyebrows. "At least grant me the honor of treating you to supper soon. I'm sure Amanda would enjoy the visit, too."

Hillyard shook his outstretched hand. "Judge, if we stop any place long enough to eat a decent meal, we'll take you up on it."

"Actually, I brought my own cook with me. I was thinking of us eating in my car."

"Amanda Sue said you had a private car," Hillyard replied.

"I'm sure that sounds quite snobbish."

"Snobbery is not limited to a particular class," Catherine said. "We'll be happy to join you."

As the train rattled west through the night, black air raced around them as if late for an important meeting. Catherine leaned against Race's shoulder. "I wonder what else this train holds that we don't know about?"

"You can check it out when you get to your Pullman compartment."

Catherine tried to brush a smudge off her blue-gray sleeve, but only lengthened it. "I'm beginning to question that decision. But I will never admit it to you, Race Hillyard."

Hillyard pulled off his worn suit coat and slipped it over her shoulders. "I don't know. Having you in a safe Pullman compartment might be best. Don't you think your Phillip would want you to have the best?"

She pulled the coat tight. It reeked of dust, gun-powder, sweat and leather. *Catelynn used to say that's the smell of "man."*

"I believe you are right about that. But the judge and Amanda Sue weren't any safer in his private car than we are back here. At least we have the soon-to-be legendary Race Hillyard."

He laughed. "Sometimes, Miss Catherine, you make my heart happy."

"And other times?"

"I'm tempted to throw you off the train."

The prairie sprinted by them. "Please wait until we slow down. I know I can be difficult. My poor parents had to put up with two of us."

"I am sure you two were the delights of their lives."

"Race, I hope so. I do wish . . ." She brushed her eyes.

"I know . . . I know . . . we were robbed of our families."

"You have a mother."

"Who refuses to write to me. And you a sister."

"Whom I don't speak to."

When the train hit the bend, she grabbed his arm.

"Shall we go back inside?" he offered.

"The cool air feels good out here, now that I have a jacket."

"Don't you think your reputation might be hampered, standing out on this platform for such a long time with the likes of Race Hillyard?"

Catherine poked him in the ribs.

No fat . . . just muscle.

"Listen, Hillyard, like it or not, we are linked already in everyone's mind in that train car. I'm sure the gossip is flying around about us even as we speak."

"Then let's head back."

She blocked his way. "Are you afraid of the dark?"

"I'm afraid of the things I think about in the dark." He held the door open for her.

A faint, dim glow greeted them as they re-entered the car. Passengers coughed and snored as the train car shook and rattled to a steady rhythm.

"They all went back to sleep," she whispered.

"So much for juicy gossip."

"I didn't say anything about 'juicy' gossip. Just what were those thoughts you had in the dark, Mr. Hillyard?"

"Ah . . . now we're getting back to our proper roles."

"You mean question and accuse?"

"Something like that."

"Maybe we should try to get some rest, too."

He pointed to the seats facing each other that had been vacated by the outlaws. "You want to get that sleeping rig for these seats? I'll take the bench behind Francine and you can have this all to yourself."

"Are you kicking me out?"

He collapsed on the padded seat and slid to the window. "I'm too tired to do anything else. If there is any more trouble, I expect you to take care of it."

She slipped in beside him. "Give me a gun. I'll take the first watch . . . isn't that what you say? Then I'll wake you later, and I'll get some sleep."

"If you shoot someone, do it quietly."

99

Her bare fingers felt dry, chapped. "Did you reload both revolvers?"

"Yep."

"Will you promise to pick up the story and tell me about the armory business later?"

"Yeah. . . ."

"Is it related to why you are going to California?"

"Yeah."

"Are you really going to sleep now?"

"I hope so."

Catherine watched his steady breathing.

I have no idea why I'm learning so much about Race. I will get off the train in Sacramento and fall into Phillip's arms and marital bliss. Race is so abrupt. Almost harsh. And yet, I think I know him as well as anyone. But there is so much more hidden deep.

Someone in the back of the car sneezed. She peered around. The six teen girls sprawled on each other's shoulders. The wild man with the long matted hair waved his handcuffed hands at her and grinned. She spun back around.

Race doesn't seem to get anxious about anything. It must rub off some. I can't imagine going through all that and not being terrified to inaction. What a strange trip this is. All I wanted to do is get a Pullman compartment and ride in solitude until we get to Sacramento. Yet, there hasn't been a peaceful mile. What are you telling me, Lord?

The clatter of rails softened as the train reached a straightaway and regained full speed. She thought she heard a faint shout, but now it seemed so distant it didn't matter. Her chin slumped to her chest. She felt like she floated on the crest of a cool breeze.

"Some nights seem like years."

At the sound of Hillyard's voice, Catherine shot up. "What do you mean?"

"A man closes his eyes, listens to the clank of the rails and feels the sway of the car, then sleeps. In a little while, you open your eyes, miles have passed by unnoticed. People live out there. There are ranches, homesteads, mines and a gully full of teepees. People work and play and argue and we've just chunked by them, perhaps never to come this way again."

"Very philosophical, Mr. Hillyard."

"Just looking at myself. I go through life like a train. I ignore anything that's to one side or another, and run over anything in my way."

She leaned against the back of the seat and closed her pale blue eyes. "And you claim that's not philosophical?"

"Robert was the philosopher," Race insisted.

"He read the classics? Aristotle, Socrates . . . Plato?"

"And the contemporaries . . . Kant, Rousseau and Dr. Samuel Davidson."

"I've never heard of Davidson."

"Good. Robert claimed he was locked into his intellect and never relied on reason, common sense, nor the Holy Ghost for his writings."

"I would like to meet Robert some day. I like him already."

"I paled in his shadow," Hillyard looked away from her. "In some ways the smartest man I've ever been around."

"You're using past tense. Is he . . .?"

Hillyard jammed his thumb and forefinger in the corners of his eyes, as if to block the tears. "He died a couple months ago."

"Oh, dear Jesus. I'm so sorry, Race. I had no right to stir up your sorrow. Please accept my apology."

"I haven't been able to mention his name since his death. It's time to get beyond that."

"I will ask no more questions." She studied the dust and dirt on the cuffs of his jacket. "Would you like your coat back?"

"Sometime before Sacramento."

"I'll listen to whatever you want to talk about."

"Anything? Okay, the dog's name is Gibraltar." The words shot out like a poke in the rib.

"What dog?"

"The Mormon's."

"What Mormon?"

"The one with a beard, fat squatty dog and six daughters."

"They are his daughters? But they are so close in . . ."

"They don't have the same mamma, I reckon. Anyway, the dog's name is Gibraltar. I knew you'd want to know."

Catherine glanced over her shoulder; the girls still slept on each other's shoulders. "Yes, eh . . . thank you. I was curious about the girls. It was very brave of them to try to distract the kidnappers. What else do you know about our companions?"

"The miners will get off at Cheyenne and head to the Black Hills."

"But isn't that Sioux land that is off limits?"

"It was, but there's gold up there. They've found a way to sneak in."

"And the man in irons?"

"Being returned to New Mexico, where he slaughtered four Mexican merchants for a wagon full of guitars."

"Guitars?"

"He came across them down on the border and assumed they were bringing in some rich Spanish treasures. They were smuggling guitars instead. He was scheduled to be hung in Socorro, but escaped."

"I'm amazed at your power of observation. How did you discern all of this?"

"That last part I read in the Omaha newspaper before we left."

Catherine envisioned their meeting on the train platform. "I was a little busy in Omaha."

A smile cracked across his tanned, leathery face. "I'd say you were."

"That just might be your first big smile, Mr. Hillyard."

"It was a comedy to behold."

She raised her hands to her gritty cheeks. "If you don't mind, I'd rather inter that scene in the past."

"Not that it wasn't a fine kiss, mind you. But, some things are better left buried. Some things . . . but not all things." Race gazed straight ahead and lowered his voice. "Robert liked to take the train to San Francisco . . . on the express in a Pullman compartment. About a year ago we got a letter from Mr. Charles Crocker in San Francisco."

"Doesn't he own this railroad?"

"He and some others. He had heard of our armory and wanted to talk to us about opening one in California. So Robert came out to discuss the matter."

"And you stayed in Texas to run the business?"

"Yep. Well, it was quite an ambitious project. Crocker and some of his banker pals wanted to build a huge armory on the bay at a place called

Benicia. They would finance it. Robert and I would come out and run it for them."

"Sounds like quite an opportunity."

"Robert turned them down."

"Why?"

"He said we didn't want to work for wages, that we'd only be interested if we could invest in the plant ourselves and work out a partnership. Like I said, he was the businessman."

"And philosopher. So, what did Crocker and his pals say to that?"

"They finally went along with it. But in order for us to buy into the partnership, we would have to sell the armory in Texas to raise the capital."

"Ah, a drastic move."

"So Robert came home with a wild business plan and rose pink lipstick on his shirt collars."

"A lady was involved?"

"That's another story."

"You're right . . . I will ask no questions." Catherine scooted closer to Hillyard so she could hear his low, gravelly voice.

"Robert was all excited to sell out and move, but I refused."

"Oh, dear."

"I told him I was not going to leave Texas."

"A certain home state loyalty, I suppose."

"Nope. I tried to tell him it was too risky. We had a nice set up and lots of folks employed. But he saw through all of that."

Catherine put her bare hand on his shoulder, then pulled it back. "I suppose that's another story, too."

"Robert can be persuasive. He spent the next few months with business projections for the Texas Armory, as opposed to the one in California. He got letters from senators and congressmen about government contracts for Crocker, once the armory was built. He even had photographs of fine houses on Nob Hill, where we could raise our families."

"And you gave in?"

"I told him we'd sell the Texas business and invest in the one in California, but I wasn't going to leave Texas for a while. There were, uh, more important things."

Catherine's eyes popped open like a swing door being kicked from the backside. "I won't even ask her name."

"And I wouldn't tell you if you did."

Catherine stretched her arms straight back and felt them relax. Her right hand drooped into the aisle of the coach. "Oh!" She looked down at the floor. "Well, how do you do?"

Hillyard glanced over. "You got a friend?"

"Mr. Gibraltar is licking my fingers."

"How do you know it's Mr.?"

"No one would name a girl dog that, would they?" She studied the animal. "He is definitely a male. I wonder what breed?"

"Spoiled."

She shooed him away with a flip of her hand. "Honey, you go back to where you belong."

"You talkin' to the dog . . . or me?"

"You are not going anywhere, Mr. Hillyard. You haven't finished your story."

"Where were we?"

"You were in Texas, Robert in California. . . ."

"He was there with all our assets. I got hit by some difficult situations, so I headed . . ."

Catherine grabbed his arm. "She turned you down?"

"You promised. . . ."

"You're right. No questions." She released her grip. "I'm sorry."

"I figured on going down to Brownsville and visit some pals from the war before I joined Robert in San Francisco. In the meantime, he tried to telegraph me, but it didn't get through. I returned to Houston around the first of April to pack up my belongings."

"And Mr. Walker?"

"Yep." Race stretched his long legs out under the seat in front of them. "The morning after I got home, Robert arrived."

"What a surprise." Catherine leaned forward to check on the sleeping Francine and children.

"Shock is more like it."

"Did he have lipstick on his shirts? Sorry . . . no questions about women." She started to pull her hand back from his shoulder.

Hillyard placed his on top of hers. "Robert looked awful, like he hadn't slept in weeks. Like someone stuck in a mineshaft."

She raised her dark brown eyebrows. "I know the look."

"Yet he didn't want to talk. He was so concerned about me and . . ."

"And what's-her-name. But I'm not asking."

"Robert suggested we go out and celebrate the fact that we were together and whatever the future brought, it would be the Hillyard brothers facing it."

"Did you make a night of it?"

"We ate too much, smoked too many big cigars and drank way too much. Neither of us had ever been much of a drinker, but we both must have had a lot to forget that night."

"Wouldn't it be nice to be able to forget all the things we want to forget?"

"Sounds nice, but ever' time I've tried to play God, I just mess it up all the more."

She closed her eyes again and stretched her neck. "Yes, I suppose we would abuse the gift."

"Meanwhile, our house had been sold for cash for the California project, so I was staying at a hotel. Robert insisted on his own separate room. I woke up in bad shape the next day about ten in the mornin'. I cleaned up a bit and knocked on Robert's door. When he didn't answer, I figured he was sleepin' it off. I kicked the door open just to check on him."

Catherine sat straight up and opened her eyes. "I don't think I want to know," she murmured.

Hillyard's words lumbered out slow, as if they had been in hibernation. "He wrote me a long letter, then . . . he . . . he took his revolver and . . ."

"No, Race." Her hand flew to her mouth. "You don't have to say it."

"Maybe I need to. My brother, whom I idolized from the time I was two. My brother who was loved by all people. My brother who trusted in Jesus as Lord and Savior every day of his life, put a bullet through his brain, all because he couldn't face me."

Tears streamed down her dusty face. She couldn't look at him. She didn't want to look at anyone. She tried to think of something to say. She wanted to talk about God's love and grace and goodness. Catherine wanted to think of springtime and daffodils and smiling babies and young men laughing. But all her thoughts, all her visions, all the images in her mind turned dark, frightening, depressing. She fumbled in her valise for a white linen handkerchief with violet embroidery.

Hillyard reached his hand over and she clutched it.

The train rumbled. Miners snored. Francine

murmured in her sleep. Catherine couldn't stop weeping. "I'm so sorry, Race. It breaks my heart."

Now his voice rang clear, strong. "In his scrawling, ten page letter, Robert explained that while in Crocker's office going over the architect's design of the armory, a team of mining engineers burst in with a pile of papers, maps, deeds and a proposition. They had discovered an incredibly rich diamond mine somewhere in the Montana/Wyoming/Idaho/Nevada region. They wouldn't disclose where. They sought financing. Crocker laughed them out of the office."

She wiped back the tears, then coughed. "I didn't know there were diamonds in the West."

"Neither did anyone else."

"Oh, dear. . . ."

"But these guys persisted. They returned with New York bankers, diamond experts from Tiffany's, mining men from Amsterdam, all convinced of the mine's authenticity. Finally, Crocker put together his own team of geologists and engineers and a few curiosity seekers, including Robert, to go out and inspect the mine site. They had to wear head masks for two days during the trek."

Catherine folded the wet handkerchief and tucked it back into her valise. "An incredible story."

"The mine was deemed authentic. The potential

investors were satisfied. They kept it a secret from others in San Francisco and New York, so there wouldn't be a diamond rush. And Crocker invited Robert to join in."

"How much did he invest?"

"Robert said he prayed about it a lot and sent me a telegram."

"But you were in Brownsville, recovering from a broken romance?"

"Yeah," he winced. "The deal turned out that the mine owners did not want to sell stock. They wanted ten backers to put in $100,000 each. None could put in more. None less. They felt like they could keep it out of the public eye with such a limited partnership."

"Did you and Robert have $100,000?"

"It took every penny from the sale of the armory, houses, Texas property, savings . . . everything. Crocker had to go to Washington, so he instructed his banker to seal the deal for him. They projected that in six months the mine would pay dividends. The initial funds would be returned in twelve months. And they could expect anywhere from $500,000 to a million dollars apiece within the life expectancy of the mine, about five years."

"I've never even heard of that much money."

Hillyard sighed. "Robert had a plan. Running the armory would tie us down to long days and years. He had always been fascinated with

William Cary's missionary work in India. He carried in his wallet Cary's phrase, 'Expect great things from God, attempt great things for God.' "

"And he felt God's leading?"

Hillyard paused. "I don't know. He thought that even if we only double our money, we could live handsomely on the dividends. This, eh . . . beautiful society lady from San Francisco shared his dream and he wanted me to be able to remain in Texas with . . ."

"Don't tell me her name."

"He wanted to go to the Orient and encourage Christian mission work."

Catherine rubbed her forehead to ease the beginning of a headache. "So he invested it all . . . and it turned out to be a ruse."

"A total deception. Only six of the investors proved legitimate. Crocker, and his pals . . . and Robert. The other so-called New York bankers acted as shills. The geologists, jewelers, and engineers were either paid off or duped into writing the report."

Catherine now massaged her stiff neck. "Even the lady with the rose pink lipstick?"

"Yes. She was an actress from Denver. The main crooks were last seen on a steamer to South America."

"South America? That's a wild and faraway destination."

"And safe, I suppose. Crocker and the others

took their lumps but they had plenty of assets left. He felt sorry that he had gotten my brother into this. He offered to go ahead and build the armory as planned. My brother and I could work for wages as plant superintendents. But he wanted to keep the diamond swindle quiet so he wouldn't be a laughingstock. "

"There's no way to recover the funds?"

"That's what Robert claimed in his note. He came back to break the news. I think the drinking contributed to his action. Never in his life did he get that drunk. So, he wrote the confessional letter. He said he knew he had let me and the Lord down. He couldn't face me, and would take his chance on the grace of God."

"We all are accountable, I suppose."

"Well, both me and the Lord have forgiven him. After I buried him, I went sort of crazy and rode down a long the border. I worked some ranches this spring and then I took on a job to drive two-hundred mustangs across Texas into the Indian Nation by myself."

"That sounds impossible."

"To tell you the truth, I was hopin' to get ambushed. Mexicans, Comanches, outlaws . . . anyone. I was prayin' that someone would shoot me out of the saddle, but had bad luck that way. By the time I delivered them in the Territory, I made up my mind what to do next. I took five of those mounts and rotated them, riding straight up to Omaha without sleeping. When a horse broke down, I just turned him out. That's when I first met you at the depot. I know I was in a lousy mood. Two old boys tried to rob me right before I saw you. Shoot, I reckon I'm still in a lousy mood, although tossin' an outlaw off the train did perk me up a little."

Catherine felt a heaviness even as she offered a half-smile. "Oh, Race, I'm so sorry. You struggled with real life while I played games at the station. I apologize for my arrogance. What will you do in California?"

"Robert wrote that several of the side characters in the charade, including the woman, remain still in the San Francisco area. I figure I owe them a visit."

"Are you going to kill them?"

"I doubt it. But I'd like to get a lead on those in South America. I'd might kill them if I found them. I won't be able to rest until there is some justice meted out." He stopped to stretch his arms and legs. "I've never told any of this to anyone."

"Not even. . . ."

"Not even Miss Charity Ann Johnson." He stared out the window. "A fascinating woman can make a man do dumb things."

"Hmm . . . beautiful and fascinating, I'm guessing."

"You know, in the moonlight of Galveston

Bay, her hair looked like . . ." Hillyard gaped at the window. "Hey, daylight's breaking across the prairie. Makes me want to sip strong, boiled coffee around a campfire and ride and ride and ride."

"Whoa, wait a minute. I feel like I've just got bucked off a horse. I thought we were talking about the fascinating Charity Ann . . . and now we're boiling coffee?"

"I changed the subject."

"I see that. I just need to brush myself off and get back on. I didn't anticipate that sudden turn."

"Catherine, do you like to ride horses?"

"I've been around horses my whole life. I love to ride. Can I tell you a secret that no one but Catelynn knows?"

"I'd be honored."

"I love straddling a horse and riding bareback."

"Heavens! How shocking," he grinned.

"I know, I know. Did you ever ride a horse sidesaddle?"

"I don't believe I have."

"It's the most uncomfortable and stupid way to ride ever proposed by mankind. And I do believe men invented it."

"I'll take your word on it."

"If daylight was breaking, and you were out by that campfire, and you mounted a good horse, where would you go?"

"Doesn't matter. Sometime you just have to ride hard and try to leave the past behind."

"I've never done that, but there are times to run away."

"Isn't that what you are doing right now?"

She thought of Phillip's last letter and the glowing description of the home being built for them. "I suppose I am running . . . but I do have someone waiting for me."

"For that, Catherine Goodwin, I envy you. As far as I know, there is no one, anywhere, that's waiting for me."

"How about your mother?"

"We didn't part with pleasant words."

"Did you tell her about Robert?"

"I sent her a short telegram."

"How short?"

"Two words. 'Robert died.' "

Francine sat up and spread her massive arms. "Good morning. I trust that was a bad dream last night. Or did you two kick a half-dozen gun-slingers off the train?"

"Race did the hard part."

"You rushed that old boy with the gun as if you knew it was going to misfire."

"Race removed Cantu's bullets earlier."

"You knew it was empty?"

Catherine nodded.

"Well, ain't you two the clever ones. It was as if I was in one of them dime novels." Francine propped a wide-eyed Preston in the corner of the blanket and stood in the aisle brushing down the wrinkles in her dress. "My Farley says I ought to write a book about the things I've done, and if I do, there will be a chapter on you two."

"Don't use up pages on us," Hillyard said.

"Oh, it will be a big book. Farley says everything I do is big."

Hillyard winked at Catherine.

The now clean shaven conductor strolled into the car and pushed his hat back. "Folks, we'll be stopping at Harrison's Siding in about ten minutes. You can buy breakfast there. Mrs. Harrison is one of the best cooks on the line. I'll give you forty minutes this time. I need to file some reports about last night's ruckus."

"Raw eggs. Solid fat bacon. Gritty coffee. Undercooked, bitter potatoes," reported Hillyard.

"Yes, but the rest of the meal was quite nice," Catherine teased. "After all, she's one of the best cooks on the line."

"Makes a person want to fast."

"Perhaps we'll have a decent meal with the judge."

"You don't see him and those around him enjoyin' Mrs. Harrison's fine cuisine."

"Do you think we have time for a stroll?" Catherine asked. "Sitting on a hard leather cushion for twenty-four hours seems to stiffen everything."

"I think so. Of course, you could have had a luxurious sleeping board and pillow."

"Don't start that again, Mr. Race Hillyard."

The muddy North Platte River paralleled the train tracks and scattered buildings at Patterson's Siding. Mountains of firewood blocked her view of the river, but as they strolled west, the river and the bluffs behind it appeared. To the south, short, dry, brown grass sprawled for miles across treeless, rolling prairie. Occasional wagon ruts recorded the direction of an intrepid pioneer.

The morning sky flashed a deep, royal blue, with high streaks of white clouds that looked like thick paint slung across the sky. A slight breeze drifted towards them as they trekked across dusty, rocky trail that served as Patterson Siding's only road.

Catherine's high, lace-up leather shoe slipped off the gravel. She grabbed Race's arm.

"Excuse me, Mr. Hillyard. I twisted my ankle." She stopped and stretched her foot.

"You're just trying to butter me up for a loan."

Catherine bent her finger, poking him in the ribs, then pulled her arm away. "You better be teasing me."

He reached over and slipped her arm back in his. "As long as the good Mr. Phillip Draper won't mind, I'm happy to assist a pretty lady on a walk."

"Hmmm . . . a compliment from Mr. Race Hillyard. Should I be suspicious?"

He continued to lead her along the train cars. "I'd be disappointed if you weren't, Miss Catherine Goodwin."

Catherine studied the faces in the train car looking back at them. "You know, Race, yesterday I held you in deep disgust."

"Has that changed?"

"Yes, today I hold you in mediocre disdain."

"I'm glad my charm is growing on you."

"I wouldn't call it charm. You are quick to speak, opinionated and quite thoughtlessly blunt."

His wide grin startled her. "And what are my negative qualities . . . besides being dirty, unshaven, and poorly dressed?"

"I must admit, I would enjoy seeing you cleaned up some time. As, I'm sure, you would me."

"Nope. I like you dusty and droopy."

Catherine's back stiffened. She jerked her hand away from his. "I am not droopy."

"All tall ladies tend to droop their shoulders."

"But I most certainly do not. I have been disciplining myself not to slump my shoulders since I was eight. I do not droop." She stomped several steps ahead of him.

"Whoa, I can see that is a sensitive subject."

"You have no idea how sensitive tall women can be about their height." Catherine strolled along the train cars in front of him, nodding to passengers who stared out.

Hillyard scurried to catch up. "I suppose it's too late to say that you carry yourself well and that I believe a tall lady stands out like a queen in a crowded room."

She pointed her small nose up at the pale blue Nebraska sky. "It is entirely too late. As long as I live, I will never forgive you for calling me a drooper."

Hillyard pushed his hat back. "I reckon this means you will not be taking my arm any time soon."

"I most certainly will not." With a curled lip and a smirk, a tall, mustached man on the train with a three-piece suit and a crisp black bowler caught her eye. *Zane? Matthew Zane? What is he . . . ?*

She twirled with her back to the train and slung her arms around Race Hillyard's neck, planting her full lips against his narrow, chapped ones.

CHAPTER FIVE

Catherine's lips slid next to his ear. "Nothing personal," she whispered.

"It's personal to me," he said.

"Take me back to the train car without letting anyone on the Pullman see my face," she insisted.

"You're hiding this time?"

"Yes."

"So, I get a kiss because you want to hide from someone. If I had been a bale of cotton, you could have ducked behind me without kissing."

"Please, Race, I can explain later. And you can tell me what I should have done. Please."

Hillyard shielded her from the train car as they scurried back down the tracks. "Is it okay if I admit that I don't understand you at all?"

"Quite acceptable." Catherine glanced over her shoulder. "Most days I don't understand myself either."

They stopped near the door to their train car.

"Okay, we are out of sight. What's this all about?" he prodded.

"Wait until we get inside."

"This is crazy."

"Be patient."

He held her arm and she pulled herself up the steps. "You're trembling. Are you mad or scared?"

"Both."

Other than a sleeping prospector on a back seat, the train car was empty. The windows were down, but little breeze filtered through. The dry air felt dry, dusty, stale.

"Francine fixed our seats again. How nice." Catherine patted the saddle horn. "Mr. Walker, I trust you had a peaceful night. What? You didn't get a wink of rest? First, a little girl hid behind you. Then all night you trembled in fear that the sleeping board would collapse? I can see your difficulty. You sit right over there by the window and rest."

Race tugged off his wide-brimmed hat. "Did I ever tell you it gets on my nerves when you talk to my saddle?"

"Why do you think I do it? But I'll make you a deal. Let me sit by the window and I won't pester Mr. Walker."

"Sit by the window? Does this have anything to do with your latest charade kiss and hiding from some unknown interloper?"

Catherine sat by the window and patted the seat next to her. Dust fogged up. "Yes, but I must admit I rather enjoyed the kiss. Didn't you?"

"Enjoy?" When Race plopped on the cushion,

she bounced up an inch or two. "I was in such a state of shock, I could have been kissing a carp."

"Oh, so you think I kiss like a carp? I don't believe anyone has ever told me that before."

"Maybe you had them all buffaloed."

"I assume charm is a foreign concept to you."

"For Pete's sake, Catherine . . . skip the carp, and charm . . . and tell me what in the world is going on. Who is it that you so didn't want to have see you that you would actually go against your best interest and kiss the likes of me?"

"I assure you, it was in my best interest to hide behind your lips."

"Do I need to pull my gun and point it at you to get you to talk?"

"Why is it that you must always resort . . . yes, well . . . this is not easy to talk about."

"Nothing we have discussed of any importance has been easy."

"I agree. Okay . . . listen . . . you know about my sister?"

"You have a twin sister named Catelynn who lives in New York City and is trying to break in as an actress, but she is as tall as you are and finds parts scarce."

"Yes, well . . . Catelynn is currently . . . eh . . . she has a, eh . . . ."

"She's living with some guy she's not married to?"

"Yes, and it breaks my heart. She's a wonderful woman, and she knows better, but she's been running away from God ever since Mamma and Daddy died."

"She blames God for their deaths?"

"Catelynn blames Him for their deaths, the entire Civil War, and most of the natural tragedies of history."

"Everything bad is His fault?"

"I suppose it's that way. Oh, Race, I love her dearly. But she believes He is sovereign, so that all this could have been prevented, if He wanted it to."

"Does she believe in the sinful nature of mankind?"

"Oh, yes, and she's not sure why God allowed that either."

"But what does your sis have to do with the kiss?"

Catherine raised her rounded eyebrows. "The carp kiss?"

"Catherine, just forget . . ."

She brushed down the front of her dress. "I'm droopy and kiss like a carp. You know how to impress a girl, Hillyard."

"Catherine! I might not live long enough to find out why you kissed me."

When Francine entered the car, there was a sideways sway, as though the train were moving. "There you two are. I was looking for you. They say we're stuck here a while. We have to wait for another express train. Here, hold Preston and Nancy while I go, eh, powder my nose."

Nancy stood in Catherine's lap. "I'm hungry."

With gloved hand, Catherine tried to wipe a smudge off the child's cheek. "Didn't you just eat breakfast?"

"I didn't like it. I gave mine to Preston."

Hillyard held the little boy in front of him as if he were a leaking bucket. "I need a little help here."

"Why don't you just shoot him?" Catherine chuckled.

Nancy's eyes grew large. "Is he going to shoot Preston? Can I watch?"

"That's just a joke, honey. Of course he's not going to shoot him. He might drop him out the window, but he won't shoot him."

Nancy puffed out her cheeks, then blurted out, "Just like he did the devil?"

Hillyard still held the wiggling Preston at arm's length. "What did I do?"

"Mamma said that the bad man was acting like the devil and Mr. Hilly threw him off the train."

Catherine clapped her gloved hands. "I like that. Mr. Hilly threw the devil off the train. That would make a nice title for a book, don't you think so, Mr. Hilly?"

Race's attention fixed on Preston's sagging

drawers. "Catherine, I need some help."

She sat Nancy on the floor next to him. "Come on, Preston, let's go find your mamma. You watch Nancy."

"I don't want to stay with him," the little girl muttered. "He might throw me out the window."

"I'm not going to throw anyone out the window. But if I did, it would be a Goodwin twin. And I wouldn't do that until the train is moving."

"Come along with us, Nancy. Mr. Hilly is in a surly mood."

When she returned alone, Race was slumped in the window seat. "Are you asleep, Mr. Hillyard?"

"Of course not."

"Why are you hiding under your hat?"

He sat up. "Just hiding from the bogyman in the Pullman compartment."

"But you don't even know who is up there."

He pushed his hat back. "And at the present rate, I may never know."

She perched next to him. "Nonsense. It's Matthew Zane."

"Who is?"

"Catelynn's, eh . . ."

"The one she lives with?"

"Yes. I detest him with every bone in my body."

"The Lord can help you with that."

"Oh, He has . . . I'm much more calm around

him that I used to be."

"Calm? That panic kiss was calm?"

"What I wanted to do was pull your revolver and shoot him dead. Zane has dominated Catelynn for years. He tells her what she can do and not do, what friends she can make, or can't make. He takes every cent she earns, encourages her to drink with him, and when he's drunk tends to beat her."

"Why would she stay with such a jerk?"

"She loves him."

Hillyard tossed his hat over the saddle horn and tried to smooth down his matted hair. "And can't admit failure to her school teacher sister?"

"Perhaps. He dresses her up in gowns and jewels and shows her off around town. Says it's good for business."

"What kind of business?"

"He calls himself a promoter."

"And he promotes what?"

"Everything. Anything. Prizefights. Real estate. Art auctions. Railroads. The list goes on and on, but all seem to be on the shady side."

"So, Catelynn's the diversion?" Hillyard seemed to be studying her face. "They are all looking at a beauty, while he slips a hand in their bank account?"

"I suppose, but I've never really thought of Catelynn as a beauty."

His stare intensified. "She's your identical

twin, isn't she?"

"Thank you for the compliment, Mr. Hilly."

"It was just a statement of fact. Nothing personal."

"It was personal to me."

"So, you spotted him on the train, don't want to see him . . . and used the old kiss-a-cowboy diversion?"

Catherine tugged off her soiled, pale yellow gloves and fiddled with her fingers.

I can't wait to have a ring to wear. Oh, Phillip, you promised a gold ring with a large stone. Right now I'd settle for a small band of gold and a hot bath.

"Right after Christmas, I traveled to New York to inform Catelynn what was happening with the family estate in Virginia. When I saw her situation this time, I couldn't hold back. I railed at her."

"About all the things you didn't like in her life."

"The list started with Matthew Zane. Then her weight gain. And how she lived a life that would have grieved Mother and Daddy. She let me know with a choice variety of words, that I knew nothing about all that she faced. After our screaming fight, I stormed out. I haven't spoken to her since then. I sent a note of apology last February, but didn't hear back. I don't know why I had to say all those things. They were true, but not helpful to either of us. I talk too much and am way too tactless."

"I've been accused of being insensitive and blunt."

"I'm sure you have." She didn't smile. "Then I met Zane in the hall as I left the building and told him what I thought of him."

"You didn't shoot him in the leg?"

"That's not funny, Race Hillyard. I detest the man. I don't trust him. And hate what he has done to my sister. I don't want to ever see him again."

"How do you know your sister isn't with him now?"

"He goes to San Francisco often and she's never allowed to accompany him."

"I wonder why that is?"

"He's crook and a liar. She'd be in his way on one of these trips, I suppose. He would only bring her if it was to his advantage."

"Maybe he has, eh, you know, other living arrangements out west. He doesn't seem to worry too much about gettin' married. I've heard of that kind of thing."

"I've thought of that, too."

"So, when he's gone, Catelynn has a little time to herself?"

"Not really; his associate, Chet Pinehurst, keeps an eye on her."

"Doesn't sound like a happy life."

"When she's out on the town, she loves it. Catelynn loves the social functions, and pretending she's someone important. I don't think I'm much better than she. I said all of those things and made her hate me for life. So, where does that put me? Race, I love her and we aren't even speaking. Isn't that pathetic?"

"Is that why you are dashing off to your beloved Phillip?"

"I am attracted to the idea I can start over. Maybe I can. I also realize all of those things hold a lingering effect on me. I have to get away. But, I need to know how to make things right with Catelynn. I'm not that wise yet."

"And seeing good old Zane today reminds you of the whole mess?"

She bit her lip and looked him in the eye. "Sometimes my failure at Christian charity is so appalling I wonder why the Lord doesn't give up on me."

"I reckon if he was only lookin' for perfect people, he wouldn't have many to choose from. So, the kiss was not only so Zane wouldn't see you, but so you wouldn't have to face your own failures?"

"Yes, I guess that's it."

"That will make your beloved Phillip's arms even more tender. He's the haven from all your strife."

"Well put, Race. For someone I hardly know,

you have become a good friend."

Hillyard cleared his throat. "Hardly know?"

"It's only been a day or so."

"Well, let's pretend you visited a friend every week. Say, you spent a couple of hours sharing things about your lives. What if you did this every week, without fail, for three months. Would you call that one a good friend?"

"Yes, I would, although I've had very few of those relationships."

"We've spent over twenty-four hours together, not more than a foot or two apart. That's like two hours a week for three months. And we've been in a number of emotional and stressful situations. I'd say we are better friends than the 'hardly know' stage."

Race, you continue to challenge my way of thinking. I think that's good.

"Bravo, Mr. Hilly. You make an excellent point. We are good friends. I'm hoping you will stop by Paradise Springs to see Phillip and me. I know you two will get along. He's much like you."

I think. I hope. Oh, dear, sweet Phillip . . . I'm not so sure I know you at all.

Two teenage girls in green gingham scooted up to them. "Mr. Hillyard, I'm Balera Jordan," the shorter one said. "You have to come quick. Papa wants you to shoot Gibraltar."

"What happened to your dog?"

"I'm Ermina. Please come quick. He's suffering a lot," the taller one added.

"The dog?" Hillyard said.

"No, Papa," Balera explained. "They are very close. But he's eaten something and gone mad. He's stuck under the train station."

"Your papa?" Catherine asked.

Ermina shook her head. "No, the dog. Calida and Damia offered to shoot him, but Papa wanted someone who . . ."

"Wasn't related to the family?" Catherine finished.

Hillyard shoved his hat back on. "I don't like shooting dogs."

"If it's something he ate, sounds like plant poisoning." Catherine shoved the girls down the aisle. "Race, you get Gibraltar out from under the station. I'll get a remedy from Mrs. Harrison."

"A remedy?" the girls parroted.

"An old Goodwin family secret remedy."

Mrs. Harrison's kitchen was a combination of three main layers of filth. Dishes and food were stacked on the floor, dirty dishes and food were piled on the counter, and dishes and food were stacked on the shelves. Open air-tight cans mixed with pots of beans and shards of hard bread. The aroma blended rotting fruit and cinnamon.

"Do you have any red apple vinegar?" Catherine asked.

Gray hair fell out of its pins. A once beige apron hung like a flag of surrender. Mrs. Harrison waved across the room. "Over there. Second shelf."

"And honey?"

"On the floor by the door, last time I saw it. What are you making?"

"A purgent, I hope. Where is your spice rack?"

"My what?"

"Never mind . . . I'll find it."

Catherine held two tin can cups when she rounded the train station. A crowd of onlookers had gathered, including six teenage girls in green gingham long-sleeve dresses. They all stared at Race Hillyard's boots. The rest of him burrowed under the building. Mr. Jordan, on hands and knees, peered low beside him.

Catherine bent low. She spied Race in the dirt, with a rope loop tied to a four-foot stick.

"Haven't you got him out yet?" she queried.

"He's not exactly cooperating. He keeps biting the rope," Mr. Jordan explained.

"Don't hurt him," Ermina wailed.

"Hurt him?" Hillyard grumbled. "You want me to pull him out and shoot him, but I shouldn't hurt him?"

"I think we should pray," one of the girls suggested.

A sister jabbed her with an elbow. "That's all you ever do."

Catherine stooped over again. "What's taking you so long?"

There was a growl and a frightened yip.

"He clamps onto the loop with his teeth, so I can't get it over his head," Hillyard roared.

"Drag him a little at a time," Catherine suggested. "When he chomps down, pull him towards you slowly . . . then when he turns loose, go for the loop around his neck again. He'll be so busy he won't realize you've moved him little by little."

"How did you figure that?" Mr. Jordan asked.

"It's how father used to get raccoons out from under the store," she explained.

"Did it work?" one of the girls pressed.

"Oh, yes."

The girl with her hands folded in front of her stepped forward. "What did he do with them when he got them out?"

"He shot them. He just didn't want dead animals decomposing under the store."

"Hey, it's working," Hillyard called out. "He slides fairly well in the vomit."

"I'm going to be sick," one of the girls whimpered.

"You always get sick," another replied.

Catherine motioned to one of the girls. "Get a wet sack to wipe him off. And grab that stick.

No, the big one. We have to shove it in his mouth so he can't bite anyone."

"Here he comes," Mr. Jordan shouted.

"Grab him," Hillyard called as he scooted out.

"He stinks!" one shrieked.

"Don't let him bite you," Catherine warned.

Mr. Jordan staggered to his feet. "There he goes."

"I'm not going to touch him." One of the girls backed away.

Hillyard tackled the panicked dog.

"Jam the stick in his mouth," Catherine called out. "Hold it there."

She poured a full tin can cup of liquid into the dog's mouth.

Covered with dirt and slime, Hillyard looked up at her. "How long do I hold him?"

"Until he's swallowed it all."

"Oh, he's swallowed it." Hillyard turned the dog loose.

Gibraltar threw himself into the dirt and wallowed in the muddy paste, then bolted towards the train. He stopped halfway, spun around six times, let out a tail-curling belch, and fell over on his side.

He didn't move.

"Is he dead?" one of the girls asked.

"No, he's quite well." Catherine brushed hair out of her eyes. "The medicine is doing its work."

Mr. Jordan waved his hands. "Girls, take the wet towels and go clean him up."

"All of us?"

"Yes, Adora, all of you."

Hillyard retrieved his hat. "I'm quite impressed, Catherine."

She shaded her eyes with her hand. "Thank you, Race. Not bad for a droopy woman who kisses like a carp."

"I need to clean up. What a mess." He brushed the dirt off his britches. "I don't suppose we could just forget all of that droopy stuff."

"Not in a hundred years. I am sure I'll go to my grave remembering those two things you said about me."

He took a couple steps towards the train, then wobbled. "Why don't we just get back on board? I can sleep and you . . . can . . . whew . . . wow."

She held his arm. "What is it?"

"It's like someone kicked me in the gut." Hillyard stumbled to the train platform and collapsed on a small wooden barrel. "Mrs. Harrison's plate wasn't that bad, was it?"

One of the girls followed them. "You've lost color in your face. You don't look so good."

"What is this? Oh, man . . ." Race scooted over and laid on his back on the rough wooden train platform. He glanced up at Catherine. "You have my permission to shoot me."

"Maybe Mr. Hilly should have the rest of the medicine," the girl suggested.

Catherine nodded. "You might be right."

He waved them off. "That's for dogs."

"You're sick as a dog. Drink it." She bent down and lowered the cup.

Hillyard held up his hand. "Will I run around in circles and fall over?"

"No, but you might belch. Drink it."

"What is it?"

"Slightly fermented red apple vinegar, honey and a couple of spices."

Hillyard held his stomach and rolled back and forth on the platform. "Are you sure it's fit for human consumption?"

"Shall I get the big stick and push it in his mouth?" the girl pressed.

"Grab his nose and yank it back quick."

The teenager pinched his nose and jerked it back. "Like this?"

"Wait!" he protested.

Catherine poured the entire contents of the can in his mouth. "Drink it all, Mr. Hilly!"

Hillyard gurgled and coughed. The girl let go of his nose. He laid still, wiped his mouth on his sleeve, and sat straight up. "I was going to take the stuff. You didn't have to . . ."

The belch started out deep and exploded so much that the girl in gingham jumped. Somewhere in the distance, Gibraltar barked.

"Excuse me ladies. That was rather . . ."

"Purgitive?" Catherine asked.

"Eh, yeah . . . I reckon."

"Do you feel better?"

Hillyard stood and took a deep breath. "Yes, but I can't believe . . ."

She patted his arm. "Oh, ye of little faith."

"But I just drank the stuff, it can't . . ."

"It did, didn't it?"

The other girls crowded around.

"Oh, goody," Balera clapped. "Gibraltar is alright and Mr. Hilly is alright. What a glorious day."

"After a very horrible night," Calida added.

Damia smiled. "I thought it was quite exciting."

"You would," Adora added.

"Now, if you ladies would excuse me, I've got to clean up and find some fresh clothes. Although what I feel like doing is falling over in the dirt like Gibraltar and sleeping it off."

Everyone was reloaded in the coach when Race Hillyard pulled himself back on board.

"You look very nice, Mr. Hilly." Catherine said as she motioned him to slide next to the window.

"This is my last clean shirt and coat. Actually, the only ones. I tossed my soiled ones."

"Are you still sleepy?"

"Compared to how I feel now, being dead would be a picnic."

"Try to nap. I'll wake you if there is anything important."

"I think I'll give up eating and just live on air and water."

"That bad?" Catherine started kneading his neck and shoulders.

"You don't have to do that."

"I'll stop when it doesn't feel good anymore or you fall asleep."

Catherine stopped in less than twenty minutes.

Hillyard sat up quick, as if awakened by a pan of snow melt.

"It's dark?"

"You slept through the day."

He looked out the window. "I don't sleep like that."

"Well, you did. You missed seven long, tedious sidings, five stops, and Nancy singing 'Amazing Grace.' Other than that, it's been a delightfully dull day. No one was shot, kidnapped, or tossed off the train."

Francine leaned forward. "Did you know that Catherine can recite the entire alphabet in French?"

"As I said, a dull day."

"But aren't we suppose to have supper with the judge?"

"I postponed it. Seems Amanda Sue was a little sick also. We've got a long lay-over in Cheyenne. The judge offered a meal with them then."

"I'm wide awake," he announced.

"Good, we can talk about Texas."

They visited about battlefields, baseball, bulls, Boston and buffalo, but nothing personal. Once again, Francine and the children took the sleeping board seats. Catherine and Race sat behind her.

"Go on," she encouraged. "What happened next?"

"Like I said, Robert was fourteen and I was twelve. We'd never been to a city that big before so we . . ."

"Mr. Hilly?"

A gingham dressed young lady hovered beside him. "Does Adora stand for adorable?" he asked her.

Her face turned bright red. "Oh, no. Father just found old names that matched all the letters in the alphabet."

"Does he have twenty-six children?"

"Not yet."

"What can I do for you?"

"We are all tired, but we don't want to go to sleep and miss some of your stories. Would it be possible for you to wait and finish them in the morning?"

"You could hear me way back there?"

"I think everyone in the coach hears you."

"I'll try to be more quiet."

"Oh, no. We want to listen. But we want some sleep first."

The breakfast stop was early and they had only fifteen minutes. Hillyard drank a cup of steaming black coffee and munched on a wedge of sourdough bread.

"The eggs were tough," Catherine admitted. "You have the best part."

"I think my stomach still needs to calm down a tad. Another relaxin' day would help."

"Mr. Hillyard! Mr. Hillyard!"

The conductor trotted towards them.

The winded man in the dark serge uniform stopped to catch his breath. "Mr. Hillyard, I need your help. Johnny Socorro has escaped."

"The long-haired outlaw?" Hillyard pulled his gun and checked the cylinder.

The conductor waved toward the south. "He dove off into the brush."

"Where's the deputy?" Hillyard asked.

"They say Socorro knocked him out by slamming his head into the freight door."

Catherine took the coffee cup Race handed to her. "But they were handcuffed."

"Socorro threw the marshal across his shoulders and staggered off into overgrowth. As far as I know, they are still cuffed together."

Hillyard stared across the brushy prairie. "Does he have a gun?"

"And a knife, but no keys," the conductor explained. "The marshal didn't have any keys to the handcuffs. So he can't go far, all strapped together."

"If he has knife, he could get free," Hillyard said.

"You don't think that . . . oh, my word," the conductor slapped his hand over his mouth. "I think I'm going to be sick."

"Miss Draper knows how to cure weak stomachs. I'll go see what I can do, but I don't plan on gettin' shot over this."

Catherine watched Race duck between the train cars.

I don't think I've ever known anyone quite like him, Lord. He seems to attract crisis, yet never starts the trouble. He never backs down. I don't know if he's reckless or brave or just doesn't care about his life very much. I pity the woman who marries him. She would be in constant worry about his safety. On the other hand . . . on the other hand, I have no business thinking about his future wife. What I really want to know is, was that truly Matthew Zane? If so, what is he doing on this train?

"Was Mr. Hillyard ever a lawman?" the conductor asked.

"Not to my knowledge," she replied. "He fought in the war then owned an armory in Texas, until recently."

"He handles a gun and some tough men as if he had done it before."

"Some men are just that way."

"I suppose. I sure don't know what to do about Johnny Socorro and the marshal. Here comes the express. I need to get the train back on schedule."

"You can't go off and leave Mr. Hillyard."

The conductor pushed his cap back and scratched his head. "Quite right."

The passengers on the siding watched the express train rattle past them. Most of the blinds on the cars were pulled shut.

"Load up!" the conductor called.

"Mr. Hillyard is doing you a favor. I wonder if you could do me a favor? I need to know if there is a Mr. Matthew Zane from New York City on this train."

"I can't reveal passenger lists. It's a company policy."

"And it's a very fine policy, I'm sure. But this is a rather delicate situation."

"Delicate?"

"Yes. I noticed a man who looks a lot like a friend of my sister's. A very good friend, if you know what I mean."

"Oh, yes. Train conductors are very discreet."

"Well, if it is this friend of my sister's, I need to say something to him rather personal. But if it isn't, well, I can't be confused about it. I don't need to see your passenger list. Just read it through and nod your head if there is a Matthew Zane on the train."

"Really, I can't . . ."

Catherine touched his sleeve, then tilted her head. "I know I have no right to put you in such a bind. I don't want you to reveal anything more than a nod. Just think of me as your spoiled daughter."

"I'm not that old, lady."

She yanked her hand from his arm.

He tugged a list from his vest pocket. "What name?"

"Matthew Zane from New York City."

He looked around as if expecting someone to be spying on them, studied the list, then rubbed his chin.

"Well?" she asked.

He nodded his head.

Zane is on the train. What's he doing here? I need to know how Catelynn's doing . . . and why he's going west again . . . without him knowing that I'm on the train. Perhaps she's travelling with him this time. That would be a wonderful answer to prayer.

"There you are." Francine Garrity waddled up, a child in each hand. She shoved Nancy over to Catherine. "This delay is quite something. Most times we never have enough time to eat. Now, I got a little peckish and had another helping. That Indian lady is quite the cook. Are you getting back on board?"

"Yes, the conductor said it's time."

144

"It's all right with me. I've seen all of this part of Nebraska I want. Have you ever been to Cheyenne?"

"I've never travelled anywhere west of Pittsburgh until this trip."

"I've gone all over. That's before I hitched up to my Farley."

They settled back in their seats on the train. While Preston slept, Nancy studied a ladybug crawling on her arm. Francine leaned forward while Catherine sat across from the saddle.

"I hear that Mr. Hillyard was sent to apprehend that man in irons."

"I believe so."

"He's really something, isn't he?"

Catherine wrinkled her nose. "Mr. Hillyard or the man in irons?"

"If I weren't a married lady, I'd wrestle you for Hillyard."

Catherine gritted her teeth as she thought about wrestling the very large lady. "Well, you are married and I'm going to Sacramento to marry my Phillip, so I suppose other women will have to fight over him."

"That's right . . . I forgot about your Phillip . . . what with you and Hillyard being so chummy and all."

Catherine rubbed the bridge of her nose. "We have become friends, that's all."

Francine rocked back and forth. "That kiss up

there by the Pullman cars looked more than chummy."

"It was a diversion. I was hiding from someone. At least, I thought I was."

All the train car windows stood open, as the passengers filed back into the car. Adora, Balera, Calida, Damia, Ermina, and Faustina Jordan each stopped to curtsey for Catherine. Finally, Mr. Jordan strolled down carrying a sleeping Gibraltar.

He tipped his hat. "Once again, special thanks to you and your husband for rescuing my dog yesterday."

"I'm glad we could help, but he's not . . ."

"I bought Gibraltar when wife number one died. Gave me comfort in my loneliness."

After he had passed by, Francine whispered, "Didn't his other wives give him comfort?"

"I was wondering the same thing."

Francine sat back and folded her bare arms. "Now, tell me why that kiss with Race Hillyard didn't mean a thing."

"Only if you promise to keep it to yourself. And you have to help me do something."

"I promise."

Catherine whispered most of the account about Matthew Zane and his relationship with her sister.

"What can I do for you?" Francine asked.

"I need you to positively identify Matthew Zane for me."

"How am I going to do that? I've never met the man."

"He's wearing a red silk vest and has a thick, black mustache that is rather lopsided. He's six-foot tall, with hazel-colored eyes. You can't miss him. Check out his scar."

"What scar?"

"Upper lip, right side. He got hit by a sad iron."

"Your sister hit him with an iron?"

"No, I did."

"Another reason you don't want to see him, I suppose. What shall I say if I find him and he admits to being Matthew Zane?"

"Tell him you spotted him at the station and wondered whether Catelynn was with him."

"What if she is?"

"That would be far too great a coincidence. But if she is, you'll spot her. She looks just like me, only better dressed."

Francine brushed down her skirt, then stood. "You babysit. This trip has turned out to be more exciting than pullin' calves in January."

A gunshot from the brush along the south side of the tracks sent everyone scurrying to the other side of the train car, to peer out the windows.

"Mr. Hillyard?" Francine asked.

"That would be my guess," Catherine added.

Everyone at the windows began to cheer and clap.

Catherine picked up Nancy and carried her

across the car. By the time she shoved her way to a window, a dirt-covered Race Hillyard dragged an unconscious Johnny Socorro and the marshal next to the car.

"Are they dead?" someone shouted.

"They are just sleeping," Hillyard gruffed. "A couple of you fellows help me load them up so we can leave."

The westbound train was up to speed by the time Hillyard washed up and returned to his seat next to Catherine.

"I trust you are okay?" she asked.

"Yep. But I don't have any more clean clothes. Are you babysitting again?"

"Francine is doing an errand for me."

"Does it have to do with Mr. Matthew Zane?"

"Why did you say that?"

"Why did you avoid answering me?"

Catherine sat back and grinned. "Isn't this marvelous?"

"What?"

"The way we harp at each other. Do you have this same adversarial relationship with anyone else?"

"Nope."

"Neither do I. Don't you think it was rather ironical of the Lord to place each of us on a train, sitting next to someone so entirely different than ourselves?"

"Entirely different? I thought it was because we are so much alike," he grumbled.

"Mr. Race Hillyard, you and I have so very little in common."

"Besides being stubborn?"

She slipped her arm in his. "Yes, besides being bull-headed, pushy, blunt, soft-hearted, creative, courageous in the face of danger, handsome, and totally self-centered, we hardly have anything in common." Catherine laughed and laid her head on his shoulder.

"You forgot two things."

"Only two? What were they, besides both being pals of Mr. Walker?"

"We are both running away from something. And we are not sure of what lies up ahead."

"That's not true. I know what's up ahead for me. My precious Phillip will be there at the station to whisk me off to paradise."

"If you truly believed that, you wouldn't have you arm tucked in mine, or your head resting on my shoulder."

Catherine sat up quick and dropped her hands to her lap.

CHAPTER SIX

Francine Garrity sashayed down the aisle as if she were the prime exhibit at a county fair. "Matthew M. Zane, mining consultant and attorney."

Catherine studied her face. "Zane said he was an attorney? That's a new one."

"Yes, and Catelynn is not with him." Francine checked on the sleeping children before she wedged herself into the train seat. "I didn't speak to him direct. I spoke to his shadow, Chester Pinehurst. He said that . . ."

"Pinehurst is on the trip?" Catherine's hand flew to her chest. "He always stays in New York to watch Catelynn."

"Well, he's here now and he carries a sneak gun in his trousers."

"He told you that?"

"Of course not. But a woman can spot such things, if you know what I mean. To him, I'm Francine Garrity, an actress from Atlanta."

"Actress?"

"There are more big girl parts than tall girl parts."

Catherine noticed how Francine's amber eyes were deep-set in her round, full face.

Such pretty features.

"Perhaps you're right about that."

Francine folded her massive arms across her lap. "I told Chester I had been in a couple of plays with Catelynn and thought his boss looked a lot like her husband."

"Husband?"

"I didn't know what else to call him. Pinehurst told me Zane was a mining consultant and attorney from New York and wasn't married."

Catherine looked straight at Francine. "That's right, but he didn't acknowledge Catelynn at all?"

"Not to me. But Zane had the sad iron scar under the mustache."

"How did you get that close?"

"When I stooped to retrieve my handkerchief, he peeked at me then looked away. Men do that when I stoop. While his eyes focused elsewhere, I studied his upper lip. It's your Matthew Zane, alright."

"I just can't figure why Pinehurst is with him."

"Maybe he got a promotion and has someone else to watch your sis."

"Or perhaps, she ran him off like you suggested," Hillyard interrupted. "And there is no more relationship."

Catherine leaned her head back and sighed. "That would be too good to believe."

He tossed his hands in the air. "Is it that unreasonable possibility?"

"Knowing Catelynn, it is. She will hang in

there with a jerk, just to prove something to me. Being a twin is a blessing and a curse."

"Then why not think of it as a blessing?" he chided.

"You are an optimistic fellow all of a sudden."

"It's easier to be optimistic for someone else than for yourself."

Catherine shook her head. "You are pessimistic about your prospects of finding the men associated with the diamond swindle?"

"I know it's just ridin' blind. But the big disappointment is up ahead, so I pretend I'm doin' somethin' important and it helps me make it through the day."

Francine breathed on her with peppermint breath. "What are you goin' to do next, Catherine?"

"Try to stay away from Zane . . . and just ride it out until Sacramento. But with Pinehurst along, now I feel like I want to know about what's going on."

Hillyard slouched down in the seat and leaned against the backrest. "Why don't you just march straight up to him and say, 'Zane, you miserable snake, did my sister finally have enough good sense to kick you out on your cheatin' rear?' "

"I'm not sure he'd answer me even then."

"Then yank your gun and threaten to shoot him." Hillyard pulled his revolver. "You could tell him, 'I've shot crooked lawyers before, I can do it again.' "

"You've shot lawyers?" Francine gasped.

"I'm not confronting him with a gun. I really think I could get angry enough to pull the trigger. There must be some other way. We have time. I'll think of something."

"Just like that Goodwin woman, you shot a lawyer?" Francine pressed.

"We'll have that stop in Cheyenne. Why don't you send your sister a telegram from there? You could pick up her reply on down the line," Hillyard suggested.

"Both you and her are from northern Virginia and you both shot lawyers." Francine rubbed her chin. "Must be a nice place to raise girls."

"That would work, if she replied. You don't know my sister. She's as stubborn as . . ."

Hillyard raised his eyebrows. "You?"

"Wait a minute," Francine blurted out. "Your name can't be Draper. Not until you marry your beloved Phillip."

"Unfortunately, you are right. Patience died off with Mother and Daddy. Catelynn and I are very much alike at times."

"My brother and I weren't alike at all. He was more trusting. More theoretical. He drew motivation from grand ideas and themes. You know why he wanted the South to win the war? Not because of economics or to maintain the caste system or slavery. Robert's dream? Win the war. Chase all the Yankees north. Then, with complete independence, abolish slavery on our own. He thought we should do it because it was the right thing to do, not because we were made to do it."

The big woman scrunched her amber eyes. "You are that Goodwin woman."

"Eh, yes, Francine, but it's not what you think." Catherine turned back to Hillyard. "That's very noble. But I don't think it would have happened that way."

"Nor do I. But that was Robert. He believed not only in the sinful nature of mankind, but in the redemptive nature of God. He always elevated my thoughts about what God could do in this world . . . and in our lives. How I miss him."

"Glory, hallelujah. Thank you, Jesus. I got to meet that Goodwin woman. I'm so happy . . . so happy . . . I could . . . eh . . . tinkle. I'll be right back." Francine scurried down the aisle.

Catherine grasped his arm. "In a way, we have both lost our siblings . . . only there is a glimmer of hope that I can one day be reconciled with Catelynn. That's a good idea for me to telegraph her at Cheyenne. I wonder what it costs? My funds are limited, as you know."

"Slip your hand in my coat pocket."

"What?"

"Do it."

"Coins? I shall not take money from your pocket."

"Catherine, how I would love to telegraph Robert and tell him everything is okay, that it's not important about losing our funds. I'd like to tell him that the two of us will be brothers and good friends for our whole lives and nothing can come between us. But I can't do that. It's too late. But it's not too late for you and Catelynn. If you won't take the coin for my sake, do it in memory of Robert."

Catherine dabbed her eyes. "Race, that's the most eloquent eulogy I've ever heard. Yes, I will take the coins for Robert's sake. Sometimes you amaze me, Race Hillyard."

"And other times?"

"You annoy me beyond belief."

"But you aren't bored?"

"Never bored."

"Maybe I can do something about that."

"What are you going to do?"

"Sleep."

"Ah, sweet slumber. I believe Mr. Walker and I will do the same. He didn't get much rest last night."

"So I heard."

"If I nod off and my head bumps your shoulder, you won't think it improper."

"Of course not, but what would your beloved Phillip think?"

"You are right. I shall spend the day proper, rigid and restless."

Phillip . . . oh, my Phillip. I boarded the train with only you on my mind. How I longed for our life together. How I longed for an escape of the past. The trip getting to you has surprised me. It's like a test. Challenges to my character. To my bravery. To my past. I want to nap thinking of that beautiful little New England style house you built for us. The white fence, the manicured garden, the front porch . . . the big mirror above the entry table . . . the grand staircase up to the bedrooms . . . the oak, four-poster bed and thick comforters.

Catherine could feel her face flush.

No, perhaps I should not think of the upstairs rooms.

Stale air. Rumble of the rails. Rocking of the car. A sleepless night. Catherine awoke with her head snuggled against Race.

"Oh . . . I must have dozed off a little."

Hillyard sat up and shoved his hat back. "Two hours."

"Please forgive my impropriety."

"I didn't notice. I stirred only a couple of minutes ago."

He stood straight up, hat tumbling into Catherine's lap.

"Are you alright?"

"A cramp in my leg. Got kicked by a mule in the army and sometimes it locks up on me. Let

156

me out to the aisle and I'll walk it off. I might have to ride standing for a while."

Catherine rose up to let him pass. "Let's go out on the platform. Some fresh air would be nice. It's a little hot and sticky in here. I wonder if we ever have a lay-over long enough for a bath?"

She led the way to the front door of the car and stepped out into the wind and bright sunlight. "Look at this country. Just rolling prairie and thick grass as far as the eye can see. Such an empty land."

"I suppose some day it will be filled with people."

"What kind of people?"

"Ranchers, mainly. Maybe some homesteaders, if they find water."

Catherine studied the barren prairie. "Such a lonely place. No one for miles and miles. What kind of person could live here?"

"Lonely people, maybe. I like it. I'd build a cabin down in one of those draws. Hunt up there in the cedars. Maybe raise some horses to sell to the people movin' in. I could see doing it."

"So, are you one of those lonely people, Race Hillyard?"

"It's gettin' that way." He held up his hands as if to say "whoa." "That sounds way too melancholy. No self-pity here. I just don't have any plans beyond this trip to California."

Catherine grinned and pushed his hands down. "It sounded more like self-evaluation than pity.

Besides, I imagine your future wife will have something to say about where you live."

"Wife? I don't think so. But I'm not complainin'. I had my chance."

Catherine admired the way the wind made waves in the brown prairie grass. "Charity Ann is a beautiful name."

"She had sisters named Faith Mary and Hope Martha. But she was the beauty." He closed his eyes and smiled as if reviewing a file full of photographs. "Not sure there is any prettier in east Texas. But that's just one man's opinion."

"Blonde hair?"

"No, she was a radiant brunette, just like you. But her eyes . . . those blue eyes would . . ."

"Don't tell me she had 'dancing blue eyes,' " Catherine huffed.

Hillyard coughed. "What?"

"Every man describes the woman of his desires with 'dancing' eyes. What is it with men? Eyes don't dance. They don't bounce up and down. They don't sway to and fro. They don't bow and curtsey. They don't dance."

"I wasn't going to say anything about dancing eyes."

"Oh, well," Catherine sighed. "Forgive the outburst."

"I was just going to say they were so bright, so focused at times . . . well, when she looked at me, my heart danced."

"Ah, there it is. Hearts don't dance either, Mr. Hillyard."

"Mine did. It leaped. It swayed. It bowed with delight. She's graceful, intelligent, charming."

I wonder how my Phillip describes me?

"My, you are a poet today. How long did you know her?"

"We met in Sunday school. I was seven and she was four."

"Oh, my, childhood sweethearts."

"Nope. She was fat and dumpy and I was obnoxious and rude."

"You? A seven-year-old that was obnoxious and rude?"

Hillyard glared at her.

Catherine punched his arm. "Please go on."

"We were only casual family acquaintances. She went away to private school in New Orleans and lived with an aunt when the war broke out. I didn't see her again until after Dad died. She and her folks came to his funeral. So we struck up a friendship. One thing led to another."

"Your heart danced."

He stared right into her eyes. "It didn't seem to turn serious until Robert and I started doing well with the armory. As we became more prominent, we garnered invitations to more and more social events. Her father was a state senator from Houston. We got to meet a few important people at those parties."

159

"Which led to more contracts for the armory?"

"Robert reigned as king of that. He could talk to a person for three minutes and they loved him for life. Me, I'd just go to those big galas and hide over in the corner. . . ."

"With the Belle of East Texas?"

"Yep. That's about it."

Catherine held her breath. "Did you ask her to marry you?"

"We were getting rather too, eh, congenial and I knew I had to ask her or break it off."

"Congenial?" Catherine wrinkled her thin eyebrows. "Did she kiss like a carp?"

"Nope, her kisses tingled. Feather soft, yet enthusiastic. They made me glad I was me. You know what I mean?"

Catherine wiped her narrow lips. "I can imagine."

"This is when Robert negotiated us building the armory in California. When I finally decided to go along with the plan, I asked her to marry me and move to San Francisco."

"Where were you?"

"In Texas."

"Were you at her house? Out for supper? In a carriage? By the bay? Where were you when you asked her?"

"In her daddy's parlor with the lights out."

"Did you get down on your knees?"

"What? Of course not."

"Were you holding her hand?"

"What is this? An inquisition?"

"I just want to envision the moment. You had some tingly, feather soft, yet enthusiastic kisses in the dark. Then you held her hand and said, 'Charity Ann, darlin', will you marry me and leave your daddy and your mamma and Faith and Hope and move over a thousand miles away to California so I can run a gun factory?' "

"That wasn't quite how it went."

"But she turned you down or you would never be on this train."

"She not only said no, she was outraged that I wanted her to leave Texas. It was beyond her imagination. She took it as a personal insult to her intelligence and loyalty."

The train lunged over a short bridge. Catherine grabbed the black iron guardrail to balance herself. "So what happened next?"

"Robert sold everything we owned. Charity Ann headed to Louisiana to visit her aunt."

"Did you follow her?"

The warm wind whipped around them and Hillyard tugged down the front of his hat. "No."

"Big mistake. You should have chased after her. She wanted you to follow."

"I didn't have a pal like you to guide me. Perhaps it would have made a difference. Anyway, Robert headed to California but I waited in Houston. I wanted to talk to her one more time before I moved. She was gone for almost a month. During that time I did lots of ponderin' and lots of reading the Bible." Hillyard stared out, his eyes glazed. "I decided that I would not move to California, but get a Texas job and marry Charity Ann. She was right. I had no right to make her move. I knew I had given her my heart and I couldn't take it back."

Catherine looked down at her hands and fidgeted with her fingers.

That's why he hounded me when we first boarded. He told me I was throwing my heart away.

"What happened when she returned?"

"I was at the train station with a bouquet of bluebonnets when she arrived . . . with him."

Catherine's eyes widened. "Him? Him who?"

"She stepped off the train with a wedding ring on her finger and a husband on her arm."

Catherine's hand went to her mouth. "Oh, dear, I didn't expect that."

"Neither did I," he grimaced. "He was twenty years older than her but he controlled over two-hundred thousand acres of west Texas range-land. I couldn't believe it. She didn't even give me a chance to explain. Talk about a total fool. I just stood there silent as she waltzed by. I was still standing there when the train pulled out, wilted bluebonnets and all."

Catherine rested her hand on his. "And a wilted heart?"

"No. No, I gave my heart away. I can't take it back."

"Not ever?"

"I don't think so."

"But Race . . . life does need to go on."

"I went back to my hotel room and locked the door. Didn't come out for two days. That's when Robert showed up."

"Not a good week."

"I couldn't even think straight after I found him dead. I didn't know what to do. I felt tossed down on the moon. Everything familiar, everything comfortable, everything lovely was stripped away."

The wind whipped her thoughts. "Your story makes mine weak and toothless by comparison. So you took a job driving a band of horses up to the Indian Nation. Then rode your rage to Omaha."

"More or less. I had a few lost weeks in Texas before I left. I just couldn't believe all of this came down on me. I tried to sleep it off, hoping it was a bad dream."

"I appreciate your telling me this. I feel like I should apologize for prying."

"I needed to hear my voice explain it. It is the first time . . . and the last time . . . I intend to talk about it. Too painful to ponder. I needed to allow those words to blow over this empty prairie."

"I, of course, will mention it to no one."

The door of the car ahead of them burst open to reveal a heavy-set man with a drooping gray mustache. "There you are. Quite a coincidence we meet out here again."

Hillyard pulled off his hat. "Afternoon, Judge Clarke. I trust you and Amanda Sue are doing well."

"Quite nice, thanks to you two. She's in the bathtub right now. My chef has timed supper to coincide with our parking at the siding in Cheyenne. I believe that will be right before dark. We very much look forward to hosting you."

"We'll be delighted," Catherine said. "I'm afraid we won't be able to clean up much."

"That is no problem. I'm not half as snobbish as I seem. I dug for silver in the Comstock one whole winter, seldom seeing the light of day or a wash rag. I shall see you in my car when we reach Cheyenne."

"Thank you, Judge." Hillyard shoved his hat back on.

"Say . . . would you like white wine or red wine?"

Hillyard shook his head. "I don't drink wine, Judge."

"And I only have a sip at communion," Catherine added.

"Oh, good. I'll tell Chef Viseano to serve the red wine."

Francine was munching on a thick bread sandwich when they returned to the car. "The Mormon girls had a few of these extra. Nice of them to share. You two hungry?"

"After that stomach sickness the other day, I may never eat again," Hillyard replied.

"Well, don't get too comfy. Deputy Becker sent a note for you to step back for a visit."

"Becker?"

"He's the one chained to Johnny Socorro that you dragged back from the dead."

"He wasn't dead."

Francine brushed crumbs off her thick, full lips. "Five more minutes in the brush and he would have been handless and dead."

Hillyard sauntered to the rear of the car.

Francine leaned forward and whispered, "You and Mr. Hilly were on that platform for quite a while."

Catherine leaned her head back and lowered her voice. "He's become a good friend. Sometimes it's easier to talk to someone you hardly know and will never see again. It's those that are close to you that it's difficult to communicate with."

"I know what you mean. Sort of like you and me becoming best friends, isn't it? The difference is, this is not the last time we will see each other. I'm sure me and the children will want to come visit you and your Phillip in California."

"Yes, eh . . . you'll have to write to me after I get settled in so I can tell you all about the situation. At the moment, it's all a little confusing."

Francine sat back and picked bread from her teeth with her fingernail. "I'm dyin' to meet that Phillip. I keep thinking, Catherine has Race Hillyard wrapped around her finger but she prefers her beloved Phillip. He must be some man."

"Phillip's been a good friend for a very long time."

"But you haven't seen him since he was twelve."

"That's true."

"People do change. I'm just sayin' that a bird in the hand . . ."

"Neither Phillip or Race are birds, Francine."

"Very true." A slow grin spread across the big lady's face. "I did know some men who were vultures, however."

Catherine studied the front door of the train car as if expecting someone to crash through. "And Matthew Zane is one of them."

She heard Hillyard stop to say something to the teenage girls at the back of the car, then meandered toward them. He stepped by Catherine and plopped down in the window seat. She bounced up in response.

"How is the marshal?" she asked.

"Deputy marshal. He has a sore head. He's anxious to get to New Mexico. They'll change trains in Denver and go south. He offered me a job."

"Escorting the prisoner?"

Hillyard folded his hands behind his head. "Yeah, a hundred cash dollars."

"That's quite a sum."

"I had me a hundred cash dollars once," Francine piped up. "Right after the war I sold three of those Union Gatling guns to some rum runners on the Mississippi."

"Rum runners?" Catherine asked.

"Takin' it into the Indian Nation, I suppose. I didn't ask. I was broke and had nothing to eat."

"Where did you get three Gatling guns?"

"Don't ask about that neither. Those were the times when we were livin' one week, often one day at a time." The contagious smile dropped off Francine's wide face. "A person has a tough go of it concentratin' on moral implications when they are starvin' to death."

Catherine turned back to Hillyard. "I'm guessing you turned the marshal down?"

"Yep. Told him there were some frail women at the front of the car that I needed to take care of."

"Frail," Catherine huffed. "I can look after myself, and I am certainly not a frail woman, and neither is . . ."

Francine held up her hand. "Don't be too hasty in your condemnation, honey. Never in my life have I been called frail. I want it to sink in."

"I didn't really say frail. I told him all of us up here were headed to California and unable to go south with him. He's going to lock up Johnny Socorro in the jail in Cheyenne and telegraph New Mexico to send some help."

Catherine sat straight up. "Telegraph! Oh, yes. I'll need to telegraph Catelynn. Do you think I could wait until after supper with the judge?"

Hillyard shrugged. "I'm sure they run three clicks on the telegraph in Cheyenne."

"I heard you visit with the Mormon girls," Francine said. "Did they offer you a ham sandwich?"

"No," he laughed. "But they did ask if I was married."

"Married?" Catherine said. "They are too young to be thinking of marriage."

"I don't think so," he replied. "They all expect Daddy will find them a husband within the year."

Catherine glanced over her shoulder at the girls. "Which one asked you that?"

"All of them."

"Ooohwee. . . ." Francine hooted. "Race Hillyard and his harem."

Catherine tilted her head. "And just how did you get out of that one, Mr. Hilly?"

"I tried to imply . . . that you and me . . . you know. . . ."

"You used me for an excuse? How sweet of you."

"It didn't work. They all knew you were going to Sacramento to meet your beloved Phillip."

"Now, how did they know that?"

"I don't reckon there are many secrets on a train. I think when all is quiet, our voices carry quite well. They can't help but hear us."

Once they crossed into Wyoming, it was a straight track to Cheyenne. The sun eased low on the Laramie Mountains to the west and the shadows grew longer. While Race slept, Catherine gazed out the window. The last trees perched on the cliff at Pine Bluffs and now only brown grass carpeted the landscape. She thought about Amanda Sue in a bathtub on the train and tried to remember what it was like to be clean. She wanted to smell her clothes to see how rancid they had become in the dust and perspiration but couldn't think of a subtle way of doing it.

Catherine sorted through her cloth valise and pulled out a small blue glass vile with an opaque glass stopper. She poured some on her fingertips and rubbed the strong lilac aroma on her neck, ears and cheeks, then breathed in the sweet perfume.

Phillip, you will have to tell me your favorite perfume. There are a lot of things you'll have to tell me. In some ways, we know so little about who we are now. But I'm sure it won't take long to catch up.

Like fog clearing on the Delta by noon, the dream began to take shape. She stood at a crowded train depot. The sign on the red brick building read "Sacramento." Men and women in simple cotton clothing scurried around as if waiting for a signal to depart. A beautiful black leather carriage rolls up and Phillip steps down. Square shoulders. Wide brim felt hat at a rakish tilt. Wool suit starched to a stylish crease in the trousers. Vest and coat barely conceals the muscular chest and arms.

With polished black leather boots on the outside of his trouser legs, he struts like a prince as he pushes his way through the crowd. His face down, he watches his step. In the din of station noise, she hears his boots announce his arrival. She licks her lips and tastes . . . lilacs.

At last, he's close enough to clutch.

"You aren't Phillip," she gasps.

The deep reply exudes strength. "I most certainly am."

"You are not. You are Race Hillyard. What do you mean coming here and pretending to be Phillip?"

"I am Phillip Draper."

"This is not humorous, Race Hillyard."

"Who is this Hillyard? Don't you recognize me, Catherine Goodwin?"

"Go away. What have you done with my Phillip? Go away, Race Hillyard, go away."

"What are you talking about?"

"You are not suppose to be here and you know it."

"Be where?"

"Catherine! Catherine!"

A rather large lady shook her shoulder. "Catherine, wake up. You're mumbling in your sleep."

Catherine sat up and wiped the perspiration at her neck. "I must have been dreaming."

Francine sat back. "We're coming into Cheyenne."

"Did you hear anything I said?" Catherine took her linen handkerchief and patted her forehead.

"Not a thing," she pouted.

Catherine glanced over at Race. "Did Mr. Hilly hear anything I said?"

Francine whispered, "Oh, one of those dreams, was it? I don't think so. His mouth was open like a beached bass and he snored like a moose calling for his mate."

"What delightful images." Catherine grinned in relief. "I trust I can remember them."

Polished oak paneling and thick green carpeting greeted them as they entered the judge's train car. A large, well-set, oak table stood under a gas operated, hurricane lantern chandelier. Four black leather and oak chairs circled the table. A polished wooden desk and bookcase with glass doors divided the dining room from the rear of the car.

Lace curtains hung from the train windows. Crystal goblets, hand-painted china plates, and silver utensils adorned the table top. As far as Catherine could see, there was no dust anywhere.

The judge moved between them. "Rather exorbitant, isn't it?"

"It's beautiful," Catherine said. "It might be the loveliest room I've ever seen."

"It makes me feel a bit uncomfortable to tell you the truth."

Hillyard, hat in hand, rocked back on his heels. "I feel the same way, Judge."

"Amanda Sue likes it, don't you, honey?"

"Oh, yes. When we don't have company, Father lets me go barefoot and the carpet feels warm and tickly on my toes."

"Don't wear shoes for our sake, darlin'," Hillyard said.

"Oh, Father, may I?"

"Do I ever tell you no?"

"You did about the baby buffalo." She kicked off her shoes. "I wanted to take one home with us. There are so many, one wouldn't be missed. I think he would be a delightful pet. I'd take care of him and raise him and teach him manners."

The judge snorted. "Even indulgent old fathers have their limits."

"But buffaloes already have manners," Hillyard said.

"They do? Oh, goody . . . then I can . . ."

"But they aren't our manners." He squatted down eye-to-eye with the girl. "The Lord created them just like He wants them with their own set of manners. He doesn't want them to learn some other ones, just the ones He gave them."

Amanda Sue wiggled her nose. "I don't understand."

"Just suppose a young buffalo took a look at you and said, 'Oh, what a cute girl. I'd like to keep her for my own.' And what if that buffalo's daddy said it was okay? Now, if you were out with a buffalo herd, you'd have to eat grass, sleep on the ground year round, and not wear any clothes. You'd need to run for miles and miles during lightning storms and drink water from muddy streams. You'd have to roll in the dirt to try to get the ticks off you, and stick your head in the water to keep the swarms of flies and gnats from choking you."

"Yeuw! I don't want to do that."

"You'd feel very out-of-place, wouldn't you?"

"It would be horrible."

Hillyard patted her shoulder. "That's exactly how that little buffalo would feel trying to learn human manners. He would be miserable. The Lord didn't create him to be a yard pet."

"Well spoken," the judge replied.

"But . . . then . . ." Amanda Sue tucked her hand to her chin. "I . . . I've decided I don't want a buffalo."

"A very mature decision." Hillyard stood.

"I want a bobcat instead."

"Oh, dear," Catherine said.

"Fortunately, it's time for supper," the judge announced. "Miss Draper, if you'd sit over here . . . and Mr. Hillyard across from you."

"You do names very well, Judge," Catherine responded.

"A politician must remember all names."

The meal consisted of steaming hot watercress soup. Cranberry salad Florence. Roast loin of pork with prune-apple filling. Brown rice and baby carrots.

For over an hour, they ate and visited about railroads, politics, and baseball. After that, dessert was served.

Viennese apricot torte, assorted chocolate dinner mints, then coffee and tea.

The judge pushed back his empty plate. "I don't usually travel in such elegance. The car belongs to a friend of mine, Leland Stanford. With all the trouble and litigation with the silver mines and this threat upon my life, Leland insisted we take his car. He claimed that any who sought to harm me would expect me on the express. I would be overlooked on this train. We all know how well that worked."

Hillyard poked his calloused forefinger into the handle of the china coffee cup. "What exactly is the trouble in the mines?"

"Most all of the good claims are secure. Now there has been a rash of promoters selling worthless mining claims. They swindle and cheat in the most horrible ways. Much of which is difficult to prove. So, there is violence. Vigilante attacks. I have some litigation tied up for over five years. I don't know if it will ever be sorted out."

Catherine sipped African red bush tea. "It sounds like a lot of greedy people."

"Quite right. And the bench is required to state what is legal, even if it seems to support the morally wrong. Some of the cases are quite troubling."

Hillyard carefully set down his cup. "Did you ever hear of a case concerning a bogus diamond mine?"

"Heavens, there are no diamond mines in the West," the judge muttered. "At least, none that I've ever heard of."

"No, but someone could claim to have found one," Hillyard added.

"I suppose, but who in the world would believe him? Gold mines and silver mines, that's the swindlers' territory."

Catherine interrupted. "What a delightful meal, Judge."

"The least we could do. Are you sure you don't want any Beaujolais? It's Arthur Barolet et Fils, 1871."

Hillyard shook his head. "Judge, you mention fancy wines and I feel as out-of-place as a buffalo in your backyard."

"I am learning to be quite a snob. I need my wife to keep me humble."

With a linen napkin, Amanda Sue smeared chocolate across her lips. "My mother is a doctor and sometimes she gets blood on her hands."

"I suppose so," Catherine replied.

Amanda Sue tossed her napkin onto her plate. "When I grow up, I'm going to have a big ranch and raise . . ." she stole a look at her father ". . . bobcats."

When Catherine stood, the men rose too. "Judge, thank you again for your gracious hospitality. This is the place in the evening where the ladies retire to one room, and the men go to the den and smoke dreadful cigars. The truth is, I need to go to the station and send a telegram before we pull out."

"Yes, of course. I just can't show my appreciation enough for how you rescued my Amanda Sue. God is gracious to a rather pompous old judge, isn't He?"

"He's gracious to all of us," Hillyard offered. "Did it work out for you to hire a little more protection?"

176

Catherine started toward the door. "I really must get to the station."

"The ex-Pinkerton man adds another wall of security. Perhaps you noticed him checking in on us from time to time?"

"Tonight?" Hillyard asked.

"Yes . . . I asked him to be discreet. I don't want someone hovering about."

"I didn't notice him at all."

"Splendid. Perhaps you'd like to meet him."

"If you men will excuse me," Catherine said. "While you talk security, I'll slip out and send my telegram."

Hat in hand, Hillyard turned towards her. "Wait, I'll walk with you."

"I'm quite capable of finding the station on my own. Really, it's no bother."

Catherine slipped out the door, just as the judge led Hillyard across the car.

"You see, Leland had this mirror installed. It's a special kind of glass where someone can look through from the other side. That's where Chet Pinehurst spends most of his time."

At the sound of the name, Catherine spun back, but the polished oak door had swung shut.

CHAPTER SEVEN

The lights from the stars blanketed the night sky north of the train station. As Catherine hiked the wood plank platform toward the brick building, she heard the shouts and tunes of a city relaxing its morals.

Lord, I think maybe the things that go on in the dark prove that people believe in You. They are afraid to do those same things in the blaze of daylight. Afraid You will see them. Ashamed. But at night, well, they think Your vision or concern is somehow limited. May I only do those things at night that I would do in the light of day.

She heaved open the heavy wooden door to the lobby of the train station.

Come to think of it, my daylight activity is not always that great either. You will need to help me with that, as well. Perhaps I need an angel looking after me.

Inside the terminal, a dozen people lounged on long, high-back wooden benches. Most had a valise or bundle near them. Some talked. Some dozed. Others stared out at the immobile train. The air smelled stale; tasted used. Her clothes felt sticky, dirty. Yet, the tart taste of the Viennese apricot torte swirled in her mouth. She smiled at the "train food" she had just enjoyed.

Catherine strolled towards a Dutch door marked "Tickets: Times: Telegraphs."

A dark-skinned girl about eight-years-old with a smudged long yellow dress and tangled, thick black hair accosted her. "Excuse me, ma'am. I couldn't help but notice that you are all alone."

Catherine glanced around the room, as if expecting to spy her parents. "Yes, honey. I just stepped off the westbound train to send a telegram."

The girl shuffled the heels of her very dusty, black, lace-up shoes. "Are you reporting good news or bad?"

Catherine peered into the girl's large, round eyes. "What?"

"In the telegram?" The girl shifted the burlap bag she carried from one shoulder to the next. "Do you have good news or bad news to report?"

Catherine paused and bit her lip. "That is to be determined."

The girl rubbed her nose with the back of her hand. "Are you married?"

Catherine tried to suppress a smile. "No, I'm not. But I'm on my way to California to get married. And you? Are you married?"

The little girl grinned, revealing straight, white teeth. "No, I am not married. But I have been thinking about it."

"You have?"

The girl picked at one of the soiled spots on

the front of her dress. "Yes, you see, Cheyenne can get dangerous at night for beautiful single women like you and me when we go out alone."

Honey, you are a jewel. Does all of this come natural, or do you practice these lines over and over?

"Oh, is that so?"

The smile melted to scorn. "Only last night a man chased me for two blocks. It is lucky I am quite fast as well as pretty."

I must fight the urge to comb her hair and wash her face.

"That is a good combination. Perhaps you should stay home in the evenings."

"Perhaps, but sometimes I need to work. You see, my mother died when I was very young. I know she loved Jesus and is in heaven, but my father works at night at the jail. He doesn't make very much money and he must buy medicine to help him breathe better."

Catherine rubbed her chin.

I do believe I'm getting suckered into something.

"What kind of work do you do?"

"Ah . . . I was going to tell you." She glanced around the terminal. "But I don't want others to hear. Step over here, if you will."

The little girl took Catherine's gloved hand and led her to an empty back bench. She dropped her burlap sack with a clank on the worn wooden seat and held out her small brown hand. "My name is Angelita Gomez."

"And I'm . . . eh, Catherine Draper." She noticed her glove seemed to stick in the girl's grasp.

"Pleased to meet you, Catherine Draper." Angelita climbed up on the bench seat. "I believe it is important for single women like us. . . ."

"Single, beautiful women. . . ." Catherine interrupted.

"Oh yes," Angelita grinned. "For single, beautiful women to have some protection on them at all times. Do you carry a revolver?"

"A gun?" Catherine glanced around but spied no threats. "Heavens, no."

"That's what I was afraid of." Angelita folded her arms. "It is really quite dangerous to live that way. You are headed west, no?"

"Yes, I am."

"Everything gets very wild as you go west. Laramie is much worse . . . and Ogden. Reno Station is a violent place. And Rawlins . . . well, respectable women are advised not even to depart the train. It is very dangerous indeed. Your sensitive ears should not even hear what goes on there."

Catherine studied the smudged face, the alert, dark brown eyes.

Where does she get these lines? Even Mark Twain could not write a script this good.

181

"Thank you, Angelita, for being so considerate."

"You are welcome." She reached over and put her hand on Catherine's shoulder. "But there is a solution to this threat of violence."

Catherine rested her hand on Angelita's. "I should start carrying a revolver? You don't happen to have one to sell me, do you?"

The little girl's eyes widened in delight. "Oh, yes . . . I have a very fine Colt 73, peacemaker .45 caliber revolver with a five-and-a-half inch barrel and shiny bore." She pulled the revolver out of the burlap sack. "It fires a standard 255 grain, blunt nose bullet with 40 grains of black powder. It is very powerful, yet sleek, don't you think?"

Is this girl eight or twenty-eight? How does she know all of this? Why does she know all of this? She might be the most interesting character in Wyoming.

"Thank you, honey, but I'm really not looking to buy a firearm." Catherine turned toward the telegraph office. "It was so nice to visit with you."

"But, wait," Angelita jumped off the bench and grabbed her arm. "I haven't told you the exciting part."

"Oh?"

"This very revolver was once owned by none other than the legendary Stuart Brannon himself. You have heard of Brannon, no? Of course, everyone has heard of him."

"A Stuart Brannon gun? How rare. How did you come by it?"

"Well, you see, I often come to the train station. There are such interesting people here. Some real characters, if you know what I mean. Sometimes they need a quick meal. So, I bring some sandwiches or cheese to sell. I make my own cheese, you know. It is slightly sharp and zesty."

"Zesty?"

"I put just a few hot peppers in it. Some say it is the best cheese in Wyoming, but I do not know that for sure. Anyway, an old man came up on the train from Ft. Collins. He looked like a prospector who is down on his luck. He wanted to buy my whole bag of sandwiches and cheese."

"He must have been very hungry."

"He was very thin. Like a coyote in August. But it was early on a Saturday and the east and west trains had not arrived. I had a very large sack of sandwiches and . . ."

"Hot, spicy cheese?"

"Yes. I had a lot of food in the bag. I was look-ing forward to selling them one by one. Then he tells me he has no money, but he will trade me this gun he received from Stuart Brannon down in Arizona Territory. He wanted to trade this very gun for the food."

"But you already had a revolver, didn't you? A beautiful lady like yourself needs protection."

"That is very true. I do carry a sneak gun at all times. But I felt sorry for the old man. I believe it is my duty as a Christian to assist the hungry."

You carry a sneak gun? Honey, that seems incredulous, yet somehow, I believe you.

"So you traded for the gun and now want to sell it to me?"

"Yes! And since we have so much in common, I will sell this historic gun for only six dollars." Angelita licked her full, pink lips. "Gold or silver coins, please."

"You don't like greenbacks?"

"There are some shops that devalue them."

Am I really listening to a little girl?

Catherine looked down at her purse that she clutched in front of her. "I'm afraid I can't afford . . ."

"Did I say six dollars? Tsk. Tsk. What am I thinking? Us beautiful women must help each other whenever we can. Only four dollars for you, but don't let anyone else know I sold it so cheap."

"Honey, I know a little about guns. My father sold them in his store. I have read several times that Stuart Brannon only carries a Colt .44 to match cartridges in his Winchester 1873." Catherine waved her gloved finger like a schoolteacher giving a mathematical lecture. "How can a .45 caliber gun be his?"

"Oh . . . oh . . . well," Angelita pursed her lips.

184

"I can see you are very well read. That is excellent. Yes, that is very true. Mr. Brannon only carries a .44." Angelita regained her wide, dimpled grin. "That is why he sold this revolver to the old man. It was the wrong caliber. That makes it very rare, indeed. Imagine a .45 caliber gun belonging to Stuart Brannon. And I did not even add to its value for rareness."

"How considerate of you. Angelita, even though it is very exceptional and unique, I can't afford to . . ."

"Did I mention it comes with five bullets, no extra charge?"

"Five? I thought a Colt held six."

"Of course it does, but you do not want the hammer sitting on a live cartridge. There is a danger of an accidental discharge. Five bullets will be sufficient to slow down any attacker."

"I suppose you are right. But I still . . ."

"Imagine, five bullets that the legendary Stuart Brannon slipped into this very gun. It just sends goose bumps up your spine, doesn't it?"

"Honey, I just don't have the money."

Angelita puffed out her cheeks, then let the air out slowly. "I must not go home empty-handed tonight. I will sell you this fine, historic pistol for only two dollars, but that will include merely one bullet."

"You are a very good saleslady. But you picked a very poor customer. I spent my money on a train ticket to California. The man I will marry is waiting for me there, and I only have enough funds on me right now to send a telegram."

"How much do you have?"

"Only fifty cents, and I need it . . ."

"You are sending a telegram to your fiancé in California? That is only thirty cents, which means . . ."

"I am sending a telegram to my sister in New York City."

"Oh, New York. I think I will go there one day and become a famous actress. Do you think I could be an actress?"

"You already are quite good."

"And beautiful."

"That goes without saying."

"But a telegram to New York is only forty cents, if you keep it to twenty-five words or less. That means you will have change left. Now, mind you, I wouldn't do this for just anyone." She flipped open the cylinder and pushed out one bullet. "For my good friend, Catherine Draper, about to be wed in California, I will sell one genuine Stuart Brannon bullet for only ten cents."

Catherine smiled. "Angelita, I have never met anyone quite like you."

The little girl rubbed her nose with the palm of her hand. "My father says I am quite special. Then you will buy the bullet?"

"Check with me after I send the telegram."

"Yes, yes." Angelita studied the lobby doorway. "But you must act quick. Pappy will be making his rounds soon and I'll need to go home."

"Your father is coming by here?"

"No, my father watches the jail. Pappy is the sheriff. I must leave before he, eh . . ."

Catherine laid her hand on the girl's shoulder. "Runs you off?"

"It is better to say, before he escorts me home."

She read the message over again:

"Catelynn, forgive my impertinence at our last meeting. I want the best for you. Love blurs my wisdom. Telegraph me at Reno Station, Nevada. Catherine."

"Did you say this would be forty cents?"

The chubby clerk with a weak mustache sat on a stool behind a solitaire card layout. "Yes, ma'am. Twenty-five words or less, forty cents."

She plucked up two nickels change. "And you'll send it right away?

He pushed his green isinglass visor to the top of his forehead. "Yes, ma'am. As soon as I'm finished with this. . . ."

"The eight of diamonds does not belong on the nine of hearts."

"What?"

"You're cheating at solitaire. Send the telegram now, please."

"Yes, ma'am." He turned toward the idle telegraph key.

Catherine sauntered half-way across the lobby before she heard the familiar voice behind her.

"I wonder if they have one my size?"

She turned around to see Angelita and the gunny sack following her. "Your dress is beautiful. I would like to have one just like it. As I mentioned before, just one dime for a genuine Stuart Brannon cartridge."

The evening air whipped Catherine's face like a fan. Her eyes had barely adjusted to the darkness when another familiar voice struck her ears like an unwanted slap.

"Catherine, it is you. I can't believe this. Chet said you were with the judge tonight, but I thought there must be some mistake."

She could make out his tall shadow and natty, tilted hat, but not the slicked-down mustache nor the narrow, piercing eyes. "Mr. Zane, I think I adequately expressed my opinion of you at our last meeting. I do not want to see you or talk to you now. Please excuse me. I must get to the train."

He yanked her arm. "Catherine, I need to talk to you."

She shoved him away. "Don't touch. We have nothing to talk about." *Now I wish I did have Angelita's gun.*

"It's about Catelynn," he began. "Have you had contact with her lately?"

Catherine spun around. "You were there on the day of our last meeting."

"Then you don't know?" He sounded puzzled more than startled.

"Don't know what?"

The man in the shadow rubbed his chin. "Eh . . . it's rather private."

Defused light filtered out of the station windows. "There is no one on the platform."

"It could take me some time to explain everything. Perhaps we could step back on the train and you could come to my compartment."

"I do not trust you."

"I don't blame you for that. But once you hear what I have to say, you'll understand my discretion. Please. For Catelynn's sake."

Catherine stormed toward the train, with Zane following her. "If you want to tell me about my sister, you can do it now . . . or in the presence of my friends, but not in your compartment."

He remained on the platform when she pulled herself up on the step of her car.

"If you won't come talk to me for Catelynn's sake." His voice tightened. "Then come talk to me because of her daughter's sake."

It felt like a blow to the side of her head. She spun around and grabbed the iron railing to keep her balance. "Daughter? Catelynn doesn't have . . ."

"Little Marie DuClare. . . ."

"Our mother was named Marie DuClare."

"Yes, indeed. I'm in compartment 3C. Try to be there within fifteen minutes."

He strutted towards the front of the train as Catherine blinked her eyes in the pale darkness.

A baby girl? My sister doesn't . . . she would have told me . . . she isn't even married . . . she wouldn't . . . but . . . she might. I called her fat. Oh, no, no. Was she pregnant and I was too pompous and pious to tell?

Francine and little Nancy drew a picture on a brown paper when Catherine returned to her seat.

Race sat up and pushed his hat back. "Me and Mr. Walker were gettin' worried about you. I should have escorted you to the telegraph office."

Catherine rubbed her forehead and tried to quiet the chaos in her mind. She glanced across at Race's saddle. "Mr. Walker, I trust you, at least, had a peaceful evening."

"I'm guessing you had a less than pleasant experience at the telegraph office," Francine suggested.

"I just had a most disturbing conversation with the most despicable man on earth. Race, do you still have that extra pistol?"

"So you ran across Matthew Zane?" Francine asked.

"He came looking for me. His pal Pinehurst is the judge's new security guard. Which, in itself, is a suspicious arrangement."

Hillyard dug into his saddle bag. "You plannin' on shootin' someone?"

"Do you have the gun?"

"Yes, ma'am."

"May I borrow it? And five bullets."

"Five?" Francine questioned.

"One must leave the hammer set on an empty chamber, isn't that right, Mr. Hillyard?"

"Eh, yeah, that's best. Do you really want this gun?"

She clutched the revolver. "Yes, I do. I need to go talk to Mr. Zane. He has some private news about my sister. I must find out how she is doing."

Francine handed Preston and Nancy small round crackers, then leaned forward. "I thought you hated him."

"I do. Thus, the gun."

Hillyard rubbed the back of his neck. "You promise not to shoot him?"

"I make no such promise. But whatever happens, he will only get what he deserves."

"Maybe I should go with you," he offered.

"I think I need to hear this news alone. But if I'm not back in thirty minutes or so, come and look for me in 3C."

"Guns drawn?" Hillyard asked.

"By all means."

Catherine stood and stuffed the revolver into her purse.

"I'll expect a full report when you get back," Francine insisted. "Traveling with you just might be the most exciting event in my life. Other than meeting that snake dancer in Memphis."

The aisle was crammed as the passengers re-entered the car. The conductor's familiar "all aboard" bellowed through the open windows.

The train jerked forward as she made her way through the passenger car ahead of them. Like her own, it teemed with an assortment of people, a cornucopia of aromas. She felt very conscious of the revolver concealed in her handbag. She nodded at the conductor as they squeezed by each other in the aisle.

"I've not forgotten your request, Miss Draper," he said. "Still no private open compartments. Perhaps, when we get to Ogden."

She made a quick remark and kept marching through the car. A blond cowboy tipped his hat. Her glare caused him to shove it back over unruly hair.

Lord, I don't want to talk to Zane. He always makes me angry. Why would he say Catelynn has a child? Why would he say that? Yes, things are not good between us, but that is something she would not keep secret. He has manipulated my sister for years with lies and innuendoes. I will not allow him to do that to me. This will be a very short discussion.

A well-endowed woman with thick black hair and a low neckline on her burgundy silk blouse led two laughing men into compartment 3F. Catherine paused in front of 3C .

"Yea, though I walk through the shadow of death, I will fear no evil. . . ."

Her loud knock on the door seemed to clear her head. When she heard, "Come in, Catherine," she sucked in a deep breath.

She shoved the door open, surprised at the smallness of the compartment. Two leather padded bench seats faced each other, with a fold-down bed fastened above the right seat. A narrow water-closet door was on the left. Matthew Zane and Chester Pinehurst faced each other.

Zane patted the seat next to him. "Come in. Close the door and sit down."

Out the window, the tiny, scattered lights from houses along the tracks through Cheyenne hurried by like lemmings leaping off a cliff in single file. She scrutinized the smirks on both mustached faces.

"Pinehurst, you leave. I like you even less than I like Zane. So go out on the platform and smoke. Or better yet, just hurl yourself from the train." She glowered at Zane. "I will sit in the seat facing you and you will leave the door open."

Pinehurst scooted by her and she slid in next to the window.

"I thought you might think it more prudent to have a third party with us."

Catherine pulled out the revolver. Matthew Zane flinched when she cocked the hammer and laid it in her lap. "This is the only third party I need."

"Good grief, Catherine." He wiped his forehead. "Put the gun away."

Though the air in the compartment was stuffy, it didn't account for the sudden sweat on his brow.

"Understand something, Mr. Zane. I will decide when, and if, I put the gun away." She aimed the muzzle at Pinehurst. "I believe you need to go check on the judge. Little does he know he hired the wolf to watch the chicken."

When Pinehurst was out of sight, she turned to Zane. "Now what is all this nonsense about Catelynn having a baby?"

The car lurched to the side. She feared for a moment he would grab for the gun. She regained her posture and aimed it at him.

"It's not nonsense. Now, if you'll lay that revolver in your lap, I'll explain. This is way too rough a ride to feel chatty with a muzzle pointed at me."

Catherine brushed the front of her dress, placed her handbag on her lap, and the revolver on top of the handbag.

"Last March, Catelynn birthed a baby daughter. It was a difficult delivery, as I understand."

"You weren't there?"

He avoided her eyes. "I was in San Francisco at the time."

"You had a business trip and couldn't be there for your own daughter's birth?"

"Well, there is some question of parentage."

The revolver trembled as she pointed it at Zane. "Are you accusing my sister of . . ."

"Catherine, put the gun down." His voice was tight. Almost a whine. "I'm only telling you what you would find out on your own. I do assume the baby is mine. One time, in an angry moment, your sister seemed to challenge that idea, but I assume she was just trying to get at me."

Catherine lowered the revolver, took a deep breath and raised her shoulders. "Since very few things you have ever told me are true, how could I believe you this time?"

"Would photographs help?"

A plump man, with a light gray linen suit and no tie appeared at the door. "Hey, are you the furr . . . the purr . . . Persian belly dancer?" he slurred.

Catherine glanced at the man's lopsided grin.

The train slowed and the man staggered back down the aisle out of sight.

"Maybe I should close the door now," Zane offered.

"No. The door stays open. Do you have pictures of the baby?"

"Yes, I do." Zane opened a black satchel, and pulled out a flat leather binder. "I believe little Marie is about three months in this one."

She stared at the half-smiling round face of the tiny naked girl propped up on a blanket. Catherine held her chest with the palm of her left hand as if to calm the rapid breathing.

"Oh . . . my . . . I, she looks just like Catelynn when we were young." Her right hand still clamped on the revolver, Catherine wiped a tear with her gloved left hand.

"Therefore, she looks just like you at that age, too."

She took several deep breaths. "How do I know for certain this is my sister's daughter? You are a lying and deceitful man, Matthew Zane."

"I thought it was obvious. You said you see the family resemblance."

"I love all pictures of babies. Do you have a photograph of my sister with her baby?"

He glanced down at the leather binder. "Eh, yes . . . but you don't want to see it."

"Of course I do."

"Hey. . . ." The drunken man braced himself

at the doorway. "Are you the Turkish jelly-bouncer? Eh . . . no . . eh, jelly-dancer?"

Catherine tried to smile. "I thought she was Persian."

"I don't have a prejudiced bone in my body." He staggered back toward the aisle. "I'm not sure I have any bones in my body."

"I am not a Persian, Turkish or Lithuanian belly dancer. Please don't bother us again."

"Mithuanian belly dancer? I never heard of them. I never heard of Mithuania. Say, you wouldn't happen to have a . . . ?"

Catherine pointed the revolver at the man. His bloodshot eyes widened. "I think I'll look in the next car."

Catherine turned back to Matthew Zane. "What about the pictures?"

"I will show them to you if you release the hammer on the revolver and return the gun to your purse."

"I don't understand."

"You will. I really must insist. If you don't, you may just go on back to your coach."

Catherine eased the hammer down, then shoved the gun into her purse, but did not release her hand from the walnut grip.

Zane reached in the satchel, then handed her several three-by-five-inch photographs.

Her heart raced. Her head pounded. Catherine shook her head, but couldn't speak.

With arched dark eyebrows and a dominating smirk, Zane admonished, "I warned you."

"But . . . but . . . but . . . why did you have pictures of my sister and her baby totally naked?"

"It was the 'artistic' thing to do."

"It is indecent and immoral."

"It's a popular thing among some of the theater types in New York."

"How much brandy did you pump down her to get her to agree to this?"

"Perhaps you don't know your sister as well as you think you do."

"I know my sister's heart. We have been united in heart since the day of our birth. She would not do this. You got her drunk, didn't you?"

"That is not a difficult thing to do lately."

Catherine pulled the gun back out.

"Wait," Zane protested. "Put the gun back. Let me explain the situation. You, me, and Catelynn are the only ones that have seen these photographs."

"And the photographer."

"Yes, but as I said, he does lots of these and it's of no importance to him. When Catelynn saw these the next day, she insisted on him destroying the plates, so these are the only copies."

Catherine reached her arm across the narrow aisle. "Give them to me."

He pulled them back to his vest. "Yes, I'd like to do that, however. . . ."

"You want money for them?"

"Not money . . . just a favor."

"Are you trying to bribe me?"

"It's a rather long story. Little Marie is sick. It is a lung problem of some sort. I really don't understand all that is involved. I tell you the truth, I do not always comprehend a doctor's prognosis. But the leading lung doctor in New York is Dr. Dankshiem. He has told us about a treatment that involves injecting oxygen into the blood that is working extremely well in Germany. There is no equipment or skill to accomplish this in the states. It not only makes the patient feel better, but will actually bring about a permanent cure in just a matter of weeks."

Catherine felt numb. She couldn't erase from her mind the unclad pictures of her sister and the baby. "Then why aren't you and Catelynn and Marie on your way to Germany?"

"I was getting to that. Such a trip is expensive, of course. And, to be honest with you, I've made a few foolish investments lately."

"I can believe that."

"I'm coming west to make one more deal. It's a very nice sale of mining claims and real estate. As soon as the transaction is complete, I'll have the funds to go to Europe."

"Okay, that's your story. Give me the pictures and I'll pray that your business deal succeeds."

"It's not that easy."

A commotion out in the aisle halted their discussion. The drunk man cowered in front of the large, dark-haired woman with the immodest blouse. She pounded him on the head with her small black purse.

"She's not Mytholanian," he shouted to them as they rumbled out of sight.

A shout. A crash. Then silence.

Zane turned back to Catherine. "Some weeks ago we met with the Nevada mining investors in New York."

"We? You and Pinehurst?"

"Me and Catelynn. She is quite anxious for this deal to succeed so we can get the medical attention Marie needs. In fact, it was her charisma and grace that sold the investors on the deal. She can be quite charming, as you know."

"That's the first thing we've agreed about."

"Now the investors want to meet us in Nevada to complete the transaction and they wanted Catelynn to come with me. With Marie sick, this couldn't happen. I've worried about how they will respond if I show up without Catelynn. This is a delicate transaction. Now, your presence is like an answer to prayer."

"Words about prayer coming from your lips sound like blasphemy."

"And yours show no sign of grace. The truth is . . . you and Catelynn are identical in looks.

You could pass for her, as you did when younger ladies. She's told me about those times."

"You want me to pretend to be your . . ."

"My wife."

"Did you marry my sister?"

"Not officially, but that's what we told these investors. We intend to get married before we sail to Europe."

"So, I pretend to be your wife. You make this big deal. I get these photographs?"

He patted his vest pocket. "And one hundred cash dollars."

"And you?"

"I go back to New York, get married, and book passage for the three of us to Germany."

"This is insane."

"I know it's a drastic measure. But it might be the only way to get little Marie to Germany. Will you do it? You'd be expected to stay in my compartment for the remainder of the trip."

"That's impossible. This is like a bad dream. When does it stop getting worse?"

"I don't think it's an accident that we find each other on the same train."

"You knew I was headed west. I told Catelynn last February I was going out to marry Phillip. You could have arranged all of this."

He leaned back and folded his arms across his chest. "This is one time you must trust me."

"I will never trust you. I will not consider

your proposal until I get some confirmation from my sister." She paused. "I'll telegraph her in Ogden. If she tells me about the baby and needing treatment in Germany, I will consider it."

"But that's impossible." He scooted to the edge of the seat and lowered his voice. "She heard the ocean air would be good for the baby. Some friend of hers at the theater had access to a cabin out on Cape Cod. She's there now. Just a temporary therapy until I return with the funds. I have no way of contacting her until she comes back. We were both to be back in New York in two weeks."

"You told me an incredible story . . . and expect me to believe it with no confirmation? I want to wait and talk to Catelynn. Zane, nothing you have done since I've known you has prompted me to believe you. If you are through, I'm going back to my coach and try to absorb all that you have said." Catherine stood to leave.

The drunk man blustered into their compartment, bounced into Catherine, then tottered back into Zane's lap. The man slammed the door, then whimpered, "You've got to hide me! It's a matter of wife and death."

Catherine shoved her revolver towards him. "Get out!"

"Shoot me. It would be a kercy milling."

Catherine scrambled to her feet. Zane lunged for the revolver. She slammed her elbow into his neck and hurled herself into the drunk. When he pitched forward, the door popped open under the weight of his shoulder.

"I believe the Queen of Sheba is in the last car. You should go check it out," Catherine said.

He squinted down the aisle. "The Sheen of Queba? Whoa. Thanks. I owe you one . . . if you are ever in East Alton, Illinois, you should stop by and see my ex-wife."

Catherine closed the door and switched the dead bolt.

"Are you sure you're safe?" Zane smirked.

"I'm not sure of anything except I have five 255 grain lead bullets in this Colt and I intend to use every one of them if need be."

"Sit down. I have another proposition for you to consider."

She plunked back down across from him. "I trust it's better than the first."

"It's worse, but you are forcing me to it."

"I'm forcing you?"

"I need this deal to go through, Catherine."

"For a sick baby?"

"You will not believe anything I tell you."

"You're right about that. What is this horrible proposition?"

"When we get to Reno, you pose as my wife for a day as we meet with all the investors in Nevada. I'll return to New York with the funds needed, and you go to your Phillip with one-hundred dollars to aid the new marriage."

"What makes you think Phillip will need money? Besides, I've already rejected your proposal. What will you do if I refuse?"

"Only what you force me to do. I will circulate these photos on the train, with the judge, with your friends in the coach . . . and with Phillip and the whole town of Paradise Springs. You seem to forget at times that you and Catelynn are identical twins. I will simply tell them this is you and your illegitimate daughter."

"What?"

"Do you think the judge and Amanda Sue will believe some story, 'oh, that's not me, it's my identical twin?' "

"Phillip knows Catelynn."

"Well, he'll know her a whole lot better after he sees this. And how about Paradise Springs? Will they want to patronize the store where such a woman works? They will all know every detail of your . . . eh . . . appearance. How about that Texan you've been partial to on this trip? Pinehurst has filled me in."

"Race knows I have a twin sister."

"Do you think he'll see Catelynn when he looks at this? He'll see you. Like it or not, this is you, Catherine. And your daughter looks just like you."

"She looks just like Catelynn."

"That's my point. There is no difference."

Catherine jammed her hand into her purse.

"That's it. Pull the gun and shoot me. I won't be the first man you've shot. I know all about the lawyer in northern Virginia. But you can't shoot me. Your sensitive Christian conscience will constrain you."

You think so, Matthew Zane? Just watch this. I'll pull the gun out, point it like this at your black heart, and pull the trigger. The report deafened, the recoil rocked her and deep, red blood spurted from the round hole in his chest. "I didn't believe you'd kill me," he blurted out. "It was my Christian duty to rid the world of evil," she replied. "Now, run along to the tortures of hell."

"You see, you can't do it. You sit there unable to respond."

My mind has been very active.

"I misjudged you, Matthew Zane. I knew you were a woman beater, a cheat, and a despicable man . . . but I did not know the depths of your evil."

"You still don't." He stood up and straightened his suit coat. "I want you to do this. And you will. If you don't, after the pictures make the tour of this train, I will talk to the conductor. I will inform him that you came to my compartment, showed me the pictures and tried to solicit me. I'll demand he immediately toss you off the train. That will leave you in the middle of Wyoming Territory with no money."

"You can't do that. I . . . I have friends on this train."

"You won't for long." Zane stuffed the photographs back into his satchel. "Think it over. I'll give you some time."

She stood and stepped towards the door. "I will never . . ."

"You might." Zane gripped her shoulder and pulled her back. "Ponder it a while." Then he closed the door behind him. She heard him lock it from the hallway.

Catherine stared down at her shoes.

Oh, Catelynn, my dear sweet sister. How could you get yourself into such a mess? You started to drink brandy when Mother and Daddy died in the war. You never could face things, could you? Lord, I would do anything to help my sister, but nothing for Matthew Zane. I just want to be in Paradise Springs. I need to be with Phillip . . . or even in the coach with Race and Francine. If I had the funds, I could switch trains in Ogden and get away from this ugly, horrible man.

Phillip, you need not know about any of this trip. I will show up and your strong arms will encircle me. Your love will engulf me. If I had money, I'd buy a beautiful trousseau. We'd have a very proper church wedding . . . and live in love and laughter all the days of our lives. That will all begin only three days from now. Except for the trousseau. I should have listened to Race and not squandered the twenty dollars on a compartment that never happened. Of course, I have a compartment now.

She studied the door.

It has an interior deadbolt as well as a keyed lock. Perhaps I'll lock myself in the room for three days. I'll have a comfortable bed, a private water closet . . . but no food.

She peered out the window at the black Wyoming night. She couldn't tell if they had started climbing into the mountains or not. The rhymic sway of the train leveled any incline. When she closed her eyes, she could not tell if the train raced forward or backward. Opening them, she thought she spotted a farmhouse lantern, but wasn't sure.

Some gal is at the dishpan, listening to the train whistle and wishing she was on it, headed for some distant adventure. I wish I was in the farmhouse . . . with my Race . . . I mean, my Phillip . . . settled, comfortable, secure with someone who loves me, not someone trying to manipulate me.

She eyed the door closer.

I could shoot the lock . . . and hope no one stood on the other side and the bullet did not ricochet. The conductor would stop the train to investigate and Matthew Zane would show him the picture, claim it was me and that I was trying to solicit him or kill him. Then I would get kicked off the train.

I could pull the brake cord and stop the train. Or open the window and drop down to the . . . well, I'm not sure what's out there . . . or how far down it is. I can just wait for Zane to return, shoot him dead on the spot and claim he made improper advances. They will put me off at the next stop, haul out his body, discover the photographs, and assume it is me. They will call it a jealousy slaying and only give me five to ten years at some dismal Wyoming prison for women. Which might be worth it, but Phillip won't wait that long. I just need to get out and find my way to Paradise Springs.

She tugged at the window but could only get it to open a few inches.

But what if Catelynn is truly in trouble? What if the baby does need help? I couldn't live with myself if I knew I had failed her. If my decision led to her baby's death . . . oh, Lord, I would curl up in a ball and die. I have to do it. He knows I have to help her. How can I do anything else? Oh, Catelynn, how I wish we were still giggling little girls running through Mamma's garden chasing baby rabbits. Life was good and we thought it would last forever.

The door handle rattled and she pulled her revolver. Then a knock and some muffled noises. There was a shout. She leaned her ear against the polished wooden door.

"I said, that's my compartment. What do you think you are doing?"

"Looking for a friend."

"She's not there."

That's Race and Pinehurst . . . I think.

"I didn't say I was looking for a woman." Bang, bang, bang . . . the door rattled. "Catherine!"

"I told you no one is in there," Pinehurst insisted.

"Race?" she yelled out. "There are two of them."

"What?"

"Move it, pal!"

"A little man with a knife is still a little man," Race hollered.

A knife? Race . . . no.

There was a crash against the door and several more out in the aisle.

"You broke my arm!" Pinehurst screamed.

"You'll live. Another one? What is this, the idiot train?"

There was another crash, a shout, a sickening thud after thud after thud. Then silence.

"Race?"

Nothing.

"Race, are you alright?"

Someone fumbled to put a key in the door. She stood on the seat and raised the revolver above her head.

Zane is the only one with a key. If he's injured Race, I'll shoot him. At least, I'll cold cock him.

209

I know how it's done. You won't even know what . . .

The door swung open and a dark-haired man staggered in. With all her might, she drove the barrel of the gun square into the man's head. He crumpled to his knees.

What happened to Zane's red vest?

She dropped the revolver. "Race Hillyard? How dare you come in here under false pretenses." Catherine slumped to her knees and threw her arms around his shoulders. "Race, did I hurt you?"

He leaned against the cushion and gasped. "Cath . . . erine . . ." His breath was short, choppy. "That is without . . . a doubt. . . ." He rubbed his head. "The stupidest thing I've ever heard you say . . . and I mean to tell you, I've heard plenty."

Then he collapsed in her arms.

CHAPTER EIGHT

Catherine hovered over Race Hillyard. "Are you sure you're alright?"

He grasped both hands on top of his head. "It's not the first time I had my skull creased."

She massaged his shoulders. "I appreciate very much you rescuing me."

Hillyard squinted his eyes. "What did I rescue you from?"

"I can't tell you that."

"Oh, a mystery." Francine clapped her hands. "I just love mysteries, don't you?"

"No," he grumbled. "Especially ones that give me a splitting headache."

"Race, it is a personal and potentially embarrassing matter with my sister. That's all I can say. Isn't that enough?"

The large lady brushed cracker crumbs from her chin. "No, it's not at all enough."

"I agree with Francine." Hillyard continued to stroke the top of his head. "There has to be more to the story."

Catherine's neck tightened. "I have some sensitive issues yet to be resolved. I can't say more."

He leaned forward with his elbows on his knees, his forehead resting in his palms. "Then, perhaps I didn't rescue you at all."

"Oh, no, I wanted out. But now I need to think things through."

His voice was a low rumble. "Things that you won't talk about."

She clutched her arms across her chest. "I need to step out on the platform and get some air."

He started to rise. "I'll go with you."

Catherine clamped his shoulder. "Not this time, Race. I need to have a clear mind to understand what to do."

"And I cloud your mind?"

And my heart, but I just can't admit that. Not to you. Not even to me.

A train at top speed has a rhythm. It clatters and quivers, but to a steady tune that calms the spirit and brings a kind of peace. The air that swirled around Catherine was warm, but offered a hint of coolness. Though it was dark, she guessed they must be ascending the Laramie Mountains. Dim lights in the car ahead shadowed the shapes and sizes of passengers. Within reach, the black night raced by.

She presumed the people on board longed for their destination. Those in private cars or on express trains might travel just for the enjoyment of the trip, but surely the cramped ones in the coaches could hardly wait to get to where they were going.

It seems like such a protracted trip. Just a

few days has so convoluted my life. I planned to snuggle by the window, get lost in my dream, then run to my Phillip's arms. It's like I took the wrong train. Why is Matthew Zane here? Lord, that's not fair. I'm sure You could have prevented it. And why did I sit down next to Race Hillyard? I have no idea if that was good or bad, but it has confused me, that's for sure.

The train embarked on a long right bend. She seized the cold, iron railing.

Now Zane blackmails me. Even if I could convince the entire world that's a picture of Catelynn, would it matter? I don't want my sister humiliated. And he's correct, the viewers would imagine that's what I look like . . . and they would be right.

A hulk of a man with a black coat buttoned at the neck stepped out on the rear platform of the adjoining car. She couldn't see his face, but he tipped his hat and she nodded.

"I'm a cigar salesman wanting to enjoy his wares," he called out. "Do you mind?"

Catherine shook her head.

The red glow from the cigar punctuated the night like a target at a county fair shooting gallery. She turned, but the tobacco aroma hovered around her head.

If I had not met Race, it would be an easier decision. I would just take the one-hundred dollars and get it over with. Just smile at the speculators . . . not at their tasteless stories and jokes . . . then ride over the Sierras to my Phillip. I would not be cheating anyone. I will make no claims of a mine's worth. Besides, sometimes they prove to be more valuable than previously thought. All speculators try to get rich without working for it. Not much different than Zane.

Take the money . . . destroy the photographs . . . marry Phillip and live happily ever after. That's not so tough.

But then, what will I tell Race? He will think it deplorable. And why do I care so much what he thinks? Why am I trying to impress a man I will never see again after this trip?

Catherine flinched when the train whistle pierced the night. She searched for the cause of the blast and spied a farm wagon on a dirt road, waiting to cross the tracks. Even in the shadows, it looked like a woman drove it.

What is she doing out in the middle of the night by herself? Perhaps she is a midwife hurrying to a delivery. Maybe she has to rush a sick child to town. But there are no towns. No midwives. Nothing. Perhaps all our lives defy understanding without knowledge of context.

The train slowed as the grade steepened.

I should have brought my shawl. I should go back in. But, I haven't resolved anything.

She turned her back to the breeze and noticed the man and the cigar were gone.

Lord, You are the one I must please. Should suppressing those photographs be my highest goal? They cannot be Your will. I will not do anything immoral, but want so much to do something positive for my sister and her baby.

The man who stepped out on the adjoining platform this time did not tote a cigar. He wore a conductor's hat and carried something white in his hand. "Miss Draper, is that you?"

"Yes."

"There are a couple of bruised gentlemen up in 3C. Do you know how they got that way?"

"I didn't see anything. Why do you ask me?"

"Every crisis on this run seems to involve you and Mr. Hillyard. A peaceful stretch would be a blessing. One of the bruised men gave me this note to give to you in private. I think you'd consider this private."

He reached across the railing.

"I'm sorry to report no compartments have opened up. I'm not sure it will be any better in Ogden. The westbounds have been very full all summer. I tried to warn you of that."

Catherine waited until he departed to unfold the note. Even stepping closer to the rear window, she couldn't find enough light to read it. When she stepped back into the coach, Francine and the children slumbered on the blankets and sleeping board in the front seats. Race, hatless, with blood matted in his dark hair, sprawled across the next seat.

If I had agreed with Zane, Race would not be wounded. Of course, had I practiced more self-control, he would be healthier as well. I am not sure I've brought anything positive to his life.

She scooted on the end of the bench seat. Hillyard moved toward the window, but didn't open an eye. Holding the note towards the aisle, she strained to read the neatly scrolled words.

"Catherine, you cannot escape the consequences of these photographs, no matter how many times your cowboy boyfriend rescues you. In the morning, I will protest to the conductor on how you and he tried to get me in a compromising position to blackmail me and that I was assaulted because I refused to pay. I will take my case and the photographs to the judge. I'll tell him you passed off these pictures of you, claiming the child is mine. Pinehurst will collaborate my story and reassure the judge that I've never seen you before in my life. Both of you will be arrested and jailed in Ogden. Some of the photographs will be turned over to the sheriff there. I'm sure he, his deputies, and most of the men in the saloons will enjoy looking at them and coming to the jail to see you in person. Another photograph I will mail to the mayor of Paradise Springs. I'll ask him to deliver it to Phillip with a note about your arrest and why you will be delayed arriving.

"I know you despise me, but you do know me

well enough to understand that I will do this. Be at 3C before 8:00 a.m., if you would like to prevent these consequences.

"Matthew Zane"

She read the note a second time, slowly, but the words didn't change.

Assault, extortion . . . blackmail . . . wouldn't that be a lovely Utah trial? Of course, I could have Catelynn and little Marie come out to testify as to the real situation with Matthew Zane. But, I couldn't put her through that. Neither of them must know about this. I will protect them. Lord, how can I do anything else?

Catherine eased out of the coach. She paused at the door and glanced back. She thought one of the Mormon girls nodded at her or perhaps dropped her head forward in slumber.

Lord, since the war, I have done so many things I swore I would never do. But I can't blame Mr. Lincoln anymore. I know he was right. Things had to change. But I seem to be on a downhill run ever since.

When she returned to the coach a half hour later, everyone seemed to be in the identical positions.

She sat straight up, valise in her lap, purse on top of valise, next to a snoring Race Hillyard.

There were stops in Laramie and Rawlins during the night, but Catherine didn't budge, nor close her eyes.

Race shoved his hat on his head before he opened his eyes, but flinched and pulled it off. He glanced at her. "I, eh, slept pretty sound."

She forced a smile. "Race, I can't apologize enough for hitting you. Some parts of this trip seem out of control. I seem to be doing more things without much forethought. It's not like me. Catelynn is that way, but I've prided myself in living a well-ordered life."

"You're away from Matthew Zane. I presume that's a good thing."

"You know how I feel about him. Right now the only thing on my mind is getting to Paradise Springs and being with Phillip."

He scratched the back of his neck as he studied her face. "I envy you. You have a goal, a vision, a plan. My plans seem a lot less definite than when I first crawled on this train."

"You're headed to San Francisco to find those who swindled your brother, right?"

"Yeah, but I suspect they will all be gone. Besides . . . you confused my life, Catherine."

She froze. "I did?"

"I think it's obvious how I feel about you."

Catherine gazed at her shoes. "You've complicated my life too, but I think it will straighten out soon. When you got on the train,

218

you despised me. Maybe your first instincts were correct."

"What are you talking about?"

"I really can't say any more."

"That's what you told me last night."

"You see, you're already getting disgusted with me again."

"Now my head really throbs. I think I'll find some water and wash up."

He sauntered to the rear of the car.

With considerable effort, Francine sat up on the sleeping board across the front seats. "Aren't you getting a little distant from Mr. Hilly?"

"I realize how little he knows about me."

"But he likes what he knows. Anyone can tell that."

"I don't think I like what I know about me." Catherine brushed down the front of her dress, even though it didn't need brushing. "The trip will be over in two or three days. And I do have Phillip waiting for me."

Francine struggled to her feet and covered both sleeping children with the single wool blanket. "I figured you and Race would head to San Francisco and leave poor Phillip stranded at the station."

"I could never do that. He's begged me to come out to California for almost seventeen years."

Francine stretched out her fleshy arms. "What does your heart want to do?"

Catherine dropped her chin. "I haven't followed my heart since I was twelve."

"You mean, your Phillip doesn't have your heart."

"He will have." Catherine felt her lips tighten. "I just have to get some other things done first."

"Other things besides . . . ?" Francine nodded down the aisle.

Race Hillyard strolled back, his hat perched on the back of his head. "Had an interesting conversation with two hardware drummers in the back. I overheard them mention diamonds, so I stopped to visit. Seems a pal of theirs knows someone who made some quick money in a diamond mine."

"Mine?" Catherine squeezed to the side to allow him access to the window seat. "There is no mine."

"If he made money, he's on the other side of things."

"So you have someone to go talk to."

"Mr. Legrans Degott. Isn't that a fine name? He lives out a few miles from Stockton, California."

"Interesting that you would pick up some clue on the train."

"Maybe the Lord's leading."

"I believe you have shaved, Mr. Hillyard. You look very nice."

"I borrowed a razor from a cigar salesman.

Friendly sort. Of course I had to buy two cigars and I don't smoke. Would either of you ladies care for a cigar?"

"That would be nice," Francine beamed.

"You smoke cigars?"

"No, but my Farley does. What a perfect present to take home to him."

Hillyard handed her the two El Presidentes.

Catherine watched Francine fuss with the children. "I have some news. I got to talk to the conductor last night. He believes a Pullman compartment will open up by the time we get to Ogden."

"Then you'll be leaving us?" he asked.

Catherine refused to look at Hillyard. "I'm debating it. I'm getting used to being right here."

Race fixed his hand on her arm. "You need to take the compartment. You already spent the money and can't get a refund. At least you can be rested up when you get to Sacramento. I trust it won't be up by Matthew Zane."

She spread her hand on his. "That would be a point to consider."

Francine leaned over the seat and faced them. "You can always wander back here to see the poor folks from time to time."

"I just wish this trip was over," Catherine sighed. "Life is too bewildering on a train."

"That's why I love taking the train," Francine

said. "It's a break for me. If it weren't for the hogs, my life at home would be quite boring."

"The, eh . . ."

Hillyard motioned for Catherine to be silent.

"Looks like we're stopping again. Is there a restaurant?"

Francine stooped over and peered out the window. "Nothing but a water tank."

The conductor strolled through the car. "Everyone stay on board. It's just an express train. We're going to couple one of our cars to it, then we'll be off."

"How about this one?" Francine suggested.

"No, we're going to . . ." The conductor looked around at the people in the car. "Eh, it won't take long. Everyone stay on board."

When the conductor exited, Francine leaned forward. "Perhaps it's a freight car with a payroll or something important. It took us three days to cover one day's track in Nebraska."

"This is a simple train. I don't think there are any treasures here," Hillyard said, then nodded to the seat ahead of him. "Besides Preston and Nancy."

Francine beamed. "You're right about them. Children are a treasure. But maybe a plain old train is the best place to hide riches."

In less than fifteen minutes, the express train pulled alongside them. Catherine studied the faces in the other train car that also assessed her.

"Do you see the one with the purple ostrich feather hat?" Francine blurted out. "My Farley bought me a hat like that, but I never had the nerve to wear it. At least, I think it was a hat. Do you like big hats, Catherine?"

"I don't like any hats at all, but they seem to be the badge of civility. If I must wear one, I'd rather display a small, unassuming one."

Francine straightened her own beige hat which looked like an inverted salad bowl with most of the salad missing. "I like your hat. Sort of an Italian design, isn't it?"

Catherine nodded. "Yes, it is, thank you. I've had this ever since I started teaching school."

"Did you like being a schoolteacher?"

"Some days I did. Other days, I got frustrated."

"I reckon kids can be squirrely."

"Oh, the kids delight me. The frustration was trying to convince the parents the importance of an education. Some wanted to pull their sons out early to work on the farms. Others were convinced girls didn't need to know anything but how to cook, sew and clean."

Hillyard waved towards the window. "Looks like the express is pulling out."

Catherine leaned against him. "What car did they attach?"

"Easy to spot. They hooked the judge's car behind the caboose."

Catherine continued to lean against him as the other train pulled away. "I don't think I've ever seen one hooked behind a caboose."

"I suppose they were in a hurry." Hillyard patted the top of his head as if trying to calm a frightened dog.

"It still hurts?"

"You are very good at what you do."

"Thank you. But why did the judge leave us?"

"He must have decided since a lot of folks knew he was on the slow train, he might as well take the fast one."

Catherine pulled away. "You'd think he would have mentioned that at supper."

When Race slapped down the sleeves of his coat, dust fogged up. "Then it wouldn't be a secret. That's why no transfer in Cheyenne."

"I like him . . . and Amanda Sue."

"They will be in Nevada in twenty-four hours," Francine said.

"We can only dream," Catherine replied.

Francine tied a ribbon in Nancy's hair. "Race, do you think girls should get an education?"

"Educated or not, I've noticed most gals are smart."

Francine grinned. "A true diplomat."

"Not very wise," he added, "but smart."

Catherine felt her neck tighten in her collar. "A prejudiced diplomat. And he didn't answer your question."

"I reckon every girl should have the opportunity to learn as much as she needs in order to accomplish God's calling for her, what he created her for. Same as men. In either case, wisdom is more important than knowledge."

"And how does a woman gain wisdom?" Catherine probed.

"By asking a man."

"I should clobber you, but that is one of the few grins I have seen on you. You have a very disarming smile."

"And you have a strong right arm," he said. "You already clobbered me. Women get wisdom in the same way men do. By living a decent life in front of others and learning from their mistakes."

She focused on the back of the seat ahead of them. "That sounds very prudent."

"That's because I've made lots of mistakes."

"Lately?"

"I busted down a train compartment door without knowing what's on the other side."

"Totally foolish."

"But I won't repeat that mistake."

Once the children had been washed and dressed, they switched back to their original seats. Hillyard, Catherine and Mr. Walker moved up, with Francine and the two little ones behind them.

He slouched down by the open window as the train rumbled west. Dirt and bugs blew in, but he seemed oblivious. The Mormon girls took turns walking Gibraltar up and down the aisle. They appeared to take careful note of the dozing Race Hillyard and curtsied to Catherine.

He's way too old for you, girls. But he does offer a whirlwind of adventure. In comparison, life with Phillip promises to be such a . . . a peaceful dream.

Nancy fussed with her two dolls and Preston consumed a steady stream of small round crackers as Francine rocked back and forth humming a tune at an unrecognizable but annoying level.

Buildingless sidings with names like Tipton, Red Desert, Latham, Creston, Rawhide and Walcutt sprinted by. They stopped for tasteless potato soup at a place called Mrs. Mustard's Table Rock Emporium, but reboarded the train in less than twenty minutes.

Catherine sat with her gloved hands folded in her lap.

Hillyard, hat pulled down over his eyes, leaned against the now half-open window. He rolled his coat up for a pillow. Francine rocked Preston, then pressed forward with a groan.

"That soup was rather, eh, rank, didn't you think?"

Catherine nodded. "Three spoonfuls were all I could handle."

"Preston liked it." Francine wiped perspiration from the boy's forehead. "But he's paying for it now."

Catherine surveyed the coach. "Where's Nancy?"

"She's visiting with the Mormon girls. She can be quite sociable when she wants." Preston let out a low cry. "I think I'd better get him somewhere safe to heave. He'll feel better with an empty tummy. Wouldn't want him to lose that awful soup all over Mr. Hilly."

Hillyard didn't stir.

"I think he's still recuperating from the blow you gave him."

Catherine lowered her chin and her voice. "It was quite by accident."

"You know that and Race knows that. But the barrel of your revolver and his head don't discern such." Francine toted the whimpering Preston to the back of the car.

Catherine surveyed the two bench seats formerly occupied by the cowboys. An elderly Chinese couple, traditionally dressed, sat at the windows. Each had a wooden cage on the seat next to them. One held a colorful bird that looked like a very small peacock. The dark blue, green and turquoise feathers caught and held her gaze for a moment. The other cage held, what looked like to Catherine, a giant rat. It lay on its side and didn't move. She wasn't sure if it was dead or alive.

They got on at a place called Salt Walls. There were no buildings, just a wood and water stop. They had no carriage. How did they get there? Wherever they came from, I'm sure it's better to be going west.

For what seemed like a very long time, she stared out the window at the sparse brown grass in the Divide Basin. No houses. No fences. No cattle. No roads. A string of ten foot tall telegraph poles that ran like a little brother, alongside the tracks.

She focused on the saddle. "You know, Mr. Walker, when I close my eyes for any length of time . . . then open them again . . . it is as if we haven't covered any ground at all. This scenery is identical to that one an hour ago, or yesterday. Have you noticed that?"

She paused as if listening to the silent saddle.

"You're right. You can't see much from your position. But you have noticed how slow time becomes when you ride a train? I wonder if time slows the faster one travels. What if a train could go one hundred miles per hour, would time stop? I suppose that's quite preposterous, but it's the kind of thing one thinks of on a long trip. I'd certainly like to get this trip over."

She fixed her gaze out the window at a herd of pronghorn antelope that numbered over one hundred, then turned back to the saddle.

"It's a big, empty land, Mr. Walker. I can't tell if

the emptiness attracts me or frightens me. It would all depend on who was with you, I suppose. I'm sure you and Mr. Hillyard would have no trouble out there. I'm glad my Phillip owns a store in the thriving town of Paradise Springs. I won't have to face an empty land."

The Mormon girls giggled and Catherine noticed that Nancy was dancing in the aisle for them. "Mr. Walker, I remember being a giggly girl. Catelynn and I liked to tease each other. I don't know when or why we lost that. How sad. I don't suppose you have a brother or a sister."

I'm talking to a saddle. Get some rest, Catherine. You will have little or no sleep after Ogden. I can't believe I agreed to help Matthew Zane. Yet what were my choices? Go to sleep. Don't wake up until Sacramento.

Catherine roused when Race tripped over her to get to the aisle. "What is it?"

"I'm going to see." He set his hat lightly on the back of his head. "We stopped in the middle of the tracks."

She gawked at giant granite boulders. "Where are we?"

"Nowhere, as far as I can tell." He waved at the windows. "It looks like we're on a big bend and there's a trestle up ahead."

As passengers lined up to peer out the windows, Catherine followed Hillyard outside. He helped her down off the last step. Then they trudged through the weeds and dry dirt to the trestle where a half-dozen men leaned over the canyon rim. Above them hovered white, streaky clouds which looked as if they were swept onto the pale blue sky with a heavenly paintbrush.

"What's down there?" Catherine asked.

A short man with a bowler, suit coat and no shirt, spat a wad of tobacco into the dust, then kicked dirt on it with his boot. "A train car. One of those fancy Pullman cars."

"A fancy one?" Hillyard stepped closer to the cliff edge. "You mean like the judge's?"

The shirtless man scratched his chest and shrugged. "Yep, I reckon that's it."

"Oh, no." Catherine's hands gripped her temples. "Not the judge and Amanda Sue! No . . . no . . . everything is going wrong. First, my life has a train wreck, and now the judge? I just can't do this."

Hillyard hugged her shoulders tight. "We don't know for sure. That may not be their car. Nothing is confirmed."

She slipped her arm around his waist, but pulled her head back. "It's his car and you know it."

"It does look like it," he admitted. "But it's tough to identify all smashed up like that."

"Why did they hook up to the express? Why were they behind the caboose? Why did the train go off and leave it down there? This can't be. Things like this shouldn't happen."

The conductor in his blue wool suit and cap hiked over with an overall-clad engineer. "We need to check out the wreckage before we can resume." He nodded at the man in overalls. "Monty will climb a pole and telegraph the company about it." He glanced around at the crowd, but settled his eyes on Race Hillyard. "I need a couple of men to go down and check out the damage and look for, eh, survivors."

Hillyard surveyed the canyon. "You got any ropes?"

"We got a hundred foot coil in the caboose," the conductor said.

Race yanked his hat off and handed it to Catherine. "Let Mr. Walker guard my hat. I'm going down."

"It looks dangerous," Catherine cautioned.

"I was rather fond of the judge and Amanda Sue, also."

"I'll go with you," the man without the shirt offered. When no one else stepped forward, he tossed his coat to the dirt. As he hiked over to the cliff, Catherine spotted several deep lateral scars on the man's back. She nodded to Hillyard.

He lowered his voice. "Yeah, I'd guess he took a whuppin'. Those are old scars, someone really pounded on him. Probably in the navy. They seem to beat men more often than anywhere else."

The man marched over to them. His round face looked staunch and stern. "Who did you say was in the car?"

"Judge Clarke, his daughter, and his cook," the conductor replied.

"How about Chet Pinehurst, the ex-Pinkerton man?" Catherine asked.

"Oh, no," the conductor replied. "It was his idea to switch trains, but he didn't ride with them. He's still on our train."

"His idea?" Catherine sputtered. "Why isn't he here helping these men? Was there a telegraph back at Table Rock where we had lunch?"

The conductor nodded. "Of course."

Hillyard grabbed her shoulder. "Catherine, what are you thinking?"

She jerked away from him. "I want to have a talk with Pinehurst."

Race cut her off. "Give me the gun."

Her chin dropped. "What?"

"Catherine, give me my spare revolver."

She reached in her purse and handed him the gun. "I promise I won't shoot him."

"Let's make sure."

"But I might have to hit him in the head."

Race opened the cylinder. Five cartridges dropped to his hand. He handed it back to her.

She shoved the gun in her purse. "No ammunition? That was rude."

"I see fire in your eyes. But we don't know

what we'll find down in that car. I don't want you doin' something you, me and the Lord will regret."

"It's smashed to pieces. All you're going to find is mangled bodies. Pinehurst had to have something to do with it."

"You don't know that. Maybe you should wait for me to get back before you go talk to them."

"The Lord has stirred my fury and I intend to release it."

"Catherine," he called out. "Do the wise thing."

She ground her teeth and shaded her eyes with her hand. "Women aren't hemmed in by wisdom. I believe that's what you intimated."

The conductor shoved a thick hemp rope into his hands.

He turned to the shirtless man. "You ready, partner?"

"Yep." He took one end of the rope and tied it around his waist. "I'm Byron MacCay, but most just call me 'Shirtless.' "

Hillyard tied the other end of the rope to his waist. "You never wear a shirt?"

"Not since the war."

"Well, Shirtless, I'm . . ."

"I know who you are, Race Hillyard."

"Have we met?"

The man rubbed his unshaven chin. "Only at

a distance. During the war, I was aboard ship down off the south Texas coast."

"Did we serve on the same . . ."

"I was on the other side. But we all knew your name. There was a $500 reward for anyone who could shoot Hillyard out of the crow's nest."

"A reward? By name? How come I never heard about that? I was just doin' my job. But to tell you the truth, I never liked it. You ready to go?"

"You want to lead?"

"Yep."

"You trust me to keep you safe?" Shirtless queried.

"Yep."

Shirtless coiled the excess rope around his shoulder. "Yeah, Hillyard, we were impressed how good a shot you were." He worked his way around several boulders. "We all wanted to learn to shoot like you, but at the same time, we wanted you dead."

Hillyard turned his back to the canyon, then lowered himself over a shed-sized boulder. "I still have nightmares about those days. War makes a man do a lot of things he regrets."

The man held the rope taut until Hillyard reached the bottom. "Don't worry. I don't hold a grudge," he called down. "I did for a long time. You see these stripes on my back? You're the cause of them."

Hillyard held up his hands to catch the man's feet as he skimmed over the giant rock. "How?"

Shirtless rubbed his bare shoulder when he reached the ground. "I was on the Hampton, trying to blockade the entrance of the Rio Grande. It was a foggy December morning and I was up in the loft, trying to spot you Reb ships. I couldn't see anything. Then it was two bells on the morning watch. The captain insisted we sounded bells, even in thick fog. When the second bell sounded, the captain's dog keeled over as a rifle report pierced through the fog."

"I shot the captain's dog? I remember that morning. Captain King didn't think any Union ships were within ten miles. I knew better. I thought I heard the bells and just took a chance. When you fired back with a cannon, we turned and ran back out to sea." Hillyard gripped a sage and lowered himself on down the canyon.

Shirtless followed. "Well, the captain's dog got killed and I was in the lookout. So, it was my fault."

Hillyard stopped and leaned over, his hands on his knees. "And he lashed you for that?"

"It was suppose to be only a dozen. But he did the beating himself. I passed out around fifty. I've been shirtless ever since."

"Partner, I'm truly sorry I caused you that much pain." They worked their way down to the mangled train car.

Shirtless stood by the busted back door. "The good news: we all hated the dog. No one but the captain mourned him. I only hated your guts for five, maybe ten years." He worked his way over to Hillyard. "Can you see anything? Anyone? Any bodies?"

Hillyard climbed up on the crumpled black iron railing of the deluxe train car. "I'll search inside the wreck. You look around outside. Look for any signs of blood, torn clothing. . . ."

"Arms, legs, feet?"

"Anything."

Shirtless wiped the sweat off his forehead. "It's like the war, isn't it?"

The car lay on its side and Hillyard trudged through broken glass, busted chairs, and scattered furnishings.

Lord, I really don't want to find anyone down here. Don't know if I have the moral strength to carry a broken little body all the way to the top.

He shuffled through a pile of books and waded toward the kitchen area. Fancy silverware scattered among air-tight cans of peaches and a busted twenty-five pound bag of rice.

"Judge! Amanda Sue? Is anyone here?"

On his way back out, he inspected an empty clothes closet. A voice from outside drew him to the door.

"Shirtless, what did you find?"

"Nothing, Hillyard. No bodies, britches or blood. Did you find anything?"

"Everything inside is busted up, but no signs of humans when they hit bottom."

"I reckon folks could have been tossed out up on them rocks at the west rim. How did one car cut loose?"

"Look at the grade up there. It just keeps climbing as it circles south. If you send one car rolling back down, I suppose it would gain so much speed it would jump the track just before the trestle."

"And land about here. Wouldn't you expect that express to stop and investigate the wreck?"

"Maybe they did and got back on their way."

"Did it look like anyone had been searching the car before you?"

"Nope. Did you find any tracks around the car?"

"Nothin'."

"My guess is that no one was in the car when it hit bottom. All the clothes and personal items were missing. But that doesn't explain much. You go on and lead the way up."

Shirtless grinned. "And I'm suppose to trust a Rebel sniper to catch me if I fall?"

"Don't think of me as a Johnny Reb. I'm just the one who eliminated the captain's dog."

"In that case, I don't mind going up first."

• • •

It took a half-hour to reach the train and another twenty minutes to explain what they found to the conductor.

The engineer blasted the horn and the passengers filed back into the train.

Shirtless pulled his coat on. "Hillyard, I'll ride the river with you any day."

"Same to you. But those stripes you wear just remind me of my failures."

"I know. It's my revenge."

Hillyard waved a salute. "Fair enough."

He brushed dust off his coat when he returned to the car.

Francine examined him up and down. "I hear you didn't find any mangled bodies down there."

He grabbed his hat off the saddle horn and shoved it on his head. "I'm glad about that."

"Do you reckon the judge and the little girl got kidnapped?" Francine quizzed.

"I've been ponderin' that idea. We know someone was after the girl. Maybe they hijacked the car, kidnapped all of them, then let it roll into the canyon. But they were a careful lot. All the clothing was taken out of the car. Why would kidnappers do that? No way of knowin' until we get to Ogden."

The train began to chug over the tall trestle. Hillyard surveyed the car. "Catherine hasn't come back yet?"

"Oh, she's been back. She said a compartment opened up in one of the Pullman cars, so she gathered up her stuff and left us."

He stared at Francine. "What?"

"Yep, she's gone. Too genteel for us back here, I reckon."

Hillyard stalked up the aisle waving his hands. "How does a compartment open up in the middle of nowhere?"

"I was wonderin' that too. Maybe she explained it in her note."

"Note?"

Francine fanned her face with the envelope. "This is for you and I haven't even read it. I had a mind to, but the Lord's hand constrained me."

He took the brown, stiff envelope and opened the paper folded inside.

"Race, I must do what I must do. Some day I hope to explain. Don't come looking for me. It would make matters worse. Take care of yourself. We need men like Race Hillyard. You enriched my life and I will always be grateful for that. Catherine Goodwin."

CHAPTER NINE

Arms clasped across her chest, Catherine tried to control her breathing as her lips were tight, her face flushed. "I will parade on your arm and smile. I will answer to the name, Catelynn . . . and I will try not to shudder when called Mrs. Zane. But I will not lie about a mining claim."

Zane's face was expressionless, like a snake with eyes barely open. He brushed his mustache with his fingertips. "Just refer all mining questions to me, although your sister knew much more about my dealings than you might expect."

Catherine raised an eyebrow. Her heart chilled. "Knew?"

"I meant, knows. I was thinking back on the previous meeting with the investors in the spring. She charmed them all with her words and disarmed them with her . . ."

"Smile?"

"Of course. It's your smile, too. You just don't use it as much."

It's like I'm viewing this from a distance. It's not really me, just a play, a skit. I have a part to perform. It's a tragedy. I wish I would hurry up and die.

"You have never given me anything to smile about."

"Catelynn wanted . . . wants to be wealthy again. This transaction will accomplish that."

"I thought she needed the funds to take baby Marie to Germany."

"Yes, that is the first priority. But there will be much more. She longs for the affluent life like you had as children."

The image of a sprawling northern Virginia estate rolled gently on her mind. Green fields. Stately trees. Happy childhood. "I didn't think of us as wealthy. We had what we needed."

Zane shoved the knot of his black silk tie higher against a starched white shirt collar, then straightened his red silk vest. "In elegant style."

"I suppose." The reflection in her mind darkened to the coal black ruins of burned-out buildings. "But that's all gone. For me. For Catelynn. For everyone south of the Mason-Dixon Line. I don't need that now."

"You don't think of your precious Mr. Draper as rich? I thought you went to California to renew the Goodwin splendor." Zane's voice spewed sarcasm and manipulation.

"I'm sure Phillip's prosperous. We'll not be in need." When Catherine closed her eyes, she could not imagine Phillip as a grown man, only a reflection of a twelve-year-old boy who was now man-size. "But it's a mining town prosperity. I

241

have no inflated illusions. It won't be the antebellum South. Not elegant. Not refined. Just comfortable. That's what I want, that's what I need . . . a comfortable life."

"That's why you're here now . . . to get comfortable with the arrangements." Zane slid a telegram out of his pocket, then unfolded it as if it were a map to a secret treasure. "Daily, Longtire and Woolsey will be joining us in Ogden. That's why you had to move up here at this time. They'll be in the compartment next to us."

Catherine tried to fade into the pale green, wooden wall in front of her. "I thought all the compartments were taken?"

"That one was reserved back in Omaha," Chet Pinehurst said.

"And this one is in the name of Mr. & Mrs. Matthew Zane."

"And friend," Pinehurst added.

"You didn't know I was on this train."

"We planned on Catelynn coming along. It was a last minute decision to send them to the Hampton Beaches."

"Cape Cod."

Zane shot a look at Pinehurst. "Yes, of course. Cape Cod. The point is, the three of us will have to work out accommodations in this compart-ment for a day or so. We'll worry about sleeping arrangements tonight."

Catherine closed her hands together in prayer-like fashion against her lips. "There is nothing to worry about." She felt confined, hot, sticky, dirty.

This will be my last train trip ever. A buggy or stagecoach or even a freight wagon will be sufficient.

"I will sit right here fully clothed with my hand on a revolver all night. And you two will stay right where you are."

Perhaps Phillip will allow me to purchase a tall, black stallion. I'll straddle him and ride the wind along the foothills of the majestic Sierra Nevada Mountains. They sound so grand.

Matthew Zane stood and pounded on the curving light green metal door above the seat. "These bottom seats adjust into one bed, and this top bunk folds down."

"I really couldn't care less what it does."

Never, not even for one minute, have I been able to recognize what my sister sees in you. How can identical sisters possess such opposite tastes in men?

"You two may sleep up in the club car or out in the aisle. The beds in this compartment will remain unfixed."

When we were girls, we always competed for the same boys. But the loser always ended up happier.

"How will I explain that to Daily, Longtire and Woolsey?"

"I really don't care. I am not sure you need to explain sleeping arrangements to anyone on this train." The image of a scowling Race Hillyard emerged from the recesses of her mind. "For the sake of my sister and her baby, I will follow this charade, and at Reno Station you will give me the prints and one-hundred dollars."

For several minutes nothing was said, then Zane's eyes moved up from her shoes to her hat.

"Is that the nicest dress you have?"

Catherine threw her shoulders back. "I have one nicer, but I'm saving it to wear when I meet Phillip."

"Put it on now. I need my wife to dress better than that."

Her throat tightened at the sound of the word "wife." "They will have to accept me as I am."

Zane punched his fist in the air. "They already accepted you as Catelynn dresses. You know she wears nicer things."

The Planter's Annual Ball.

Catherine had no idea why it came to mind. But the white silk gown Catelynn wore had fired the "want to" in every young man in northern Virginia and the "hate you" in every young lady.

"You're right. She does dress nicer."

"I will give you ten dollars more so that you can buy another dress in Ogden that you can save for Phillip."

"You mean, you'll give me another fifty dollars for a new dress."

His face reddened. "You can buy an exclusive gown from Paris for fifty dollars."

"I believe you're right. I was just contemplating, 'What would Catelynn do?' "

He tossed his hand in the air and searched the compartment as if looking for reason from the green walls. "You two are identical in more ways than you know. Okay, okay, fifty dollars for a dress. Just put on the nicer one now."

"Not until you two leave the compartment."

"No reason to leave, we know what you . . ." Pinehurst's leer reminded Catherine of a dog who thought a rattlesnake would make a great toy.

She turned to Zane. "So no one has seen the photographs but you, Catelynn and me? And this snake of a pal of yours. And who knows how many other cronies." She glared at Pinehurst. "You have seen Catelynn, not me."

He leaned forward as if revealing a long hidden secret. "But you are Catelynn now."

"Only for the next day-and-a-half. I do not change with men in my dressing room."

"Okay, okay," Zane tugged at the man's shoulder. "Come on, Chet, let's take a stroll. Maybe we'll hike back to the coach cars and see how your cowboy pal is doing without you."

Catherine remained seated. "Yes, you did so well with him before. I believe Chet's arm is still limp. Hillyard has tossed better men than you off this train."

Pinehurst waved a finger at her. "Maybe we should show him some photographs?"

She jammed her hand into her purse and pulled the revolver out and laid it on her lap. "And perhaps I should put a bullet through your head."

"You can't threaten us with that gun," Pinehurst announced. "You might not like me, but I did learn a few things at Pinkerton. And that gun isn't loaded."

Catherine glared at the man's squinty eyes. "Did you learn how to sabotage the judge's train car?"

"I told you, I had absolutely nothing to do with that. The judge did not even tell me about the transfer. He sent me up to ask the engineer a couple of questions. By the time I returned, the car had been switched."

"That's not what the conductor told me."

"Well, he got it wrong. He assumed I had something to do with it. I didn't argue with him, I figured it made me look clever. But it was the judge's doing. He paid me good wages. Why would I send him off?"

When Catherine rubbed the bridge of her nose, she realized how tired she was. "If you aren't a part of that, why did you saddle up to the judge in the first place? You must have had a reason."

Zane brushed the scar hidden in his mustache.

"Clarke is a friend of Judge Kingston in Carson City. It's my understanding that the final approval of the transfer of the mining claims will need his approval. Or someone he appoints. We figured any way we could improve our image would be good."

"And you had nothing to do with the attempted kidnap of Amanda Sue earlier?"

Pinehurst pushed his coat back to reveal a holstered revolver. "That was an amateur job. If kidnapping had been my goal, it would have been much easier."

"In a treacherous way, that makes sense."

"Are you going to change dresses?" Zane challenged.

"Not until two things happen."

"Yes, yes," Zane's head bobbed like a spring-loaded target at a county fair. "We need to leave the compartment. What else?"

"And you will surrender all the photos except for one as you promised."

He reached into his vest pocket and pulled out a handful of three-by-five-inch photographs. He spread them like a hand of Whist, then plucked one from the center. "This is the one that I keep."

She yanked the rest from his hand and laid them face down in her lap. "Yes, I supposed it would be. Now, go."

The men paused at the doorway.

"How long will it take you?" Zane asked.

"An hour."

"To change your dress?" Pinehurst coughed.

"Obviously, you have never been married."

With the door securely locked from the inside, Catherine sat down next to the window and examined the photos. Two were of the baby by herself. And three of Catelynn with the baby. She began to rip up those with Catelynn into very small pieces.

Catelynn, maybe Zane is right. Maybe you like these, maybe they are "artistic." But they are obscene to me and to all that I know. I will destroy them for your sake. I believe it best.

She tore the scraps until none measured more than a quarter-of-an-inch square. Then admired with a bittersweet emotion the pictures of the baby.

Marie DuClare, you are a cutie. It is not obscene to have a naked baby photograph. Aunt Catherine is going to keep one of these. Some day, when you are twenty and come to California to see Uncle Phillip, me, and your three cousins . . . a boy and twin girls, I presume . . . I will give this picture to you. You will be embarrassed, but you will treasure it. How I wish I could hold you in my arms right now. How I'd like to sip tea in northern Virginia with your mommy on the veranda of your grandma and grandpa's house. You would have liked it there. So peaceful . . . so perfect. Your grandmother and grand-

father would have spoiled you rotten, of course, but that's why the Lord created grandparents. But I have no idea why He took them away. Oh, honey, those days are . . .

"So gone," she cited aloud.

Catherine tore the second photograph of the baby in a similar fashion as the others, then mixed all the pieces together in her lap. With some effort, she slid open the compartment window about two inches. It wouldn't open any higher. Plucking a half-dozen tiny scraps at a time, she sprinkled them along the Wyoming prairie. It took several minutes and several miles to empty her skirt of the fragments. The remaining photograph got tucked down inside her handbag, next to the unloaded revolver.

Thank you so much, Mr. Hillyard, for disarming me. You took the cartridges out of my gun. But I am a little more resourceful than you imagined.

With great care, she pulled the pale orange silk dress from her valise. She hung it from a hook on the back of the door, then shook, beat and smoothed the wrinkles.

Well, Phillip, of all the dresses I owned, I only brought this one. It is as close to gold as I owned and California is the "golden" state. It is the one I'm always wearing in my dreams when I meet you at the station. It is the one I wear when I daydream of that big church wedding.

Oh, my, I never did ask you the size of the church you attend. I trust the sanctuary is sufficient for a large wedding. "Prominent Paradise Springs businessman weds Virginia aristocrat's daughter." No, no . . . "weds New England schoolteacher." That might be better.

She let out a long deep sigh.

Okay, it should read "Prominent Paradise Springs businessman weds fugitive accused of attempted murder."

She set her hat on the cushioned seat and pulled her old dress over her head. *I need a hot bath and clean undergarments. You look neither like a Virginia aristocrat nor a criminal fugitive.*

"But that's the beauty of the West," she confided to the image in the mirror. "We get to start all over."

The pale orange silk dress stretched snug in the chest, but felt fine in other places. She studied the mirror. "Well, Catelynn, I know what you would say. If I didn't wear underwear on the upper part of my body, if I followed your example, it would fit fine. I am not you, honey. I never will be. I think that's our biggest problem. Neither of us can quite accept our non-identical parts. Well, I will wear a dress slightly too tight, because that is me."

With the dress hanging in style, she brushed her hair, then set it behind her head with pale orange combs. She posed in front of the small mirror and glanced from side to side.

Zane's right about one thing. I do look more like Catelynn when I dress like she does. I don't have that husky laugh of hers that turns every man's head in the room. Well, maybe I do, but I've never known how to use it. She tried to teach me once when we were sixteen, but gave up saying I sounded like a mule with a cold. That was the time you convinced me to go to the regatta with J. Hubert Sluman, because you found a better date with Randall Billings. Poor old J. Hubert . . . he never knew it wasn't you. I shouldn't have let him kiss you . . . I mean, me. It was rather pathetic. A two at best. But I thought it was one way to get back at you for sticking me with such a bore.

"Now, Mr. Zane, bring on the suckers, I mean, bring on the 'potential investors' and watch me charm them all."

The compartment door was unlocked when Zane knocked. He led the way as two men entered. His manipulative smile widened.

"Look at that, Chet, is that Catelynn or not?"

The shorter man plopped down across from Catherine. "To tell you the truth, identical twins bother me a little. When I was young, we had neighbors who had sickly identical twin boys. Never saw them out much. One was a pretty nice fellow, the other a complete jerk. Years later I found out they didn't have twins, just the same kid who had been touched in the head. You never knew who he was going to be on any given day."

Catherine plastered on her fake smile. "Thank you for those reassuring words."

Zane sat down next to her. "You look the part. Now, smile and lean forward when you talk and they will be charmed."

"I do not lean," she snapped.

Zane glanced at the ceiling as if expecting an angelic idea to float down. After a moment, he spoke. "Maybe we should stroll around the train arm-in-arm to get used to it."

"I don't want to ever get used to it."

Zane laid his hand on her knee. "I can't just show up with a wife in Ogden, whom none on the train has seen."

She shoved his hand away. "Tell them I was sick most of the journey."

He pointed to his vest. "You don't want me strolling around the train by myself with this picture in my pocket, do you?"

"No, I'd rather you threw yourself off the train over a deep ravine, but since that is hardly likely . . . I will walk with you . . . but only through the Pullman cars. Don't go back to the coaches."

Matthew Zane stood and offered his hand. "Are you ashamed to be seen all dressed up?"

She refused to touch him. "None of your prospective investors will be back in those cars. It would not be productive. I don't need practice to be among those kind of people. If I need practice, it's up here among those almost as phony as you, Matthew Zane."

"Catelynn, is that any way to talk to your husband?" Pinehurst said.

"I am not Catelynn. . . ."

"Yes, you are," Zane insisted. "From here until after the court hearing in Nevada, you are Catelynn. You need to get used to being called that."

"Yes, but only in the Pullman section."

The DeVeres chattered about their trip to Australia.

Gen. VonKlimmer berated the incompetence of Napoleon III as a military leader.

The Bettersons showed off a hundred photographs of their dog, Ginger, ignoring the fact that the golden retriever stood by their side.

Carlos Regetta droned on how he owned the largest gunshop in Peru.

The Trichots spoke only in French, but seemed to be the most pleasant of the lot.

While Catherine knew the Bible only recorded the sun stopping once in history, for Joshua over the Valley of Aijalon, the phenomena seemed to repeat itself as the afternoon dragged by with annoying slowness. A myopic joy trickled in her as the sun lowered in the west.

Pinehurst waved his half-limp arm at them. "Conductor says we'll be stopping in Rock Springs for supper."

Catherine stared at the setting sun. "I'm not getting off."

"You have to," Zane insisted. "All who met you this afternoon will expect to see you with me. I think you made a hit with them."

She tried to rub the wrinkles from her forehead. "Tell them I don't feel well."

Zane tapped her shoulder. "Need I remind you of our arrangement?"

"Don't touch me."

He pulled back his hand.

"I agreed to play the part in front of your potential investors, not for some greasy supper in the middle of Wyoming."

"We're just about out of the Territory," Pinehurst said.

"Tell them I have a headache, that I'm not used to the altitude or something. Tell them I'm basking in the splendor of such wonderful conversations this afternoon. I don't care what you tell them."

"You have to eat," Zane said.

"Bring me a cup of tea and a biscuit. I don't want to see my friends in the coaches. This situation is too impossible to explain."

"Are you saying you're ashamed to be seen with me?"

"That's exactly what I'm saying."

She received two sourdough biscuits, a large wedge of sharp white cheese, and a glass jar with tepid tea. The train had propelled into Utah Territory before she finished the meal and picked the crumbs from her dress.

Zane and Pinehurst wandered towards the front of the train and Catherine washed her face, neck and arms in the tiny basin of water. She was startled to hear someone in the next compartment cry.

I didn't know you could hear between compartments. How much do they know what has been going on in here?

She leaned her ear against the cold, slick wall of the compartment. Feeling a sharp pain, she reared back, removed her earring, then leaned again to the wall. She discerned a slight whimper and a deep voice of comfort, but otherwise the sounds were so muted she could not tell what was being said.

I didn't hear a word, yet I sensed sadness or fear. All of that going on only a few feet from me. That's the way life is, Lord. A few feet away broils an entirely different crisis. In a crowded room, or on a crowded train, I believe mine is the only drama that matters. That's one of the

255

many lessons I've got to learn. Catherine Goodwin's melodrama might not be on the center stage of life. That's a rather humbling thought. Lord, bring some peace and joy to those next door . . . and get me to Paradise Springs, quick.

She was reseated by the window, fastening her earring, when the men returned.

"Several asked about you. You Goodwin twins are both quite charming, when you want to be." Zane hung his crisp, black silk hat on a hook behind the door. "Are you going to wear that dress all night?"

"I trust, Mr. Zane, no one has ever made the mistake of calling you charming. I informed you before, I will sit right here, fully dressed, all night."

A hint of lilac tonic water drifted across the otherwise stuffy compartment.

Zane slid next to the window and she tucked her feet to make room for highly polished black boots. "You might be fearful for nothing. Aren't you presuming a lot? What makes you think either of us have any desire to take advantage of you?"

"You have both proven yourselves to be despicable men." She tried to concentrate her gaze out the window, but the glass reflected both men's images. "Why should I not assume that?"

"I will be just as glad as you are when this is

over. At times, you remind me too much of Catelynn."

She talked to the reflections in the glass. "I take that as a compliment."

Zane ignored her comment. "As long as we are to sit up all night, you need to know what happens tomorrow."

"I do not want to know any details about the mining claim transaction. I want to look all parties in the eyes and truthfully say, 'I don't know anything.' I told you, I will not lie."

Still wearing his slouch hat, Pinehurst sat next to Zane. "Your sis knew plenty. You should have seen her get excited about the Law of Apex litigation."

"Yes, but she knows nothing about how to teach thirty fourth-grade students to divide fractions. We have our separate fields of interest. I will smile and nod and act demure at tasteless humor. But that is all."

"You will need to know the schedule," Zane said. "We will be in Ogden at noon to meet three men there: Mr. Cyrus Daily, Mr. Edward Longtire and Mr. Bertram Woolsey."

"Will their wives be with them?"

"I presume not. But you made a hit with the wives in New York in the Spring."

"I didn't. Catelynn did."

"Of course. They will ride with us to Reno Station. Be pleasant to them."

"Did I make a hit with the men as well?"

"Oh, yeah," Pinehurst smirked.

"Catelynn and I met with them several times. They are New York industrialists with friends who made money in western mines. They want in on the action, but know very little about mining."

"And it's your job to give them an education?"

A grin pasted itself on Zane's face. "Exactly. The other three men . . . Worthington, Hall and Fryberg . . . will be joining us at Reno Station. They consider themselves experts in the business because they have a little copper mine on the south end of Lake Superior. In fact, they are confident that they are pulling something over on me."

"How frightfully slack of them."

"It's the nature of this mining speculation business," Zane continued. "At Reno, we will all take carriages to Carson City. And, I presume, appear before the judge to get the documents finalized. At that point, I get their investment funds. I give you your money and you are on your way."

Catherine again studied his image in the window. "And you give me that final photograph."

"Of course."

"And fifty dollars to buy a dress in Ogden."

"I agreed to that. Whether you buy the dress in Utah or Nevada doesn't matter to me."

If Matthew Zane never talked or moved, you could call him a handsome man.

She turned back to face him directly. "Do I need to go to Carson City?"

"Yes."

"But if I go with you, I'll miss my train."

"I'll put you in a Pullman on the very next one."

"I will have to telegraph Phillip and let him know which train I'm on."

"You can telegraph Leland Stanford for all I care."

She turned back to the windowed image. "You are wrong about one thing. You will in no way be as happy as me to get all of this over."

Why doesn't someone tell men with sagging jowls they should never grow drooping mustaches. So comical looking, yet impolite to laugh. I must be polite. I must. I must.

". . . well, I chuckled about that for weeks. Speaking of Henrietta, she told me I must insist that you come out this fall to our place on Long Island. She so enjoyed that luncheon you gave at the Crystal Ballroom. She wants to have a little affair in your honor. You know, an afternoon tea with a few dozen of her dearest friends."

Catherine patted his arm. "Cyrus, you tell her I'll be there." She nodded over at Matthew

259

Zane. "I'll make Mattsey buy me a completely new wardrobe for the occasion. Not, of course, that I need a reason for new clothes."

Cyrus Daily's smile revealed a wide gap in his upper front teeth. "No wonder you and Henrietta get along so well. You shop alike."

A tall man wearing a beige linen suit and battered flop hat strolled across the platform. "I say, Daily, you don't intend on monopolizing all of Mrs. Zane's time, do you?"

"I intend to monopolize silver production in Nevada, but not our Catelynn."

Catherine slipped her hand into the arm of the beige linen suit. "Edward, Edward, I've been meaning to ask you ever since last spring, what is the origin of such an intriguing last name as Longtire?"

He held the knot of his brown tie as if it gave more authority to his words. "It's Scottish. A proud name that goes back hundreds of years. There have been Longtires leading Scotland for centuries."

She tilted her head and grinned her charming best. "Why, Edward, do you mean you have one of those cute little wool plaid kilts?"

"Well, eh . . . yes, of course." His face reddened. He let her arm drop from his. "But I don't wear it often."

"I am going to insist you wear it for me."

"I'm not sure where Pearline has put it."

Catherine clutched his arm again. "Do you by any chance play the bagpipes?"

"No, I do not."

"I've always wanted to know a person who played the bagpipes. There is a burning question I'd love to ask them."

"What is that?"

Catherine wrinkled her nose. "Why do you do it?"

"Yes," Longtire chuckled. "Pearline says the pipes bleat like a herd of young goats, but they are a way of life to me."

Broad-shouldered Bertram Woolsey slipped his arm in Catherine's. "Mrs. Zane, allow me to escort you to the carriage. The train won't leave until 2:00 p.m. and there's a fine restaurant on the south side of town. You will be our guest."

"Is there a nice dress shop near it?"

Woolsey cleared his throat. "Well, eh, I'm not sure at all. You need to do a little shopping?"

"Bertie, Bertie, Bertie, did you ever know a woman who didn't need to shop? It's in our bones. We just can't help it."

She turned back to a cluster of men on the train platform. "Sweetheart, we're going out to lunch. Are you going to join us?"

"Yes . . . yes. . . ." Matthew strolled towards them. "I was just reading over these final purchase papers."

Cyrus Daily jammed his hands in his pockets.

"I trust everything is what we agreed on in New York."

The creases on Zane's forehead relaxed. "Seems to be in order. I'm just working my way though the 'misinterpretation clause.'"

"That's standard in all contracts," Longtire insisted.

"Well, you boys know I'm a small town man who's spent most of his life out here in the West scratching for a living from the hard dirt. My legal training was by the only barrister in Tuolumne County . . . but I'll trust you men." He folded the papers and slipped them into his coat, then offered Catherine his arm.

She stared across the station at a young boy chasing a thin rooster.

Zane, if I can continue this charade without gagging, I will consider it my greatest performance.

Zane patted her hand. "But if I have any trouble with this contract, boys, I'll send Catelynn to visit with your wives. I imagine they could straighten it all out."

"Now, wouldn't that be a fine pickle?" Longtire chuckled. "Maybe the wives should draw up the contracts. Could make for a happier home. Except for Bertram, the old bachelor."

"When Berty gets rich with this mine, no telling how many women will be flocking to his side," Daily commented.

"There have been plenty of opportunities over the years," Woolsey huffed. "But I always thought I was the one who ought do the asking."

Catherine clapped her hands. "Well said, Bertie. Don't let these old bears badger you. I do hope the restaurant has fresh strawberries. I haven't had a fresh strawberry since the day we left New York. Mattsey fixed me a delightful breakfast that morning of berries, fresh, thick cream and Swedish crepes."

"Your husband cooked your breakfast?" Longtire asked.

Catherine laid her head against his sleeve. "Oh, he does it all the time on the maid's day off, don't you dear?"

She couldn't tell if he look more startled or just annoyed.

"Catherine, I need to speak to you." The voice broke across the train platform more like an alarm than a friendly greeting.

She turned to see Race Hillyard, hat in hand, twenty feet away.

"Eh . . . excuse me?"

"Catherine, we need to talk!"

Cyrus Daily stepped forward. "Who's Catherine?"

Matthew Zane shoved Catherine behind him. "Mister, my wife's name is Catelynn."

Hillyard stalked forward waving his finger.

"Zane, I took care of you in the Pullman car yesterday, but I can do it again."

Catherine turned to Daily and Longtire. She lowered her voice. "My identical twin sister is named Catherine. He must have me confused."

"Rather a rude chap," Woolsey mumbled. "Perhaps we should contact the marshal."

"You're giving the rest of your heart away, Catherine Goodwin," Race shouted. "You can't do that. You won't have anything left."

Matthew Zane herded the others toward the carriages. "He's a drunk. Just ignore him. Let's go eat."

Hillyard lurched closer, waving his finger. "Catherine, we need to talk and you know it."

She spun around. Zane grabbed her arm, but she broke free.

"My name is Catelynn Zane. If you would address me by my proper name, I will take a moment to chat with you."

Race dropped his hands to his side and let out a deep sigh. "Mrs. Catelynn Zane, may I please have a word with you?"

"Are you sure you'll be alright?" Daily cautioned. "He looks a bit rough."

She lowered her voice. "I'll be fine. I've dealt with this type in my work down in the Bowery Mission."

"You do charity work there?" Daily twisted his drooping mustache. "My, you are an amazing lady."

Zane sidled up to her and whispered, "Do you have any idea what you are doing?"

She spoke softly, without moving her lips. "I'm trying to save your miserable hide."

Catherine marched past Race to the other side of the platform. He trailed behind. She stood where she faced the others, but with Hillyard's back toward them.

"This is absurd," Hillyard fumed. "I can't believe you are doing this for money, like that phony kiss in Omaha."

She brushed her bangs back and took two pinched-lip breaths before she spoke. "I am not doing this for the money. You don't know the story." She pointed at him as if identifying the guilty party in a courtroom drama. "Don't judge until you know all the facts."

His shoulders relaxed as he shoved his hat back on. "Then, for the sake of my sanity, tell me the facts."

She looked away at the steam drifting out from under the locomotive. "I can't."

He leaned his head closer. "You can't or you won't."

"Both." She didn't back away, but did drop her chin. "I don't want to do this, but I have to.

It's not for me, it's for others. I must do it. That's all I can say."

Hillyard slapped his hands on his hips and shook his head. "It's not enough, Catherine. I have to know what's going on."

"It has to do with my family. Actions in the past. A myriad of worries. My only chance to simplify it, is to do things this way. Believe me, I have considered all the alternatives."

He reached out his hand. "We're not just walking away from each other."

"Of course we are." She refused to take his hand. "We both knew that would happen when I get to Sacramento. It just happened sooner."

He dropped his hand and stared at his boots. "I told you this would happen."

His voice was so low, she stepped closer. "What would happen?"

"You have given your heart away so many times, you have nothing left. You have no feelings because your heart is gone."

"That is not true, Race Hillyard. I do have a heart and what's left I intend to give to Phillip."

"You don't have anything to give him. It's gone. Look at you. There you are standing between a worm and a cockroach, smiling at some rich old saps. Good grief, Catherine Goodwin, you've lost your soul as well as your heart."

The slap across his face stung her hand. The

sound silenced all conversation on the train station platform.

Bootheels striking the worn wooden deck caused her to spin and point a finger at the approaching Matthew Zane. "I do not need your help. Go back."

"We need to get to lunch."

"I will be there when I'm through."

She turned back to the piercing eyes of Race Hillyard. "You have absolutely no idea of the anguish I am going through with the Lord, trying to do the right thing in this matter. You don't have a clue as to the horrible complications and shame it will bring to others, whom I love dearly, if I don't do this." Warm tears rolled down her cheeks. "If I had an alternative, I would do it. The only reason I didn't throw myself off the train last night is because I could only open the window a couple of inches. So, how dare you judge my relationship with the Lord."

He took a deep breath. "You're right. I thought we might be close enough that I could . . . well, you are right. I regret causing those tears. I will have prayers of repentance because of them."

"Perhaps we don't know each other all that well."

"Well, here's what I do know, Miss Catherine Goodwin. In the few days that we've been acquainted, you have revived my dead heart. My life was without purpose. You gave me hope

267

that I might be able to survive this crisis with Robert. I will always be grateful."

"I am not sure I get any credit for that. Much of what you despise in me, I despise also. Pray for me, Race. Pray that I will do what is best for those I truly love."

"And I'll also pray for a day to come that you can explain it to me. Don't tell me that will never happen. My faith is just naïve enough to believe that miracles can happen."

"Knowing you has changed me. You might not see those changes, but they are there. The last few days have made me feel truly alive. I haven't felt that since before the war." She leaned over and kissed his cheek. "Goodbye, Race Hillyard. Thank you for putting up with me."

Catherine wiped the tears from her eyes before she strolled back to the men.

"What was that all about?" Cyrus Daily asked.

She refused to look back across the platform. "He's a man my sister, Catherine, used to know."

Zane led the way toward the waiting carriage.

Edward Longtire strolled beside her. "But you slapped him, then kissed his cheek."

"Yes, of course I did, Eddie. It's the same way I'd train my dog. Punishment, then reward. Don't you do it that way?"

"Eh, well, I suppose so." He held the carriage

door open for her. "I never thought about training men the way one trains dogs."

Catherine turned on the carriage step, a foot
above the men. "Why, little girls learn that when
we're six."

CHAPTER TEN

The gray-headed man tugged at the knot in his crisp black silk tie. "I really feel quite awkward imposing on you like this."

Catherine surveyed the three well-dressed men who filled the compartment. They sat stiffly as if waiting for bad news from a doctor. "Cyrus, I told you it is quite alright. You men are very pleasant company and I'm sure Matthew and Chet don't mind sitting up with the porter for one night."

Edward Longtire tapped on his knee. "My word, I think it strange that a compartment we had Mr. Zane purchase in Omaha was no longer available in Ogden. It's a blemish on the Central Pacific, that's for sure. Crocker and Hopkins will catch my wrath when we attend that Nob Hill gala in San Francisco."

Bertram Woolsey brushed at his thick, straight mustache. "The conductor could have been a little more helpful. He made it seem like some secret negotiations were going on in that compartment."

"Calling it a matter of 'life or death' is quite dramatic." Cyrus Daily flipped a speck of lint off his polished black boots. "You'd think there was some deposed Russian princess in the next compartment. You haven't got a glimpse of who took it?"

"I haven't seen anyone," Catherine said. "It does seem strange. I hope you men don't mind staring at this same old dress all night long."

"On the contrary, it is your presence that will make the overnight trip bearable," Longtire said.

Daily cleared his throat. "The organdy dress you purchased in Ogden is beautiful as well."

"I have you men to thank for that. Normally, I don't buy a dress that costs seventy-five dollars, but your insistence seemed to shame Mattsey into buying it for me."

"Nonsense," Longtire insisted. "A man who quibbles over a few more dollars for a dress that makes his wife happy, well, he hasn't learned much from his marriage."

"Eddie, how long have you and Pearline been married?"

"Thirty-seven years next spring. Smartest thing I ever did."

"The fact that her daddy owned a wholesale hardware business didn't hurt, did it?" Woolsey chided.

"Let me tell you about that. The day before we married, Pearline's father took me aside. He said, 'Longtire, I need to be honest with you. The business is going through a rough time. The decline after the Mexican war has left us without

271

much operating capital. We could have reverses, and I want you to be aware of that.' I told him I wanted to marry his daughter if I had to grow potatoes in New England rocks."

Catherine clapped her gloved hands. "Good for you."

Longtire assumed the voice of one addressing a convention of young businessmen. "With some smart decisions and lots of long days, we turned it around. Her daddy died during the war, but by then we had a prospering business."

Catherine wanted to stretch the stiffness from her arms, but felt awkward doing so. "And now you want to invest some of that prosperity in western mining?"

"Yes, but to tell you the truth, I'm a little more apprehensive than these other chaps. I suppose I have some romantic notion of 'seeing the elephant' and cashing in on western treasures. But I know so little about mining. It's quite an adventure for a hardware man."

"That's where you have to trust us, Edward," Daily said.

"I know, I know. I've been through this before. But I feel like a ten-year-old looking at algebra for the first time." He searched her eyes. "Catelynn, just for the sake of a nervous old man from New York, could you reassure me that your husband is a knowledgeable and reputable mining expert?"

She avoided his glance by staring at the fading Utah sun.

Reputable? He's a liar, cheat, swindler, wife beater, blackmailer and a disgrace to God's creative power. But . . .

"My word, Edward, you don't ask a wife such a question," Daily huffed. "Of course she will tell you he is. She loves the man. As far as a person's honesty and business acumen, we will have to judge that for ourselves."

"Quite right, Cyrus," Longtire concluded. "Let me apologize, Mrs. Zane."

"It is understandable, Eddie." She sucked in a deep breath, letting the words swimming in her head line up in sentences. "From my limited knowledge, many quite honest, sincere and intelligent mining investments don't return the dividends hoped for. I know nothing of this present situation . . . eh, other than what I mentioned to you in New York this spring. But in my opinion, mining speculation is always a rather risky venture."

Daily grinned. "High risks. Higher rewards."

"I do hope this turns out well for all of you. Many of the ones I talk to have come home empty-handed. But the more prosperous are still out here getting rich, or so Mattsey tells me."

"I'm hoping we don't spend the night talking about mining claims." The tone that Woolsey took had a St. Nicklaus type sound. "How dreadfully boring for Catelynn. Say, did you and Matthew get to the Kentucky Derby this year?"

Any subject but Zane's integrity will be just fine.

"Not this year. How was it?"

Cyrus Daily crossed his arms. "I don't think we should talk about it."

"Oh, it was delightful," Woolsey beamed.

Catherine covered her smile with her hand. "I believe you two backed different horses."

"It was a foul," Daily growled.

"Nonsense." Woolsey shook his head. "That's horse racing."

Catherine held her palms together but clapped her fingers. "Oh, my, a controversy. How exciting."

"My money was on Kimball, of course. He was the favorite," Daily announced.

"And I took a chance on Fonso," Woolsey said.

She studied Woolsey's putty-like face. "Fonso? That's an unusual name."

"And a wonderful champion. He's a handsome chestnut colt sired by King Alfonso out of Weatherwitch. Well, you see, the track was dry and dusty." His lips and square jaw seemed expressionless, but his dark green eyes sparkled with zeal.

Daily held his hands several feet apart. "Five inches deep in dust."

Woolsey leaned forward, as if discussing the

battle at Gettysburg. "Fonso broke to the lead and, naturally, kicked a lot of dust up for those behind."

"It was unfair." Daily seemed stiff, professorial in his assessment. "The others couldn't see their positions for most of the race."

Woolsey waved his hands high as if announcing the birth of his first son. "Fonso broke across the finish line, a full length ahead of Kimball."

Daily pushed the arm out of his way. "The other owners protested the race, but to no avail. The mint juleps had already soused the judges, no doubt. Such a shame. A travesty of justice."

Woolsey leaned back in the seat like a man who just finished off the last piece of fresh peach pie. "Now, that is the portrait of a sour loser."

"Did you two have a little side wager with each other?" Catherine asked.

"Yes. And I still have that five-dollar gold coin in my top desk drawer at home."

She laughed. "You bet a whole five dollars?"

"It's not the amount. I don't like to lose." Woolsy patted his vest pocket as if indicating the location of his wallet. "Not at horse races and not at mining. But I must admit, I got a good tip about Fonso."

"You did?" Daily's deep-set eyes widened. "You never told me."

"You'd be even more perturbed if I mentioned

who gave me the tip," Woolsey said. "The very same man who sold you the plans for concrete ships."

"Concrete ships?" she asked. "But wouldn't they sink?"

"Lucky Kynwal? You believed a tip from that wild, unscrupulous Welshman? I wouldn't believe him if he gave me directions to the men's room."

Woolsey leaned his head back and rubbed his neck. "None other. He always seems to know where to put his money. Catelynn, he's the only one I've met who made money speculating about diamond mining in the West."

She could feel her eyes widen, but tried not to show surprise in her voice. "Diamonds? I understood there were no diamonds in the West."

"So far, none have been discovered, but that doesn't keep people from seeking them. Anyway, Kynwal did quite well," Woolsey reported.

Catherine tugged at an earring. "Where is he now? Did he build one of those fancy houses in San Francisco that I've read about?"

"Last I heard he went down to Argentina to raise more race horses. He claims they raise a tougher, faster horse down there. He wants to train them and bring them back as three-year-olds to run in the states. Knowing Kynwal, he'll probably make a killing."

If Race Hillyard finds him, there will be a killing. I'm not sure if I should tell him this . . . but I must. I know I must get word to him.

She surveyed all three men, then stared out at the black western night. "I trust you won't think of me as being ungracious. But I'm worn out. I think I'll just close my eyes and try to sleep. Please go ahead and visit."

"We'll try not to rattle on about mining details," Longtire said.

"Actually, a boring subject might put me to sleep."

"If you want a tedious subject," Daily chuckled. "I'll tell you about Bertram's wardrobe."

Woolsey rose and retrieved his top hat. "This is where I get up and go smoke a cigar."

Minutes faded to hours. Darkness to dawn. Even when the train parked at a siding or station, Catherine could feel the sway of the car and the clatter of the rails. Her throat dried out. The silk dress felt coarse on her arms. The air was stifling as if living in a box. Her only consolation: twelve hours closer to Phillip.

The train station at Reno was newer than the one at Ogden, but also smaller and crowded. Several people lined up at the telegraph office.

"Catelynn, dear . . . please hurry." Zane's voice crashed like a command, not a request.

Catherine turned to see him and a half-dozen other men, most in top hats and cutaway coats clustered next to two black leather carriages.

She shaded the sun from her eyes with her hand. "Just a minute. You knew I needed to send a telegram."

When a thin lady in a navy serge dress swished out of the small room, Catherine stepped up to the desk. "I want to send a message to Phillip Draper in Sacramento. Actually, he's from Paradise Springs, but he's meeting me in Sacramento. Just say, 'Phillip, I've been delayed in Nevada. Will be there by tomorrow evening. Catherine.' "

She glanced at the filed messages behind the desk. "I'm expecting a telegram from my sister in New York. Do you have one for Catherine Goodwin?"

He sorted through both the C and the G files. "Nope."

If she's at Cape Cod with little Marie, she couldn't receive my telegram. I find it difficult to believe that story of Zane's. Or, she could be just ignoring me. Dear Jesus, how I would like to hear how she is doing.

"Thank you. I'll check later when we get back from Carson City. It's rather important to me."

"Mrs. Zane," Cyrus Daily bubbled. "I was sent to fetch you."

The telegraph clerk scratched the back of his neck. "Mrs. Matthew Zane?"

She turned back to the counter. "Yes?"

"I do have a telegram here for your husband." He handed her the beige paper.

She took the telegram and nodded. "Thank you."

He pointed toward the telegraph key. "I'll be looking for the one from your sister, Catelynn."

Daily coughed. "My word, this lady is Catelynn."

The clerk hesitated. "But, I thought . . ."

"Don't be concerned." Catherine waved the telegram like a Spanish fan. "Lots of people get us confused. We're identical twins."

She slipped her arm into Daily's as they exited the office.

"I trust you took care of your business," he said.

"Indeed, Cyrus." Catherine folded the telegram and slipped it up her sleeve. Edward Longtire greeted them.

"Are we ready to go down to Carson City?" she asked.

"We are now waiting for Montigue Hall," he said. "He wandered off. Something about purchasing a revolver. His first trip west, also. It will just be a moment."

She glanced around the station and spied Race Hillyard helping Francine and the children off the coach.

I must tell Race about Lucky Kynwal.

Zane's back was turned to her. She lowered her voice as she spoke to Longtire and Daily. "I'll be right back. I need to speak to a couple of friends. I'll be right over there."

The big lady beamed as Catherine approached. "Catherine, my, how beautiful you look. Pullman car riding agrees with you."

She hugged Francine. "Thank you, but I really want to be back with all of you in coach. It's a difficult situation to explain. I need to speak to Race for a moment."

"No problem. The children and I are a bit peckish. We'll look for a grocery."

With Francine out of sight, Race turned to her. "They let you out on a long leash."

She refused to look at him, but kept watch on the movements of the men by the two carriages. "I probably deserve that cutting remark. I am here because I overheard a name that will interest you. A casual reference to a man who recently moved to South America after making a fortune in some sort of diamond mine speculation."

"Zane told you that?" Race said.

"No, a man from New York mentioned a horse racing pal. The combination of South America and diamonds caught my attention."

"What did he say?"

"A Welshman by the name of Lucky Kynwal made a fortune and moved to Argentina, supposedly to raise horses. He seems to have a reputation for luck, but not for honest dealings."

"Maybe I'll need to go to South America."

"That's all I know, but I wanted you to . . ."

"Are you Catherine Draper?" A man with a badge had the voice which was more of a school principal than a favorite uncle.

"Yes . . . and you are?"

"Washoe County Sheriff, William Walker. I'd like you to step over here so I may speak to you."

Race strolled at her side. "Mind if I come along?"

"Who are you?"

"Race Hillyard, a friend."

"Hillyard?" The sheriff nodded. "Yeah, I was going to fetch you next."

He led them through a sliding wooden door at the west end of the station marked "Freight."

As her eyes adjusted to the shadows, she noticed a young blonde-headed girl. "Amanda Sue!" Tears welled up as she stooped and opened her arms to the smiling girl. "What a delight! I was so worried about you and your father when we found the wrecked train car. How did you get out of it?"

The little girl clung to her neck. "We were never in it."

"But . . ."

Judge Clarke appeared from the wooden packing crates. "I'm afraid it was all my charade.

We stayed on the train, but sent the car with the express. This old judge knows a thing or two about avoiding enemies. A wrecked train car can eliminate one's enemies. At least for a while."

"That's an expensive solution," Hillyard said.

The judge nodded at Amanda Sue. "No price is too high for some things."

Catherine stood to hug the judge, but he held back. "Is there a problem now? Were you still on our train?"

"We were in the compartment next to you and those other men," Amanda Sue blurted out. "Did you know the walls are very thin? You can hear what other people are saying?"

I hoped that was not the case. What all did I say? What did Zane say?

"I thought maybe I heard a little girl cry one time. It must have been you."

Amanda Sue clung to her. "I was pouting. I didn't like being stuck in there all that time."

Catherine stood up. "What exactly did you hear, Judge? I presume that's why you and the sheriff are here."

"Who are you?" the judge asked. "When you had dinner with us, you were Catherine Draper. In the compartment, you seemed to go by the name Catelynn Zane."

She peered at Race, then back at the judge. "It's rather complicated. I am Catherine Goodwin. I called myself Draper, because I'm

282

engaged to Mr. Phillip Draper of Paradise Springs, California, and will have that name by week's end. However, I have been impersonating my identical twin sister, Catelynn."

"She's the one married to Zane?" the judge asked.

"I'm not sure they are married."

"From what I overheard, Zane has something that he is holding against you to make you do this."

Her chin dropped to her chest. "Yes, I am being blackmailed."

"May I ask what he has on you?" the judge pressed.

"No, you may not. It involves my sister, Catelynn, and is delicate in nature."

"I can arrest him for blackmail," the sheriff said.

"But I would not press charges. The evidence is too damaging to be made public in a trial. I'm trying to protect my sister and her infant daughter."

"Daughter?" Hillyard coughed.

"What do you know about this mining claim sale that Zane's involved in? Through the wall, it sounded like part of the deception," the judge asked.

"I know nothing. I avoided learning details. I don't think Zane is being truthful with those men, but I have no proof. It could have something to do with apex litigation, whatever that is."

"It's a four-year lawsuit, that's what it is." The judge took Amanda Sue's hand. "And where do you fit in this, Hillyard?"

"This is the most I've heard of blackmail and this farce. I don't know what's going on, but I wish I did."

"This might be the time to put an end to the entire mining scam," the sheriff said. "I'll go arrest Zane."

"You can't," Catherine protested. "He possesses damaging evidence against my family, and he'll reveal it, if apprehended."

"There's another reason to wait," the judge added. "At this point, he is just trying to deceive the investors. If we wait and have him arrested after the papers are signed, he would be guilty of mining fraud. That's a serious crime in Nevada."

Hillyard hooked his thumbs in his belt. "Catherine, where does Zane keep this evidence he has against you?"

"In his suit coat pocket."

"He has some letters or papers?"

"Something like that."

"Sheriff," Hillyard rubbed his chin and pointed to the lawman. "You can wait all you want to arrest Zane, but I'd like to pull Catherine out of the fire first. If she suppresses this blackmail and goes to Carson City, then it will look like she impersonated her sister in order to swindle the men. She could get caught up in the arrest with Zane. A Nevada jury wouldn't think kindly of her, would they, Judge?"

"I'm afraid not." He pulled off his gold-framed spectacles and rubbed the bridge of his nose. "But what is the alternative?"

"Give me a chance to relieve Zane of the blackmail evidence."

"You aren't going to shoot him, are you?" the sheriff pressed.

"Nope. But I request you and your deputies stay away. There's going to be a fist fight at the train station and I don't want anyone stopping me."

"How do you know you'll prevail?" the judge asked.

"I don't have to win the fight, just recover the documents. But don't interfere."

Catherine tugged at his sleeve. "Race, you don't have to do this for me."

"I know you are in a hurry to get to your Phillip. And besides, mining swindlers bring out the fury in me. It will make me feel better to put one conniving charlatan in his place."

"Just how are you going to provoke this fight?" she asked.

"You don't want to know."

"Can I watch?" Amanda Sue called out.

The judge grabbed the girl's shoulder. "We will stay right here out of sight."

"Hillyard, this goes against my judgment," the sheriff huffed. "I'll not let this turn into a riot."

"Arrest me. Shoot me. I don't care what you do, once Catherine gets her letters."

"Or something like letters," she replied.

Race nudged her to the freight room door. "Hurry out. They will be searching for you. Stall for several minutes at the carriages."

Matthew Zane stalked towards her. "Catelynn, this is incredibly rude. I hunted all over. We almost had to send for the sheriff to find you. You knew we were leaving. Where have you been? I insist on knowing."

She cast a smile at the well-dressed investors. "I had to go to the privy, if you must be so demanding. I believe that is a woman's right. And I feel quite embarrassed that you forced me to say that. I trust you gentlemen will excuse my blunt admission."

"Oh, yes," Zane stammered. "But, you should have told me."

"Let the matter drop, Zane. You've discomfited Mrs. Zane quite enough," Daily insisted.

Zane waved his arms at the men huddled around him. "Then let's load up, I think five can ride in one buggy, four in the other. Catelynn, if you . . ."

She clutched her handbag. "I'm not getting in a carriage until you introduce me to these three well turned-out gentlemen. I feel like the queen of the ball amidst such handsome men."

"I'm S. A. Worthington." The shortest man removed his silk top hat to reveal a bald head. "Perhaps you've heard of the Worthingtons of Philadelphia?"

"Indeed, several women at Gloria Fordlam's Salon have mentioned you in rather, shall I say, intriguing ways."

Worthington coughed as if trying to pale his blush. "That would be my brother, Hartford, I'm sure."

"I'm M. Jenkins Hall and live a quite ordinary life, so I'm sure you've heard nothing of me."

"Jenkie just sits in his Washington Square brownstone counting money," Cyrus Daily chided.

"Yes, yes," Zane motioned to the carriage. "And this is Greenleaf Fryberg of the Pittsburg Frybergs. You know, steel and coal? Now, we really must . . ."

Race Hillyard pushed Zane so hard, he stumbled into Chet Pinehurst.

Then he grabbed Catherine, bent her back until she collapsed in his arms and crushed his lips into hers.

This is how he provokes a fight? Oh, my, on a scale of one to five, this is a definite ten. Why here? Why now? Enjoy it, dear Catherine, it might be the best you ever. . . .

"Hit me hard in the jaw," Race whispered.

"But . . ."

"Shove me away and do it."

When she thrust him away, Catherine staggered back more than he did. Her clenched right fist exploded into his chin and his head spun to the right.

I believe I just broke every bone in my hand. I will be maimed for life, Race Hillyard.

Catherine clutched her throbbing hand and fought back the tears.

Matthew Zane's revolver pointed at Race Hillyard's head.

"You have assaulted my wife for the last time," he shouted.

More than just the potential investors began to gather.

"Good grief, Zane, don't kill the man or we'll never get this deal done," Longtire complained.

"Go get the sheriff," Zane screamed.

"No need for that. Let's settle it right here, man-to-man," Hillyard snarled. "But no guns."

He unhooked his holster and let his gun drop to the wooden platform. Zane kept his cocked revolver pointed at Hillyard.

"If you want to defend her honor, you'd better pull off your coat." Hillyard yanked his off and tossed it on top of his holstered revolver. He began to roll up his sleeves. "You going to defend her or not? Shooting an unarmed man defends no one. It's murder and there are plenty of witnesses."

"Put the gun down, Zane. I'll go get the sheriff," Longtire said.

"You can't let a man do that to your wife," a portly man in a dirty sleeveless shirt shouted from the street. "Put down the Colt and roll up your sleeves."

"We got a fight here, boys," someone else shouted.

Zane glared as he handed his gun to Pinehurst.

"And the sneak gun in your coat pocket," Hillyard said.

Zane slipped a small rosewood and brass Whitneyville .32 caliber revolver out of his coat and handed it over.

"I don't trust what else you're hiding in those pockets." Hillyard waved a fist at him. "Take off your coat and roll up your sleeves. Let's settle this like men, not sneakthieves and cowards."

"I got a dollar on the tall one . . . any takers?" someone shouted.

"My word, is there really going to be a fight?" Worthington remarked.

"I wish my Mary was here," a man wearing a dirty white canvas apron called out. "She loves a good fight."

"Clobber him with his coat on. I've got to get back to the barber shop in five minutes."

Zane slipped off his suit coat and also tossed it to Pinehurst. He left on his red vest and held up his fists. "Hillyard, this is . . ."

Race's right hand cross slammed into Zane's jaw and staggered him to his knees. Several dozen bystanders crowded closer. Shouts in the street summoned others. The investors huddled to the side.

Hillyard waited for him to stand, but Zane rammed the top of his head into his chin. He bit his tongue and blood trickled from Hillyard's lips. When he tried to wipe his mouth, Zane pounded three hard jabs into his left ear. He ducked the fourth jab.

A left-handed punch caused Zane to reel back. A second left rocked him to his heels. A right uppercut dropped him like a tree in a forest. He rolled to his stomach and tried to rise to his hands and knees.

Race glanced over at Catherine. She shoved her way closer to Pinehurst.

Zane tackled him with a hard right to the stomach. Both men slammed into the rough wooden deck of the train platform.

The shouts of strangers and the rapid movement of the fight made it difficult for Catherine to reach Pinehurst. She had to slide past a man holding a small goat and Bertram, holding his top hat.

She tugged at Zane's coat. "I'll hold that," she shouted.

The crowd groaned. She looked back. Race Hillyard took a knee in the chin. More blood flowed from his mouth.

"I'll keep it," Pinehurst insisted.

"It belongs to my husband. I should hold it." Catherine clutched the smooth wool sleeve.

"My word," Woolsey shouted. "Give the lady her husband's coat."

Pinehurst reached into the inside pocket and yanked out a stiff piece of paper. "I'll keep this."

"He's going to kill him," a woman screamed.

Hillyard sat on top of Zane and pounded his chin with his fist.

She spun back and yanked at the photo in Pinehurst's hand. "Give me that." The picture ripped in two.

Pinehurst concealed his half behind his back.

"My word, doesn't anyone in the West know how to treat a lady?" Woolsey yanked the remnant from the startled Pinehurst's hand and handed it to her. "So sorry, Catelynn. This behavior is appalling."

Pinehurst lunged for her, but Edward Longtire stuck his leg out and tripped him. His face slammed into the deck.

Catherine slipped both pieces of the photograph into the sleeve of her dress and marched over to the fighting men.

"This is absolutely insane," she yelled at the top of her voice. "Stop it. Stop it right now."

"Let them fight, lady. I've got two bucks on the Texan!"

She swung her purse into Race's shoulder. "I said, stop it right now!"

Hillyard wiped his bloody lips on the back of his hand and glanced up at her. He raised a bruised eyebrow.

She nodded.

"If the lady wants me to quit, then I will," he hollered. Hillyard struggled to his feet, collapsed on a nail keg next to his coat and gun. He leaned forward and fought for each breath.

She marched over to the investors. "Gentlemen, I'm sorry for this. I'm way too upset now to travel to Carson City with you. I will stay in a hotel here overnight."

"I'm glad Henrietta didn't come with me," Daily said. "She would have fainted by now."

Matthew Zane wrestled to his knees, then pulled something shiny from his boot.

"He's got a knife," a high-pitched voice shouted.

"Race!" she screamed.

In that split second, Hillyard spun to his right. The six-inch knife blade entered the fleshy part of the back of his arm four inches above his elbow. Blood gushed down his shirt as he yanked out the blade with a scream.

"That ain't fair." The man with the baby goat kicked Zane's hands out from under him and he crashed to the platform. He mashed a dirty boot against Zane's neck, pinning him to the deck.

"Get away from him!" Pinehurst shouted while waving a revolver in his good hand.

The click of a cocked hammer and the jolt of a muzzle into the back of his head silenced him.

"Drop it, mister. This fight is over," the man with the badge roared.

Pinehurst looked over his shoulder. "If you would have been doing your job, sheriff, this would have never gotten this far."

"Holster your gun."

Pinehurst released the hammer and shoved the gun back into his holster. "Tell farm boy to get his boot off of Matthew's neck."

Sheriff Walker continued to wave his revolver. "Shakespeare, get your foot off of that man."

"He don't fight fair, sheriff."

"Let him up," the sheriff demanded.

Shakespeare stepped back to stroke the bleating goat's head. "I don't think much of some old boy who tries to stab an unarmed man in the back."

"You are under arrest for knifing this man." He turned to Hillyard. "You goin' to press charges?"

Hillyard wiped his lips on his shirt and glanced up at Catherine. "Nah, I kissed his woman right in front of his nose. I reckon jealousy made him crazy. I'll not be pressing charges this time."

"Get the doc to patch up that man's arm." The sheriff shoved his gun in his holster.

"We aren't through, Hillyard," Zane barked. "I swear, next time you won't have a woman to save you."

Blood trickled between his fingers as he clutched his wounded arm. "I thought she saved you."

Catherine fumbled in her silk dress sleeve and tugged out her linen handkerchief. "Press this against your arm until the doctor arrives."

"Catherine, I mean," Race stammered, "Mrs. Zane, you dropped . . ."

"Catelynn, are you going with us to Carson City?" Zane called out. "We have business to do and you know it."

Most of the bystanders wandered away from the station.

"I'm not going anywhere with you. I'm ashamed to be seen with you."

"I was defending your honor," Zane protested.

She tried to brush the hair off her forehead, but it drooped back down across her eyes. "You have been trying to destroy my honor."

Hillyard yelled out. "I think you dropped a couple of pieces of paper when you reached for . . ."

"We will leave you here," Zane huffed. "Chet, get them in the carriages." He slipped on his suit coat. "I'll wash up and return. I have an interesting photograph that might explain this situation."

"I agree with Mrs. Zane," Daily blurted out. "I'm not fond of backstabbing. Not sure I want to do business with someone like that. If you won't hesitate to stab with a knife, stabbing with a phony claim or false contract would be easy enough. Henrietta wouldn't like it."

"What? We have a deal," Zane screamed. He grabbed Daily by the shoulders. "You can't back out now."

"Zane, you touch that man again, and I'll arrest you for assault," Sheriff Walker declared.

Edward Longtire stepped up alongside them. "You going to stab us all in the back?"

"You too?" Zane hollered.

"Us three," Bertram Woolsey added. "I entered this for the fun and excitement. It isn't fun anymore. Plus, I've had more excitement than I want. I'll go back to my big quiet house, clip stock coupons and spend Saturdays watching my Knickerbockers play baseball."

Matthew Zane circled the investors. "You can't back out now."

"We just did," Worthington announced.

"Catelynn, explain this to them," Zane begged. "We had a deal. They don't understand."

"I'll explain it, alright." She barged over to them.

"Catherine," Hillyard called out, waving papers in her direction. "Do you need these?"

She waved him off. "I am not Matthew Zane's wife. Nor am I the one you met this spring. I'm Catherine Goodwin. You met my identical twin sister, Catelynn. I played along with this charade only because Zane held something on my sister and threatened to destroy her with the evidence."

"He blackmailed you?" Daily blurted out.

Edward Longtire stepped closer. "And you didn't warn us?"

"I am sorry for that. But it was too awful and damaging. It was wrong and I pray for the Lord's forgiveness . . . and yours."

"Maybe you gentlemen would like to see just what it is she is willing to lie to you to suppress." Zane frantically searched every pocket in his coat.

"You don't have the picture, Zane," she sneered. "I have it."

Catherine reached into her sleeve and felt nothing but a chill roll up her arm.

"Catherine," Race hollered.

She turned around and shrieked, "What is it?"

"I have both pieces of the picture."

Thank you Lord, Race has it.

Oh, no, Lord! Race has it.

She whirled back toward the investors. "The point is, I believe Matthew Zane is a crook."

"Catherine, you will be sorry. . . ."

Pinehurst grabbed his arm. "Come on, Zane. You're going to get arrested."

"What about my mining deal?" Zane bellowed.

Pinehurst shoved him past the carriages. "You can't whip a dead horse. But you can ride a different one in the next race. I've got another plan or two."

The sheriff followed them down the street.

After some mumbling among themselves, the cutaway coat crowd marched toward a hotel. Catherine continued to watch until all the men were out of sight. Then she stepped back to Hillyard. He had his shirt off and a muscular man with a black suit wrapped clean white linen around the arm wound.

She looked at Hillyard. "Do you have the . . . ?"

He motioned to his coat, which was rolled up under his arm. "Yep."

The doctor addressed her as if she were Race's wife. "Leave this on him for tonight, then take it off tomorrow. I didn't sew it up yet. I think it will heal on its own. But a little sunlight will probably take care of any possible infection, better than closing the wound."

"That was the most exciting fight I've ever seen." Amanda Sue ran up to them as the doctor departed.

Race put his good hand on her head. "I thought you weren't suppose to watch?"

"I just peeked with one eye. I cried when that mean man stabbed you."

"So did I," Race admitted.

"Does it still hurt?"

"Like someone pressed a hot coal into my arm."

Amanda Sue looked down at her dusty black shoes. "I don't think I want to be in a knife fight."

"That's a good decision." Hillyard watched the gray-haired man approach. "Sorry we didn't get them to Carson City, Judge."

"That was rather foolish of me. I miscalculated Zane's temper and violence," the judge said. "As evaluator of men's character, I failed that time. I trust the injuries were limited."

"Judge, does any of this have to do with the attempt to kidnap Amanda Sue?" Catherine asked.

"I thought perhaps it might. But the sheriff told me that the kidnapping had been planned from inside the state prison in Carson City. I convicted Hop Traver for murder last fall. He was sentenced to hang, but his lawyers have been dragging it out. Traver and one of his attorneys concocted this scheme to kidnap Amanda Sue and demand his release."

"What would you have done had it worked?" Catherine pressed.

"Judges never give in to bribes," Amanda Sue reported. "Everyone knows that. They would just have to turn me loose when it didn't work."

Catherine glanced at the judge.

He rolled his eyes. "Anyway, there is no fear now. When Judge Kingston heard of the kidnap attempt, he denied all present and future appeals and had Traver hung yesterday."

"Just like that?" Hillyard questioned.

"Nobody argues with Judge Kingston, not even the president of the United States."

"Mrs. Kingston does," Amanda Sue said.

"Quite right, sweetie. Judith will challenge him any time she chooses. Now come on, Amanda Sue. We'll go down to Carson City for a couple of days while I try to figure out what to tell your mother about all this when we get home. That might be the most important judicial decision of my life."

Only Catherine and Race remained on the train platform.

He grappled with his bloody, long sleeve shirt. "Is this where we get back on our train and go on to Sacramento?"

"I suppose so. It seems strange that I just telegraphed Phillip to inform him I would be a day late." She helped him with the shirt.

"So he won't be there?" Race allowed her to fasten the buttons.

"I suppose I'll wait in Sacramento." She

peered at his drooping shirttail. "You will have to tuck that in yourself."

"Turn around," he motioned with his good hand. "We could just get a room here in Reno . . . I mean two rooms, of course . . . and take the train tomorrow. I can lend you the money, if you need it."

"You know that would be compromising and I would never accept it. Besides, I have a very nice, unworn, organdy silk dress that I paid seventy-five dollars for in Ogden. I'll sell it for enough for a room, meals and something left over to take to California."

"Did you accept that from Zane?" He tapped her shoulder. "You can turn back this way now."

"Yes, I rather demanded it from him. He made me wear this one . . . I was saving it for Phillip."

"You will allow him to buy a seventy-five dollar dress for you, but I am not permitted to loan you five dollars?"

"That is right."

"How do you explain that?"

"I hate him."

"And me?"

"Race Hillyard, you know how I feel about you."

He stepped within inches. His voice softened. "Tell me."

"Hey, did you hear the news?" The voice

blasted across the platform like a shift buzzer in a coal mine.

Francine strolled up carrying a child in each arm. "A squall hit the summit and they closed the pass until tomorrow. No one is going to California tonight. We have to sleep on the train or take a room. I'm going for a room. How about you two?"

"We've decided on a room also," Race said.

Francine raised her eyebrows and grinned.

"Two rooms," Catherine scowled.

"I trust you feel better than you look, Mr. Hilly. If we don't get to California soon, there won't be anything about you worth lookin' at."

Francine stalked down the middle of the rutted, dirt street. Two mule-drawn freight wagons swerved to miss her.

"There is no lady on earth like Francine," Hillyard murmured.

"I like her."

"So do I, and there's a lot to like. You can go on. I need to get my bag and my saddle off the train."

She strolled with him towards the coach. "Poor Mr. Walker, he missed all the action."

"He never was much help in a fight. He enjoys the peace and quiet."

"That's exactly why I get along with him so well." She stopped. "Race, do you have that awful photograph?"

"Yep, you dropped both pieces and the telegram out of your sleeve when you pulled your hankie."

"Telegram?"

"To Mr. Matthew Zane."

"Oh, I forgot that. Did you look at it?"

"The telegram or the photo?"

She took a big, deep breath and let it out slow. "The photo."

"I didn't read the telegram, but I couldn't help but see the photo. It was face side up on the floor."

"The Lord means to humiliate me." She tried to rub the creases from her forehead. "And he's done a very exceptional job. May I have it please?"

He handed her the two pieces.

She shredded them into tiny scraps. "I can explain, if you'd like."

"It's Catelynn, isn't it?"

She let the snippets drift to the deck, like confetti on New Year's Eve. "Yes."

"And the baby?"

"Catelynn's daughter, Marie DuClare, whom I didn't even know she had."

"She doesn't look like you."

"Catelynn or Marie?"

"Your sis. I could tell it was her right away."

"She is totally naked," she whispered. "And we are identical twins."

"Yes, but she has a very tiny tattoo of a butter-fly on her . . ."

Catherine looked up. "So, you did study the photograph?"

"It just kinda caught my attention."

She ground her teeth. "I bet it did."

"And I immediately knew it wasn't you. You don't have a tattoo on your . . ."

"How do you know if I have or don't have a tattoo on my . . ."

He shrugged. "You aren't the tattoo type."

"Do you know me that well?"

"Yep."

"Okay, you are right." She stared off at the parked train. "I don't have any tattoos. I suppose you think you know exactly what I look like."

"That was your sis. Not you. And I've asked the Lord to forgive me for looking and to cleanse my mind of that image."

"Has he cleansed your mind?"

"Not yet," he grinned. "But I reckon he's forgiven me."

CHAPTER ELEVEN

The Pyramid Lake Hotel advertised itself as Reno's finest and sported a fresh coat of periwinkle paint with teal-green trim on the false façade of the two-story building. But inside, Catherine discovered another well-worn, sparsely-furnished western hotel.

The rough, wooden staircase squeaked. Loose handrail. A thin layer of dust smelled pungent, as if covering up crimes of the past. But she had not had a decent night's sleep since she left Omaha. Tonight, she hoped, would be different.

Once the pass over the mountains opened, she could be in Sacramento within twenty-four hours.

One more day and she would be with Phillip.

And only one more day with Race.

She stopped in the hallway. The door to his room was cracked ajar a couple inches. The paint at the bottom of the door showed wear as if it had been kicked at with some regularity.

A door partially left open? That could mean, "come on in" but call out first.

"Hi, Race. It's Catherine." She waited for his answer. "You'll be happy to know that I was able to sell the organdy silk dress for thirty-five dollars. I know you said I should hold out for fifty, but I think the man in Ogden overpriced it. I didn't bargain at the time because it was Zane's money and I enjoyed gouging him."

She turned her head sideways, but couldn't hear any movement.

"I know that doesn't sound very Christian, but I must admit I don't feel like repenting. Some men deserve what they get. I believe I'm still having trouble with 'love your enemy.' Anyway, I bought a simple dress, paid for my room, and still have some money for when I get to Sacramento. Isn't that good?"

She reached over and knocked on the partially open door.

"Race? Eh . . . may I come in?"

Maybe he fell asleep. Poor man, he was rather battered on this trip. I will check on him, but I will not wake him up.

She eased into the room and peeked around the door.

"Race?" she whispered.

An unused brass frame bed. One oak dresser. A porcelain basin and pitcher. Two kerosene lanterns. And a well-worn rocking chair that sported a polished leather saddle.

She strolled over to the saddle.

"Mr. Walker, where has Race gone? We were suppose to have supper together when I got back from selling my dress."

Catherine stroked the cantle with her gloved

hand. "He didn't tell you either? You just caught a nap in the rocker and when you awoke he was gone? Isn't that just like him to go off and not tell us?"

She meandered towards the open window and gazed down on the busy, dusty street. "Perhaps he found a bath house. Maybe got another shave. I'm sure he wanted to clean up before supper. I should like a bath, too, but the clean water and towel in my room provided a welcome relief. I see he had time to give you a good oiling."

As she studied the street, she noticed a crowd around the front doors of the "Dixie Saloon and Chop House."

Race doesn't drink . . . at least, I don't think he does. Of course, what he went through today might drive a man to . . . no, I'm sure he wouldn't do that.

Catherine sat down on the edge of the bed. "He's a very tidy man, in a rustic sort of way. I bet he stacks his firewood with precision. My father used to say he could tell a lot about a man by the way he stacked his firewood."

Why am I sitting on some man's bed talking to his saddle? Perhaps I'm losing contact with reality. Then again, maybe I've never had it since before the war. The months and years have gone by so fast.

She stood. "Mr. Walker, I'll go to my room and

knit a sweater for little Marie DuClare . . . if I had any wool and knew how to knit."

A least she and Catelynn are free from the clutches of Matthew Zane for a while. Oh, how I want to get a telegram from New York.

"These are not the cleanest of rooms. Mr. Walker, do you see that crumpled paper in the corner? Left from previous guests, no doubt. Perhaps this is quality enough for overnight guests, but one would not want to live in a hotel like this."

She plucked up the paper and searched the room for a trash container.

No wonder they tossed it on the floor. There seems to be no alternative. If I had a hotel, there would be a trash container as well as a spittoon in every room.

She looked down at the paper.

It looks like a telegram.

She slowly unfolded it.

It's the telegram for Matthew Zane.

Catherine hiked over to the window and held it up to the daylight that still filtered through from the street.

"Zane: wine, women and fast horses. Just like we thought. Your part of the diamond matter is the 1st National Bank in Buenos Aires. Get down here quick. You don't need another deal. This will last us a lifetime in Argentina. Watch out for Pinehurst. Rumor is that he lost his share and

is headed to Calif to sell you out to the Attorney General. Whatever you do, don't go to San Francisco with him. See you soon, Lucky"

She stared at the telegram, then at the open window.

Matthew Zane was part of that diamond swindle! Race read this . . . threw it in the corner . . . and . . .

"Oh, no! Oh, no!"

With the crumpled note still in her hand, she plucked her purse off the bed and scurried out of the room. The noise of her shoes hammering on the stairs caused several in the hotel lobby to stop and stare.

She vaulted towards the street, then made a sudden stop as a stagecoach rumbled by. The crowd of men on the boardwalk in front of the Dixie Saloon and Chop House had doubled since she spied it from the hotel window.

She grabbed a thin old man with no upper teeth. "Is there a fight in there?"

"That Texan is beatin' up on the easterner in the red vest again. And he's doing it with one arm."

She poked at two men crowded ahead of her. "I want to get in there," she demanded.

They didn't budge.

"So does everyone else," one replied.

Catherine scooted to the left. A massive man with long, thick black hair and a red bandana around his forehead blocked her way and her vision. She tapped his shoulder.

"Has he killed him yet?" she hollered above the noise of the crowd.

"Not yet, but it won't be long."

"I must get in there."

"No one will move over."

"I must get in there and stop it."

"You are a tall lady."

"Yes, and you are a taller man."

"I like tall women."

His eyes were black, intent, but not threatening. Dirty black boots stretched outside his trousers.

"I really must get in there."

"Are you one of their wives?"

"Sort of."

The man grinned. His teeth were wide, but straight. "Yeah, I have a 'sort of' wife myself."

She pulled a five-dollar gold coin out of her purse. "I'll give you this if you can get me in there next to the fight."

He plucked the coin, bit it, then slipped it into his leather vest pocket. "Hop on my back."

"What?"

"Throw your arms around my neck and whatever you do, don't let go. You might get trampled to death."

Like a snow plow leading a train, the big man shouted and shoved his way through the cluster of men. Some pulled guns or knives in protest, but the sight of Catherine riding his back made them hesitate. Once inside, the raucous, volatile crowd parted like the Red Sea.

Catherine slid down off the man, shoved a busted chair aside, and stumbled as she neared the fight. Hillyard straddled Zane, pinning his arms with his knees. Both men were bruised and bloodied.

She shoved between the final two men.

Where is Chet Pinehurst? Why hasn't he come to rescue Zane?

Hillyard's left arm hung to his side. Blood seeped through the linen of his shirt. His right fist pounded the face of Matthew Zane.

The crowd noise deafened her shouts and she couldn't hear her own voice.

"Race, stop it. You'll kill him!"

Hillyard kept beating the man.

"Race! Race!" she screamed.

Zane offered no resistance.

When Hillyard pulled his right hand back for another blow, Catherine dove on his back and clutched the arm. His forward motion slung her against the wall behind Zane.

The crowd hushed.

She couldn't breathe.

Hillyard looked startled.

"Catherine?"

She held up her hand and fought to take a breath.

"I didn't know you were here." He cocked his fist to strike Zane again.

"Don't, Race. Don't do it."

"You don't know . . ."

"I read the telegram. I do know!" She flopped across Zane making it impossible to strike him, without hitting her first. "Race, listen to me. There is no honor in beating to death an unconscious man."

"He doesn't deserve to live," he yelled. "Go back to the hotel, Catherine."

She crossed her arms. "I will not."

"Then, get out of my way. I'm killing him right now."

"I know Zane is a leech and the world will be better without him. There is no one on this planet that I hate more than him. But killing him is not your job."

"It is now. No one else seems up to the task."

"Please, Race . . . please. You chastised me for throwing away my heart. You said I would have none left. You were right. I needed to hear that. Well, you are throwing away your soul. . . ."

"My salvation is secure. Jesus made sure of that."

When Catherine shook her head, strands of hair drooped across her eyes. "But you will go through life without any soul. You will be pathetic, worthless and a mockery to mankind."

"I'll take the chance; get up."

"No. No, I won't."

"I don't care if they hang me or shoot me. I'll go to heaven a satisfied man."

"You can't go to heaven yet. This world needs men like you. Please, Race."

He grabbed her shoulder. "Catherine, get out. . . ."

She threw her arms around his neck and clutched him. Tears rolled down her face. "I need you, Race Hillyard. I need you, soul and all. Please don't do this."

He jerked his head back. His bloodied eyes focused on her.

A murmur rolled through the crowd behind them.

"I've had enough of you two. I should have locked you both up this afternoon. I won't make that mistake again."

Catherine pushed back and spied Sheriff Walker with gun drawn. He waved the muzzle at the crowd. "You men help me escort these brawlers to the jail."

Race Hillyard didn't know how long he had been standing, handcuffed to the rail at the far end of cell number two in the Washoe County jail. He had passed out or slept for some time. He did note that a lot of blood in his hair, face and hands had now caked dry.

He shut his eyes again. A holler from the

opposite end of the adjoining cell caused him to turn and survey the jail.

"That man assaulted me for no reason; I should not be in jail. Get Pinehurst. He'll pay my bail."

"Shut up, Zane," Hillyard said. "No one is listening to you."

"I'm going to bring attempted murder charges against you, Hillyard."

"If they turn me loose first, you could drop the 'attempted.' "

"Are you doing all of this over that tall Virginia spinster? You can have her. I never wanted her. I never want to see her again."

"I'm going to kill you because of that diamond mine swindle."

Most of the blood had been washed off Zane's face, but the bruises branded him. "Diamond mine? That was months ago. Are you a hired gun from Crocker and that gang?"

"No."

Zane yanked at the handcuffs locked to the iron bar. "They had it coming. They connived themselves into millions with the railroad and land deals. It didn't hurt them to be relieved of some of it."

"You cheated more than the wealthy. My brother lost every dime he had."

"Your brother? Who in Hades is your brother?"

Race felt his whole body stiffen. "Robert Hillyard."

"The Bible quoter from Houston? Hah . . . he was as greedy as the others."

"No, he wasn't." Race yanked at the handcuffs, but they held him tight. "He was a kind, educated man with a Christian heart and vision."

"Then he shouldn't have been speculating in western mining. You aren't getting his money back. He sent you to try and collect?"

"He didn't send me. Robert's dead."

"Well, I didn't kill him."

"Oh, you killed him alright. You may not have pulled the trigger, but you killed him."

"You're crazy. I was just a phony New York investor. It wasn't even my deal. Get me out of here. This man's insane!" Zane screamed.

The door between the cells and the office flew open. Catherine Goodwin crept into the hall.

"Catherine, why are you here?" Hillyard called out. "Did you talk to a judge? Did you raise bail?"

She broke into sobs.

"I know I look bad. I've been hurt worse than this. It's alright. You don't have to bawl."

"Yes, I do," she wept.

"Look, I've been thinkin'," Hillyard said, "you were right. Killing an unconscious man would have destroyed me on the inside. I think with that telegram, if Crocker and the bankers are willing to press charges, we can get Zane imprisoned for a long time. That's okay, isn't it?"

She shook her head and continued to cry.

"What do you mean, it's not okay? That's justice. That's what you want, isn't it?"

She reached into her purse as she attempted to catch her breath. "I . . . want . . . him . . . to . . . die!"

"Good grief. Get her out of here!" Zane hollered.

"Your life must be revoked, Matthew Zane, and I'm here to claim it."

Race tried to reach through the bars, but the handcuffs prevented it. "I told you. I've got it settled in my mind. It's okay, Catherine. Now go back to . . ."

She yanked the Colt revolver from her purse. "I want him dead."

"Stop her!" Zane screamed.

Race shook his head. "Catherine! You don't have any bullets. Don't play games. This isn't funny."

She marched toward Zane.

"She's crazy. Get her out of here!" he screamed, trying to pull away from the iron bars.

Race tugged again at the handcuffs. "She doesn't have any bullets in that gun."

Catherine turned back to Hillyard. "It only takes one at this range." She reached into her purse and pulled out a single .45 caliber cartridge.

"Where did you get that?" he challenged.

"Sheriff!" Zane hollered. "Deputy! Someone get in here."

"I bought it off an eight-year-old girl in Cheyenne," Catherine explained. She opened the cylinder and shoved in the bullet.

"You can't let her do this. Sheriff, get in here right now!" Zane tugged at his handcuffs that kept him bound to the iron bars.

"Catherine, don't do this for me," Hillyard said. "It's not worth it. Robert wouldn't want you to do it. Trust me on that."

"I'm not doing this for you. I'm doing it for Catelynn and little Marie."

"I don't understand," Hillyard pressed.

She pointed the revolver at Matthew Zane. "He does." Her hand shook. Her whole body trembled.

"You can't blame me for that," Zane shouted. "Sheriff, for God's sake get in here now. Hillyard, you've got to do something."

"Catherine . . . you pull that trigger and you will destroy yourself." Hillyard strained to reach through the bars, but the handcuffs still restrained him. "Killing someone, no matter how justified, changes your heart forever. You have too sweet a heart to destroy it like that."

"You said I had no heart left."

"I lied. Don't do it."

She jammed her hand through the bars and pointed the gun straight at Zane's head.

"Stop her!" he screamed. Even when he leaned away, the muzzle of the revolver quivered only inches from his temple.

"Catherine, that's cold-blooded murder!" Hillyard shouted.

"I don't care. It's justice. I will send him to hell. That's where he belongs."

"This world needs women like you, Catherine Goodwin!"

"No one in this world needs me."

"Phillip does."

"You don't know that."

Hillyard's chest heaved. He rattled at the handcuffs again. "I need you, Catherine. I need you with all your beautiful heart and soul intact. You are the only one that can keep me from going insane in this world."

She didn't take her eyes off Zane. "In twenty-four hours, we will say goodbye and never see each other again. It was never going to work. You and I both knew that."

"Miracles happens, Catherine. Don't do it."

"I've already decided."

"But, if you murder him, they will hang you. You won't get to see little Marie, and make things right with your sister."

She began to bawl.

And pulled the trigger.

Race screamed, "No!" He didn't hear the first click.

But he also did not hear a gun report.

She cocked the hammer and pulled the trigger again.

No explosion. No fire shooting out of the barrel. No black powder smoke filled the room.

Four more times she pulled the trigger with the same result.

"No! No! No!" She sobbed as she collapsed to the floor.

The sun first broke high up on the Sierra Nevadas as daylight raced down the Truckee River into Reno. Hillyard's coat felt warm on him against the chilly air. He wore a new shirt, but his wounded left arm throbbed as he carried the lady towards the train station.

Her eyes were clamped shut.

Red cheeks.

Crumpled silk dress.

"I don't have any tears left," she murmured.

"I know, darlin'. Just rest now."

She laid her head against his shoulder. "Where are you taking me?"

"Does it matter?"

"I was hoping you'd take me to a cliff and toss me off. I want to die."

"I know you do."

"Do you know why?"

"No. When you were conscious, you just blubbered and wailed. I can only guess."

She reached towards his belt. "May I borrow your gun?"

He swatted the hand away. "No."

Catherine raised her head. "Then put me down."

"We're not on the train yet."

"I don't want to get on the train."

"Phillip will be waiting."

"I don't want to see him."

"Yes, you do."

"I want to die." She flopped back down on his shoulder.

"You already said that."

"You don't believe me?"

"I believe you. That's why I won't give you my gun."

"Why are you taking me somewhere I don't want to go?"

Race hiked up the stairs to the train platform. "During extreme duress, someone who cares for you should look after you until you're able to think clearly."

"Do you care for me, Race Hillyard?"

"Yes, I do."

"Why? I've been nothing but a bother to you since the moment I got on the train and before. Isn't that true?"

"Yes, it is. And I thank you for it. Taking care of someone else does a soul good. It keeps self-pity and anger from destroying a man."

"Some day I might actually like you, Race Hillyard."

"That would be nice."

"But today, I hate you."

"I know."

She kept her head down. "I'd like you, if you gave me your gun."

"The answer is still no."

Catherine peered over at the waiting train. "Are we riding in the coach?"

"Yes. As far as I know, the compartment still belongs to Zane."

"Is he going to be on the train?"

"I believe so."

"They let him out of jail?"

"They let both of us out on the promise we would take you, leave town and not return during the tenure of Sheriff Walker."

She offered him a twisted grin. "I've never been kicked out of a town before, although I've gotten banished from a state. What was the charge against me?"

"Reckless behavior in a public place."

"I thought they'd arrest me for attempted murder."

"I convinced them that you knew there was no primer in the bullet and did it only to frighten Zane."

"No primer? It was a genuine Stuart Brannon bullet. I bought it for ten cents from a little girl named Angelita."

"She sold you a bum bullet. I don't think Brannon would make the mistake of leaving out the primer."

"Imagine being cheated by a little girl. You can't trust anyone."

"Except the Lord." Race cradled her on top of a crate, but didn't turn her loose. "I don't think He wanted you to kill Zane."

"I told you he deserves to die and go to hell. Put me down."

"Maybe the Lord wants to torment Matthew Zane here on earth a little more before judgment day."

"That's a happy thought. Race, I don't want to sit in the coach. I don't want to explain what happened to Francine . . . or Nancy and Preston . . . or the Mormon girls . . . or the Chinese couple . . . or Mr. and Mrs. Elmo Parkington."

"Who are they?"

"That old couple in the back seat that have been married sixty-seven years and call us 'the young people up front.' "

"Okay, we won't sit in the coach."

"But, you can sit there," she added. "I'll just go back to the rear platform."

"I'm not turning you loose. You'd get up on Donner Pass and decide to fly over the railing into the boulders below. Get used to these arms around you."

"You can't do this forever."

"I know," he sighed. "I know."

Race sat on a Hudson's Bay wool blanket spread on the cold painted wood of the rear platform.

Catherine perched in front of him and leaned her back against his chest. A second wool blanket, emblazoned "Central Pacific", was pulled up to her neck. His right arm cuddled her. His wounded left arm hung at his side.

"Do you think they know we're out here?" she began.

He glanced back over his shoulder. "They can't see us now, but I reckon someone spied us climb aboard."

"What did Francine tell you?"

"She heard about what happened last night in the jail. Most everyone in Nevada knows by now."

She leaned tighter against his muscled chest. "Do you think anyone in Paradise Springs will be told?"

"I'm not sure. Seems like the rumors involve several women . . . there is Catelynn Zane, Catherine Draper and Catherine Goodwin. But only one Race Hillyard."

"The world needs more Race Hillyards."

"You think so?"

When she nodded her head, she bumped his chin. "And I'm not the only one."

"Who else?"

"Mormon girls to start with."

"They are sweeties."

"Don't ever tell them that. They are at the age they don't want to be known as sweeties. Call them handsome ladies instead. That will do it." She yawned. "I'm sleepy. Are you sleepy?"

"I am, but I'll take the first shift. You get some sleep and I'll stay awake. Then we'll reverse it."

"We will not. You will not close your eyes for a second if you think I'm going to harm myself."

"You think so?"

"Yes. I'm counting on it."

"Where did those clouds come from?" When Catherine sat up, the blanket dropped down to her waist.

"From the condensation of evaporated moist air over the ocean, but I presume that was a rhetorical question."

She peered around at ponderosa pine trees next to the track. "Why are we stopped?"

"I reckon the pass had a little more snow."

"What time is it?"

"Somewhere in the middle of the afternoon."

Catherine stretched her arms. "I slept that long?"

"Yep."

"I didn't want to wake up. Did you ever want to sleep forever?"

"Yep."

"When Robert died?"

"Yep."

"I didn't wake up and tell you why I tried to shoot Zane, did I?"

"No, you didn't. Are you going to tell me now?"

"Nope."

"That's fair enough."

"When will we get to Sacramento?"

"The conductor said we have to go real slow over the top. Threats of avalanches. We'll reach Dutch Flat by daylight tomorrow and Sacramento before noon."

"One more night on the train? Can we stay out here?" she asked.

He pulled the blanket back up to her shoulders. "As long as we don't freeze."

"I'm very comfortable in your arms. Now, you need to go to sleep."

"That's true, but I can't."

"Look out there, Race Hillyard. The ground isn't three feet away. I couldn't even get a bruise if I jumped now."

"Will you promise before the Lord that you won't do anything stupid while I'm asleep?" he demanded.

"I promise to wake you up and let you watch me do something stupid."

"That's not what . . ."

"Go to sleep, Race Hillyard."

"I think I just might."

The chatter of his teeth caused his eyes to open. The dim light reflecting from the car cast a sepia tint on Catherine and the blanket.

"It's dark," he announced with the brilliance of Newton making a scientific discovery.

"You snored." She leaned back against him and sighed. "That makes me feel good."

"So, you are feeling better?"

"This is the worse twenty-four hours of my life. It wouldn't take much to improve it."

"Did it snow?"

"A little on top of the pass. We stopped a time or two but I don't know why. There was no siding or station. We're on our way down now."

He slowly stretched out his arms. "I can't believe I actually slept."

Her voice was just above a whisper. "And I can't believe I stayed right here and didn't do something stupid."

He wrapped both arms around her. "Do you still want to die?"

"Yes, will you shoot me?" she chided.

"No, but there was a lilt in your voice when you said that. I don't think you meant it like you did earlier."

"You are right. I just didn't know how to explain it to the Lord. But I did pray for an avalanche to sweep this car down the canyon and dash it upon the rocks."

"We would both die."

"I can't think of anything better than going

to heaven in the arms of Race Hillyard."

"Heaven will be a grand place. They say it will be a reunion with all of our loved ones."

"You'll get to see Robert."

"Yes, I will. Makes it a viable option."

She turned her head sideways, her ear against his heart. "That's part of the problem. There are more people I want to be with up there, than there are down here."

"Are you going to tell me what you've been going through?"

"I can't, Race. I just can't say the words."

"Okay, then get some more rest. The Lord must not want me to know."

"I'm sure he does, but I can't talk about it. You saw how I was last night. It would start all over again. But I do want you to know."

"How is that going to happen?"

"In my purse is a telegram. It was waiting for me in my hotel. From New York."

"From your sis?"

"From New York."

He reached toward her purse.

Catherine grabbed his arm. "No, not yet. You must promise me you'll not read it until I have fallen asleep. I can't bear to watch you as you read it."

"What if you don't go to sleep?"

"Then you can't read it. Is that a deal?"

"Yes, ma'am."

• • •

The chill warmed to a pleasant coolness as the train descended down the western slope of the Sierras. Race dozed off and woke up, Catherine still wrapped in his arms.

"We're getting lower, Miss Goodwin. In an hour or so, daylight will break," he whispered.

The purr from her breathing sounded like a tune long forgotten. He reached for her purse. He fumbled with his hand in the dark until he pulled out a paper. He held it high above his head to catch what glow there was from the kerosene lanterns inside the coach.

This is Zane's telegram from Lucky.

He folded it into quarters, then tucked it in his coat pocket.

When he located a second piece of paper, he held it high and squinted to see each word.

Miss Goodwin . . . I'm Mrs. Quick, manager of the apartments where your sister lived until six weeks ago. Forgive me for opening her telegram, but I've been desperate to locate Mr. Zane. I hope I'm not the first to tell you this, but Catelynn and dear little Marie perished on May 22nd, when the gas lanterns were left on, but unlit, in their apartment. The police said it was accidental. I believe they were buried in New Jersey, but I was not invited to the service. The day after their interment Mr. Zane searched the apartment, packed up and left,

*telling me he would be back in three days.
That's the last I've seen of him. I need to know
what to do with your sister's belongings. I hope
this doesn't sound callous, but I need the
income and must rent the apartment soon. May
the Lord's grace be sufficient for you in this
trying time.*

Hillyard lowered the note and leaned against
the coach.

*Catelynn and the baby dead? Catherine never
got to see little Marie. Never got to make things
right with her sis. Dead? Both of them.*

He felt tears streaming down his cheeks.

"That's not fair," he whispered. "Not the baby,
too. That's not fair."

Catherine's voice was feather light. "You read
the telegram?"

All he could do was weep.

The sun rose orange and pink behind them. By
the time it filtered through the tall pine trees,
they had washed their faces and returned to
their seats in the front of the coach.

Francine tied a bonnet on her head, then did
the same for little Nancy. "It feels like I just
watched the first half of the melodrama and had
to leave before the second act. This trip has
had more excitement than that circus train
wreck at Castle Rock. Now that was a trip. Say
did you know that elephants . . ." She glanced at

her children. "Eh, never mind. You going to fill me in on what happened?"

"Francine, it turns out that both Race and I have personal, but separate reasons for hating Matthew Zane."

Hillyard gazed out the window. "We both lost our tempers and . . ."

"And tried to kill him."

Francine slapped her hand on Race's shoulder. "I know all about that. We all heard those stories. What I was askin' . . . what happened to you two last night, all locked in each other's arms?"

Catherine glanced at Race and grinned. "I believe we took turns sleeping and crying most of the night."

Race nodded. "That's about it."

"Well," Francine sighed. "You did much more than that in my imagination."

The train weaved north at a siding and began to slow.

Francine peered out the window. "This must be Dutch Flat. I hear there is a Danish bakery here. I knew a Danish baker once, a very large lady."

The passengers exited the train in an orderly fashion. Race and Catherine were the last to leave.

"I'm not very hungry," he admitted. He stepped

down on the platform and offered her his arm.

A strong hand grabbed his shoulder. His right hand grasped the grip of his Colt.

"Leave it holstered, mister. Are you Race Hillyard?"

Race spotted three men with badges.

The tallest man pulled out a piece of paper and read it. "And are you Catherine Goodwin, also known as Catherine Draper?"

"Yes."

"I'm Placer County Sheriff, Richard Barclay. You two are under arrest for the murder of Matthew Zane."

"Zane's dead?" Catherine exclaimed.

"Pushed off the train just after midnight. We have a witness who said he saw you two do it."

CHAPTER TWELVE

Hillyard held his hat as he and Catherine stood in front of a long oak table. Sunlight streaked through the window, making the cloud of dust in the musty dancehall seem like tiny sparks of gold.

"Is this a trial?" he asked.

The gray-haired judge with a large nose and a scar across his chin peered at his gold pocket watch. "It's an inquest to determine if we have enough evidence to hold you for a trial. I have other business to attend to today. Let's try to sort this out in a hurry."

Catherine placed her gloved hand on the table, then pulled it back. "You can't accuse us because of one prejudiced witness."

The judge laid his watch down and tapped on the glass face as if attempting to make it move faster. "That is precisely what is to be determined."

She looked over the people sitting on the side bench of the dance floor. "Matthew Zane deserved to die, but we didn't do it."

The judge folded his hands. "You are not strengthening your case with such statements."

Hillyard waved his hat. "You have no case. This is an inquiry, remember?"

"Silence." The judge banged his clenched fist on the table. "I'll tell you what I have. I have a sworn statement from the witness that you two pushed Zane off the train. I have live testimony from the conductor and several other passengers and a telegram from Washoe County Nevada Sheriff William Walker. I do have reason for this inquest."

"And they all think we killed Zane?" Catherine pressed.

"Let's start from the beginning. What is your Christian name?"

"Catherine Marie Goodwin."

Hillyard turned and narrowed his thick eyebrows. "I didn't know your middle name was Marie?"

"Both Catelynn and I share that middle name. My father insisted on it."

"Silence! Mr. Hillyard, and Miss Goodwin, if you can't remain silent, I will be forced to remove you from this court and proceed without you. That would not be to your advantage."

"I apologize, your honor," Catherine said. "I think we are a little in shock at this accusation."

Chet Pinehurst leapt up from the side bench. "She's just acting, She's been acting on most of the trip. Everyone will tell you that."

"Quiet! This is the most disorderly inquest I've ever held."

A short man with a plaid shirt and Levi-Strauss

denim trousers appeared at the back doorway. "Just one question, your honor," he called out.

The judge bent his head and peered around Catherine and Race. "Mr. Achley, what do you want?"

"Are you getting back to the poker game soon, or can we just toss your cards in?"

"Don't you touch that hand. It's the first decent one I've had in a week." He waved a finger to a man on the side bench wearing a badge. "Deputy, you have my permission to shoot anyone who touches my cards." He cleared his throat. "Now, eh . . . yes, the inquest."

"I have a legal question, your honor," Catherine said.

"Yes?"

"Shouldn't we be represented by an attorney at this time?"

The judge nodded. "That is your right."

"I'll provide them counsel." The voice exploded across the room like a mamma telling Junior to quit pouring sand in Sissy's hair. Francine shoved Nancy and Preston into the arms of the Mormon girls and marched to the front of the room.

The judge leaned back in his chair. "Good grief. Do you have experience as an attorney?"

She grabbed the edge of the table and leaned towards the judge. "What experience I have, or don't have, is none of your business, shorty."

"We would like Francine Garrity to represent us, your honor," Hillyard chimed in.

The judge sat up straight and cleared his throat. "I will proceed. Here is what information I have. Mr. Matthew Zane died from multiple head wounds from striking granite boulders sixty-eight feet below the trestle over Old Swede Creek in Placer County. One witness. Mr. C. Pinehurst, said that Hillyard and Goodwin snuck into their compartment during the night and argued with Zane. They got into a fight, knocked him unconscious, and dumped his body out the compartment window."

"And where was Pinehurst all this time?" Francine demanded.

"Mr. Pinehurst?"

Pinehurst rose and straightened his tie. "I stepped on the back platform for some fresh air and a cigar. When I heard the ruckus, I hurried to the cabin. The door was locked, but I could hear everything."

"So you didn't see them toss Zane out the window?" Francine pressed.

Pinehurst glanced around. "No, but I heard him yell. Look, I know what I'm talking about, I trained with the Pinkertons and I . . ."

Francine folded her massive arms. "I thought

334

you said he was unconscious. How could he yell?"

"He must have come to." He stepped halfway to the judge's table. "When they exited the car, I rushed in. The window was open and he was gone. What else could I assume?"

"I believe it's the duty of this court to make the assumptions, not the witnesses. Isn't that correct, Judge?" Francine pressed.

"Yes, but let me add the corraborating evidence." The judge shuffled some papers in front of him. He held up a crisp, white one. "The conductor of the train, Mr. Hugo Stanfield, has stated that Mr. Race Hillyard threw other passengers off the train."

Francine pounded Hillyard on the back. "And we were glad he did. They were ruthless kidnappers and outlaws. Of course, that was onto soft Nebraska prairie."

The judge plucked up another sheet of white paper. "Plus, I have testimony from various passengers that Miss Goodwin passed herself off to be Catherine Draper and Mrs. Matthew Zane at various times on the trip."

"I can explain that, your honor," Catherine said.

"If we go to trial, you will have to." The judge waved a telegram in front of them. "And I have word from the Sheriff in Washoe County that Hillyard and Zane were in two fights, both threatening to kill each other."

"Your honor, look at Hillyard. You and I both know that's the kind of man, had he wanted to kill someone, would have pulled his gun and killed him."

"That is not evidence. I have word from the jailer in Reno that Catherine Goodwin entered the county jail and at close range attempted to shoot Mr. Zane in the head while he was handcuffed to his cell."

"The bullet didn't have any primer," Catherine murmured.

The judge looked at his watch, then stacked the papers neatly in front of him. "There is motive, opportunity and a witness. That is enough for me to . . ."

"Wait!" Francine slapped her hand on the table top so hard that the judge leapt from his chair. "You didn't give me a chance to present my defense."

"This is not a trial." He sat down. "But you may proceed with remarks."

"I'll need time. I would like a recess."

The judge's shoulders slumped. He threw up his hands. "How much time?"

"An hour," Francine said. "Go finish your poker hand and I'll be ready."

"It won't take me five minutes to finish that hand." He banged his fist down. "This inquest stands recessed for one-half hour or so, depending on how the cards run."

Francine gathered many of the passengers from their coach in a huddle in the corner of the dance hall when the judge re-entered room. He took out his watch, laid it on the table, then stacked a dozen gold coins next to it. With a wide smile he announced: "This inquest will now resume."

Francine strolled to the front. She carried Preston on one arm and led Nancy. "How did you do, shorty?"

"Excuse me?"

"The poker hand. Was it a winner?"

"Three jacks and a pair of sevens, worth one hundred and sixty-seven dollars." He frowned. "Please address me as Judge Hesley Swanson."

"Is it my turn to present some evidence, Swanny?"

"Proceed."

"My first witnesses are Adora, Balera, Calida, Damia, Ermina and Faustina Jordan."

"One at a time," the judge insisted.

"No, they operate as a unit." Francine turned to the six girls. "Would you please state what you saw last night."

Adora stood. "Mr. Hilly and Catherine sat on the back platform all night long."

"You watched them the entire time?" the judge questioned.

Balera popped up next to her sister. "We took turns."

"Why were you watching them?" he pressed.

Calida stood slowly. "We hoped they would do something more than just hug."

"But they didn't?"

"They never left the platform all night." Damia shrugged as she stood. "It was quite uneventful."

"And each of you will swear to that?"

"Oh no, Judge." Ermina shook her head. "We won't swear . . . ever."

"You will testify to that in a court of law?"

"Yes, sir." Faustina nodded.

"Thank you, girls."

"I have more testimony, your honor." Francine motioned a uniformed man to the table. "This is the fine conductor on the train, Mr. Hugo Stanfield. Will you tell Swanny what you told me?"

"Your honor, first let me say, that I was quite delighted to call on Mr. Hillyard's help during this trip. On several occasions, he assisted me. I consider him a brave and honest man. And yes, he did throw a man off the train earlier in the trip. He should have held him for arrest, but I believe he acted on what he considered the best interest of all the passengers."

Francine poked his side. "Tell him about the window."

"Mr. Zane and Mr. Pinehurst shared compartment 3C. The window in 3C is stuck and will only open about four or five inches."

"It was open wider than that when I entered," Pinehurst shouted.

"Quiet!" the judge replied.

"You can inspect it for yourself, Judge," the conductor offered.

Pinehurst rushed the table. "Just because it won't open now, doesn't mean it wouldn't open then."

"It was broken in Omaha," the conductor continued. "Mr. Zane filed a complaint with me right after he boarded the train."

The judge shuffled through the gold coins. "Does that conclude your presentation?"

"No, Swanny, it does not. Mr. J. J. Jackson, would you please stand."

A short man with a barrel chest raised up.

"Mr. Jackson is a cigar drummer who carries a valise full of samples," she announced. "Did you sell your wares to Mr. Pinehurst last night?"

"Six El Presidentes and four Conquistadors," Jackson replied.

"What do cigars have to do with this?" the judge mumbled.

Francine continued. "How did he pay you?"

Jackson nodded at Pinehurst. "With a twenty-dollar greenback he pulled out of a long, alligator leather wallet."

"Mr. Stanfield, as conductor, to the best of your recollection, who on your train carried an alligator leather wallet?"

"Mr. Zane did. That's the only one I saw."

Francine strolled over to Pinehurst. "Give me that wallet."

Pinehurst backed away from her. "This is absurd, it's all conjecture. I most certainly will not hand over my wallet to a crazy woman."

"Those on the scene at Old Swede Creek stated that the man they found dead carried no wallet or identification. For that reason, he wasn't identified until brought into Dutch Flat." She turned back to the judge. "Swanny, make him give me the wallet."

"This is an inquest. I cannot order someone to surrender potentially damaging evidence."

"You can't, huh?" Francine huffed. "Well, I can."

With clenched right fist, she threw her body into the blow that caught Pinehurst just under the chin. The crack of the punch was followed by a loud thud when he hit the floor. He didn't move.

"Swanny, could you have your deputy remove the alligator wallet from Mr. Pinehurst's coat?"

The deputy pulled out the item and handed it to the judge.

"Who do the papers inside indicate the wallet belongs to?"

"Mr. Matthew Zane." The judge flapped the wallet. "Are you saying the motive was robbery?"

Race Hillyard waved a paper at Francine. She unfolded it as she approached the judge. "This is a telegram to Mr. Zane from a friend warning him of potential treachery by Mr. Pinehurst. There seemed to be a conflict brewing between them over some previous mining matter."

"What are you implying?"

"That Pinehurst had the opportunity, motive and ability to toss Zane from the train. And more specifically, Mr. Hilly and Miss Catherine were not present when he met his demise."

The crowd broke out in applause.

The judge banged his fist. "Quiet! It is the opinion of this inquiry that Mr. Chester Pinehurst be held in jail for the murder of Matthew Zane and that Hillyard and Goodwin be released."

The crowd swirled around them and they were halfway to the train car before they were left alone.

Catherine hugged Francine. "You were magnificent."

"They got me mad. I do pretty well when I'm angry. I once leveled the Elkhorn Café when I got steamed."

"You chased everyone off? Or you clobbered everyone in the building?" Catherine pressed.

"I leveled the café, stud by stud, wall by wall. There wasn't anything left but a big pile of firewood. Now, let's get on to Sacramento.

Nothing like a little excitement to get the heart pumping. Say, I'm peckish, think I'll stop by the bakery again."

They talked non-stop for the next hour, but conversation faded as buildings began to appear.

Catherine fiddled with her valise. She looked down at her lap. "The conductor said we will be there in less than five minutes."

Hillyard reset his wide-brimmed hat. "How are we going to do this?"

"Do what?"

"Say goodbye. I don't want to make some big deal out on the platform in front of your Phillip."

She tilted her head and her voice. "Were you planning on making a scene?"

"I was planning on lots of things, but I know that won't happen. Catherine, I just don't believe in my heart that this is the last time that I'll see you. If I believed that, I would make a scene."

"What kind of sight would it be?"

"Sort of like this."

He slipped his hand behind her head, pulled her face to his, and softly mashed his lips into hers.

Mr. Hillyard, I should pull away and slap you. But this is the softest, most tender kiss I've ever felt. Perhaps I should . . .

When Race pulled back, the six Mormon girls in the back of the car cheered.

Catherine caught her breath. "Why, Mr. Hillyard, are you trying to get me to throw away my heart?"

His cheeks flushed. "Yes, ma'am, I reckon I am. But I know your Phillip will be waiting at the station."

"Would you like to meet him?"

"No. I've watched you kiss other men. I don't want to witness it again."

"Where are you going?"

"To Stockton. I have to look up a Mr. Legrans Degott. Remember?"

"I thought perhaps you'd go to Argentina."

"I might, but I have a lot of things to ponder first."

"Shall we depart separately?" she asked.

"I think that's best. Let me and Mr. Walker get off first. I'll be out of sight by the time you step down on the platform."

She held onto his arm. "Have we really only known each other for a few days? Oh, Race, this trip was too short."

"You want to do it all over again?"

"Some parts I'd like to leave out."

"Are you okay, now? I mean, with Catelynn and Marie?"

"I will never recover from that."

"If I thought you'd do something stupid, I'd just wrap my arms around you for the rest of my life."

343

She stared at him until he turned away.

When the train stopped at the station, he was the first to stand. "Well, Mr. Walker, say goodbye to the lady that gave you life. Catherine, I wish you only the Lord's best."

"And to you, Mr. Hillyard. I eh . . . eh . . . Race, please leave before I start bawling."

With the saddle over his shoulder, he exited the train.

He didn't look back.

"I'll swan," Francine sighed. "I didn't figure him walking off like that."

"He's just a friend I met on a train."

"Yeah, sure. And I weigh 106 pounds and wear a size four dress. Save that line for your Phillip, honey. Neither me, nor your heart, nor them Mormon girls believe it."

Catherine brushed the collar of her dress. She tilted her hat and plucked up her valise. "Now, remember you are going to write to me."

"And if you need me, I'll be at my sister's in Rough-And-Ready until the end of the month."

"Rough-And-Ready is a town?"

"Yep. Sounds sort of like our trip, don't it?"

Catherine waited for Francine and the children to descend. She stared around the empty coach.

Lord, I've done more living here than any-where. It's like home. All the passengers were my neighbors. And Race was my . . .

She squeezed the tears from her eyes.

This is stupid, Lord. I'm stepping off this train into the arms of my love, my destiny.

The platform at the Sacramento train station was near empty when she stepped down. Several men and teams huddled at the freight car next to the caboose. A medium-sized pig with a yellow ribbon around its neck was tethered to a lamp post.

She walked around the station to the street. Several wagons rattled past. A prospector leading two mules tipped his hat in her direction and offered a toothless grin.

This is not the way I imagined it, but little wonder. The train has been delayed so many times, the poor man probably waited at the station for days. I certainly didn't plan on spending the morning at an inquest in Dutch Flat.

I know this sounds strange, Lord. But it did help to soften the horrible blow of Catelynn and Marie's deaths. Gas lanterns can be dangerous. It could happen to anyone.

Tears stung her eyes.

But why? Why Catelynn? Why did it happen before I could . . .

She gasped back a sob.

I need him right now. He should be here. He should be wrapping his strong arms around me. He should be the one to rock me back and forth and whisper that everything will be okay. Phillip

Draper, you could learn a lot from Mr. Race Hillyard.

She cleared her throat. "Okay, Miss Catherine Goodwin. What do you do next?"

A short line formed at the ticket booth in the terminal. She waited for a couple speaking very broken English to make arrangements for a trip to "Ohgone."

She studied the half-dozen others in the station.

I'm not even sure what Phillip looks like now. He will be tall . . . taller than I am. Sandy-blond hair. Broad shoulders. Square jaw. Penetrating . . . no . . . no. I really don't know what he looks like. I've travelled clear to California to marry a man whom I do not know at all.

"May I help you, ma'am?"

"It doesn't matter what a man looks like on the outside, it's what is inside that counts," she blurted out.

The clerk blushed. "Eh, yes ma'am. Well, my wife finds me handsome."

"Oh . . . no . . . I didn't mean to say that aloud. I was thinking of someone else. Please forgive me. I'm Catherine Goodwin. I just came in from . . ."

"From Dutch Flat. We heard all about you."

"Oh? A very dear friend, whom I haven't seen in seventeen years, was to meet me here. But I seemed to have missed him. Did he leave a message?"

He studied her from boot to hat. "Lady, I'm sorry to report that hardly a week goes by when I don't hear that same story. Some woman comes west on a promise of matrimony, but the old boy just never shows up."

"That is an insult. My Phillip would never do that."

"I mean no offense. However, no one has asked about your arrival. At least, not today."

"Did he leave me a note?"

"You mean, a telegram?"

"Well, perhaps. Would you check?"

The clerk fingered through a deep file box, then returned.

"Sorry lady, nothing for you. You might try the Post Office."

"Yes. Where is it at?"

"On the corner of First and Court. But it's closed for the day. Won't be open until seven in the morning."

"Well, thank you. Perhaps Phillip's out on the street waiting for me right now. Or at the hotel. Where's the nearest hotel?"

"Are you looking for nobby or modest?"

"The kind of hotel a prosperous business owner might stay at."

"The Senator. But the American River is just as clean for a lot less money."

"Thank you."

She spotted the three story Senator Hotel from

several blocks away. The bright white paint with gold trim was lit by a flock of gas lanterns. Deep, thick gold carpet covered the surface of the lobby. She stepped to the desk.

"Yes, ma'am, would you like a room for tonight?"

"I'm looking for a man."

The clerk paused with raised eyebrows.

"Do you have a guest by the name of Mr. Phillip Draper? He's a prominent businessman from Paradise Springs."

"Is that near Marysville?"

"I have no clue."

He studied the guest registry. "We have no man by that name here."

"How about the past several days?"

He flipped back several pages and perused them. "No Draper. We had a Dryer and a Trapper."

"Well, thank you anyway."

"Did you want a room?"

"How much does it cost?"

"We have several lovely small rooms for only ten dollars."

"A night or a week?"

"A night, of course."

Catherine repeated the same routine at the American River Hotel. She didn't find any trace of Phillip Draper. The stuffy room cost three dollars. She cracked a window a couple inches, but refused to light the gas lamp. Then, she washed her face, neck, hands and arms in a small basin and twice turned the gas lantern valve to make sure it was still off. She fluffed up the one pillow on the bed, the stretched out on her back, fully dressed, on top of the comforter.

She endured a fitful night. Dozing off. Waking. Dozing off.

When awake, Catherine stared at the black ceiling of the Sacramento hotel room and thought about a man.

The wrong man.

The United States Post Office at Sacramento, California, opened at 7:00 a.m. Catherine appeared at the door by 6:45 a.m. The clerk with the visor pulled a letter from a bin marked "G." He stared at the crumpled brown envelope and handed it to her.

I knew it! I knew Phillip wouldn't forget to meet the train. I shall march over to the train station and wave this in front of that arrogant clerk's nose.

She strolled out to the boardwalk in front of the hotel. Her shoulders relaxed. She found an empty wooden bench shoved against the front of the building. She sat down and studied the outside of the envelope.

Okay, Mr. Draper, let's see what you have to say.

The lines were uneven. There was an ink smudge or two and a crossed out word.

That's just the schoolteacher in me. I don't care how he writes letters.

She took a deep breath, bit her lip, and studied each word.

"Catherine, I'm sorry I can't meat you in Sacremento. I couldn't get away from the store. It should be eassie for you to gat a ride up her. I've got things ~~argen~~ taken care in P.S. Mr. P. Dryer"

Easy to get a ride? How? Where?

Catherine spotted the Wells Fargo office a block from the Sacramento River. She studied the schedule posted in front of the white clapboard corner building.

A young man with a large, dark mole in the middle of his chin stepped up to her. "Ma'am, can I help you find a stage?"

"I need to get to Paradise Springs."

"You want to go to Paradise? That's up by Marysville, right?"

"Paradise Springs."

"California?"

"Yes, of course."

The boy shrugged. "I'll check with Mr. Montrose. He knows everything."

She watched a six-up mud wagon pull in front of the stage stop.

Lord, it would be very nice if this coach is headed to Paradise Springs, if it's not too crowded.

"Thursday."

She turned to see the young clerk.

"Excuse me?"

"Mr. Montrose says you'll need to catch the Black Butte stage on Thursday. It goes through Paradise Springs."

"There is no stage until then? It only runs once a week?"

"Once ever' two weeks. You're in luck."

"But I need to get there right away."

"I suppose you could buy a rig and take it up there, but it would be cheaper to stay in town and wait for Thursday. You got people in Sacramento to stay with?"

"I really must get to Paradise Springs. I'm going to get married."

"No foolin'?" The boy gawked at her. "I figured a woman your age was already married."

"I will ignore your impertinence and give you a dollar, if you can find me a ride to Paradise Springs."

"Yes, ma'am, and forgive my impurdiness. Come back in a couple hours and I'll see what I can do."

Catherine sipped a cup of tea and made an English biscuit with chokecherry preserves last almost an hour at the Anderson House Café. Then she walked along the Sacramento River, sat on a bench in a very small park and windowshopped her way back to the Wells Fargo Office.

She was just entering the building when the young clerk greeted her. "I did it, ma'am. I got you a ride to Paradise Springs."

"That's wonderful. Where is the coach?" She walked with him to the porch.

The clerk locked his thumbs in his belt. "No coach. Frank Utt is going right through Paradise Springs on his way to Faraway Basin."

She gazed at the men on the boardwalk. "Who is Frank Utt?"

He pointed to the street. "The teamster right over there."

Catherine hiked over to the heavily loaded rig. "A freight wagon? Where do I ride?"

The man with a black flop hat and tobacco-stained vest pointed to the wooden seat beside him.

"But . . . I can't . . ."

The clerk slid up beside her. "Ma'am, I'm honest with you when I say Frank is the only one headed up there in the next few days. Of course, the next . . ."

"Yes, next Thursday I can get a stage." She opened her purse. "What will this ride cost me?"

"Frank said you could ride along for three dollars."

"Three dollars?"

"That includes the use of two wool blankets, hard biscuits, salt pork and drinking water."

"Wool blankets?" She peered up at the grinning man with the slouch hat. "Is the trip that cold?"

Utt ran his hand across the stubble of his beard. "It is when you stop for the night."

"It takes two days?"

"If the road hasn't washed out."

"And where do I sleep?"

"Next to the campfire is best," the teamster instructed.

"For three dollars I sit on a hard bench seat, sleep on the ground, and get pulled up the hill by three mules and a swayback horse."

Utt spat tobacco into the dirt beside the horse. "Dixie will pull her weight. You wait and see."

The clerk scratched his short, course hair. "It's all I could find, ma'am."

And I promised Race I wouldn't do anything stupid.

"Where can I purchase some .45 cartridges?" she asked.

The clerk waved his hand across the street. "Right over there at Rhineberg's Hardware."

"Load up my valise. I will be right back."

"You know how to use a gun?" Utt questioned.

She turned to the clerk. "What time is it?"

"Almost noon, ma'am."

353

"I haven't pointed a gun at a man and pulled the trigger in over twenty-four hours, Mr. Utt. I don't intend on having to use it, unless I get real nervous."

Catherine folded one blanket for a seat cushion and draped the other across her lap. *It's not cold enough for the blanket yet, but I feel safer having it over my lap. Race, you knew you left your spare gun with me. I knew it too, but I didn't want to give it back. Perhaps you will come to Paradise Springs looking for it, although I'm not sure how I'll explain you to my husband.*

When Utt turned left onto the River Road, he let fly with a string of curses about the animals' ancestry and his personal view of the theology of eternity, suggesting where each animal might end up.

Catherine cleared her throat. "Mr. Utt, do you have a wife and children?"

"Nope." His answer was more a grunt than a word.

"I suppose you live in Sacramento?"

"Nope."

"It's a beautiful day. Don't you enjoy days like today?"

"Nope."

"Well, you must enjoy something. What do you enjoy?"

"I enjoy it when people don't ask dumb questions."

She looked down at her hands. "I'll make a deal with you. I promise not to talk, if you promise not to use the Lord's name in vain when you curse the animals. You can use any words you'd like. I've heard them all . . . but don't use God or Jesus in a blasphemous manner."

For six straight, long, tedious hours neither of them spoke. The only time Catherine slept was when her hand was on the polished walnut grip of the revolver in her purse.

Hard ground. Cold air. Bright stars. Catherine survived the night under a pine tree, somewhere in the foothills of the Sierra Nevadas.

She was surprised at the quality of the ham and eggs breakfast Frank Utt prepared. The strong, black coffee warmed her from head to toe.

As it steepened, the road to Paradise Springs narrowed to two wide ruts along a creek. The air chilled right after their noon stop. Catherine tugged one of the wool blankets around her shoulders.

She calculated it was mid-afternoon when they stopped at a cluster of two dozen scattered buildings, near a creek and small meadow surrounded by tall ponderosa pines.

"Mr. Utt, at least we've approached scattered civilization. How much further to Paradise Springs?"

"This is Paradise Springs." The teamster sounded triumphant, as if he just drew a fourth ace.

"No, no, no. The Paradise Springs I'm talking about has a population of over five thousand people."

"Used too. Back seven, eight years ago it boomed. Last time they put a sign up, it had three hundred and eight hearty souls. Probably less now."

"Where did the people go?"

"Most moved up to Faraway Basin when they found color up there. They just tore down their stores and homes, loaded up the lumber wagons and moved. That's the way it is around here. You got to go where the ore is."

"But, I was told it's a thriving town."

"Oh, it was a swell place in its day. Had three banks, an opera house, a fine ladies' hat shop and a half-dozen mercantiles. The real draw was the dance hall and saloons. Fourteen rowdy bars lined this street. Look at it now. There are only two saloons left and McRaffy's is only open until the old man drinks up his own liquor."

"I can't believe this."

"I know what you mean. Ain't much here. There's them two saloons. Champion's Store. Dr. Dechert's office . . . she's a fine lady. Maybe the best doc in the mountains. Back over there, Mrs. Chin still runs her laundry and Oriental medications. Behind her is the Presbyterian Church. Use to be almost as many churches in town as there were saloons. But it's all gone. Where do you want dropped off?"

"At Draper's Store."

"Draper? I don't know of any such store."

"Well, there certainly is."

"The only store in town is Champion's. I can take you down there."

I assumed Phillip's store was called Draper's. But, of course, he might have retained the name of the previous owner.

"Yes, take me to Champion's."

They rattled two hundred feet down the rutted street.

"Looks like the clerk's out there sweepin' up. Maybe he knows your fella."

She climbed eight steps up the front porch of "Champion's Mercantile and Grocery." The stairs were well-worn, as was the rest of the unpainted, wooden, one-story building. The man at the end of the porch didn't glance back as he swept and whistled.

Balding, sloped shoulders, frayed cuffs on his dingy, long sleeve white shirt. When he turned around, she spied a gold tooth in his wide smile.

"Excuse me, I'm looking for Phillip Draper."

"Catherine. You came after all." He tossed down his broom and rushed toward her.

CHAPTER THIRTEEN

No, no, no. This isn't . . . he can't be . . .

"Phillip?" she choked.

He threw his thin arms around her.

She froze in place.

He kissed her cheek. "Don't your soon-to-be husband even get a hug?"

Catherine hugged his shoulders, kissed his cheek, and stepped back.

"Phillip, I just didn't recognize you. You've . . . changed."

"Yep, I ain't twelve anymore. But you look just as purdy as ever. You sorta filled out just fine. My-oh-my, you are a true vision of feminine loveliness. How was your trip?"

"Long and tiresome." She rubbed her forehead hoping that would slow down her mind. "I expected you to be in Sacramento."

"I couldn't get away from the store." Phillip looped his thumbs in his canvas apron. "I'm the only clerk left."

"Clerk? But you own the store."

His wide smile accented the lower gold tooth. "Not yet, but I will soon."

Catherine folded her arms across her chest. "You told me it was your store. Draper's Mercantile and Groceries."

"And it will be real soon, darlin'. Mr. Champion is comin' down by the end of the month and we'll finalize the deal."

"Phillip, I don't understand."

"Well, you see, when the Paradise Springs diggin' played out, Mr. Champion built a new store in Faraway Basin. He left me in charge here. But he's been promising to sell me this store as soon as I raise one thousand cash dollars."

"When did he make that deal with you?"

"About seven years ago, when he built the new store."

Catherine peered into the shadows of the building. "And you finally have the funds?"

"I do now." He took her arm. "Let me show you the place."

The one, large room had a twelve-foot high ceiling covered with hammered tin panels and smelled of gunpowder and vanilla. Six-foot shelves displayed sparse merchandise on both sides. Empty glass cases lined the east wall. A broken chair held up by a nail keg was shoved up to a table that contained some well-worn playing cards spread in a solitaire layout.

A few signs decorated the walls, but the prices had been scratched off so many times, she couldn't tell which ones were still valid. The clothing on the racks looked used, but the ammunition boxes were new, almost dust-free.

After a serpentine stroll down each aisle, they returned to the fresh air on the front porch. "Phillip, the store is half-empty. Don't you need more inventory?"

"That's what I've been telling Mr. Champion for five years. But you and me will be getting more goods soon. I already made out an order of what we need."

He slipped his arm around her shoulder. "Catherine, you and me will get this store up and running like it was in the old days."

She scrutinized the empty street. "But if the town has changed and you lost most of the population, how can it ever be a booming business again?"

"I reckon the presence of a purdy lady will bring in a few more of the prospectors."

"You're counting on me as an attraction?"

"Well, I do have some other ideas. Ain't had many customers lately and it gives me lots of time to think and plan."

"Phillip, I just got here, but I'm wondering if this might not be the best location for a store anymore. You might want to take that thousand dollars of your hard-earned money and open a store in some other town."

"Nope. Paradise Springs is the place to be. I've lived here since I was twelve. Besides, it's not my hard-earned money. Shoot, I don't have more than eighty dollars of my own. It's your hard-earned money. At least your daddy, rest his soul, worked hard for it."

"My money? What are you talking about?"

"We're going to take one thousand from your inheritance and buy the store. Another one thousand for new inventory."

"Phillip, you don't understand. I don't . . ."

"Now, don't worry. I figured out how we can repay your inheritance, if you'd like to keep it intact. I've got it all written out on paper."

"Phillip, I don't have any inheritance."

"Now, that's a good one. You always were a tease. Or was that Catelynn? The Goodwins are the most prosperous business people in northern Virginia. I'm sure the war weakened ever'thing. But even a reduced sum will be just fine for all the things we need to do. I ain't talkin' about a lot of money."

"Phillip, look at me." She reached into her purse. "I have two dollars and eighty cents. That's all. The war destroyed everything we had in Virginia. The carpetbaggers even took away our land. There is no Goodwin inheritance except for the faith, love and laughter of my childhood."

Phillip's jaw dropped like a cannonball falling off a ship's deck. "Are you serious? No inheritance? But, you said . . ."

"I said absolutely nothing about money in any letter I wrote to you. I told you I had been a schoolteacher. And you know what kind of salary they get. That is all I mentioned."

"But I assumed . . ."

"That I would come out here and buy you a store?"

"We are goin' to get married. That's the kind of thing a wife does, ain't it?"

Catherine let out a long, slow breath. "Yes, I suppose you are right. And if I had funds, I might have been convinced to invest in the store."

"Besides, I had to use my funds to get our place. I paid thirty cash dollars each for those two lots."

Catherine's eyes searched around Paradise Springs. "Oh, yes, how is the house construction coming? You've written all about what it looks like."

"I've got the plans back there in my room. Let me show them to you."

They hiked through the store into the musty, dank storeroom at the rear.

She gaped at a bed and table against the wall. "This is where you live?"

"Yep, until our place is finished. We get free rent too."

"We?"

"Well, we'll have to stay here until the house is built. I know it's a tad dusty and all right now, but I know you'll spruce it up. There's a back door right next to the basin. The privy isn't more than ten feet behind the building. That's mighty handy in the winter."

Catherine grit her teeth. *Lord, my beautiful dream took a wrong turn somewhere. This is not what you are leading me to. It can't be.*

"I know how new all these ideas are to you. Kind of tough to take it all in, I reckon."

"I'm speechless."

"Here's the plans for the house. I bought these plans from a mail order house in Chicago. Ain't it a swell lookin' house?"

"It is beautiful. I want to see how it looks."

"This is how it looks."

"No, I mean I want to go to the site and see it."

She marched back through the store and out to the porch. "Aren't you going to lock the store?"

"Shoot, we don't get many customers. Besides, I lost the key and I ain't been in a hurry to tell Mr. Champion, if you catch my drift."

"You never lock the front door?"

"Nope. But I do throw a sack of feed against it during a blizzard."

Diagonally across the street they ran into a red-haired lady trying to harness a tall, black gelding to a black leather buggy.

Phillip yanked off his hat. "Doc Dechert, this is my fiancée, Miss Catherine Goodwin from Virginia."

"Catherine, nice to meet you. I'm Patricia Dechert." She held out her gloved hand. "And congratulations to both of you."

Phillip grinned from ear to ear. "Yes, ma'am, it's an excitin' day, that's for sure. Looks like you are having trouble hitching up your horse. Where's Marcus?"

"He decided to move to Butte, Montana. No driver, so I'm on my own now." She wiped perspiration from her forehead onto her dark blue dress sleeve. "Can you help me?"

"Sorry, Doc, I ain't never owned a horse in my life. Don't know a thing about them."

Catherine grabbed the harness and leathers. "We had many horses when I was young. I'll do it for you."

Within moments, the horse was rigged and ready to go.

The doc pulled her hair back over her ears and re-set her hat. "Can you teach me how to do that?"

"I would be delighted," Catherine said.

"Let's plan on some tea and a visit soon. I'm going to call on the Kellers at Soda Falls, but I should be home before dark."

Two blocks later, Phillip pointed to a marshy part of the meadow covered in cattails and willows. "Here it is. Ain't it a purdy location? There's going to be a street right over there one day. It's been all surveyed. As soon as the town grows, they'll put in the street."

"It's just a lot?"

"No, ma'am, it's two forty-five-foot lots with a corner location."

"But it's muddy and full of reeds growing. It's a swamp."

"That's why I bought it. It has a spring. Imagine that, our own spring. We'll rock off the spring, dry the ground, bring in some fill dirt. We can get tailings for free. And then build that beautiful house."

"Phillip, in the letters you said the house was being built."

"I got a little anxious, I reckon."

"What will we use for money?"

"That's a good question now."

Catherine rubbed her temples again. "You figured on my inheritance to build the house, too?"

"Now, it won't take long to build it. You see, this company in Chicago sells pre-cut houses. It's a package deal. They load the entire house on a flatcar and ship it to Sacramento. We just have to freight it up here. Then you and me can build it in our spare time. It said in the catalog that it came with easy-to-follow instructions. It can go up it no time. I mean, if we had the money to buy it."

They cut across another lot, then hiked towards the church.

"Rev. Whiteside said he would be proud to marry us."

She studied the peeling paint of the church. "I'd like to meet him."

"He'll be here the last Sunday of the month."

"Last Sunday?"

"Yep, he's got nine different churches he looks after. He stops by here the last Sunday of every month."

"And just where do I stay while I wait for him?"

"You stay with me, of course," he blushed. "Shoot, we're going to be married for a long, long time. Ain't no one goin' to care if we jump the gun a few weeks."

"I will care. Phillip, I will not stay with you unmarried. That would be sin. I will have no part of it."

"But Catherine, where will you go? There ain't no hotel left in town."

"I'm aware of that. I'll figure out something."

"What do you aim to do right now?"

"I want to sit on that bench in front of Champion's store and think things through."

"I ain't got nothing else to do. I'll sit there with you."

"No. I need a little time for myself."

Phillip stared down at his worn, brown shoes. "This surely didn't turn out the way I was thinkin'."

"In that, we both agree."

•••

Catherine counted fourteen people who passed the store during the three hours she sat on the bench. Four of them entered the store. Two actually bought something.

She had pulled her shawl out of her valise and had it draped across her shoulders when Dr. Dechert returned. Catherine hiked down the street to greet her.

"Catherine, good to see you. I should have had you drive me. I'm not good at making this horse mind."

"Dr. Dechert . . ."

"Patricia."

"Patricia, I'll be quite honest. Things . . ."

"Between you and Phillip didn't turn out to be what you expected?"

"Is it that obvious?"

"The way Phillip talked, I suspected expectations didn't match up with facts."

"I need time to let it all settle in."

"How much time do you have?"

"It's three weeks until the preacher arrives." Catherine took a deep breath. "I know this is being very presumptuous. Is there a possibility that I could be your driver and help you in other ways, in exchange for room and board for these three weeks? I did some volunteer nursing during the war. I wasn't sure where else to turn in Paradise Springs."

Dr. Dechert handed her the lead lines. "You're hired. Park the wagon, turn the horse into the corral and give him some oats. Then come on into the kitchen and help me fix supper. I've got plenty of room and will enjoy the company."

Catherine sensed tears welling up. "Thank you so much. I know this all sounds crazy."

"Staying with me sounds logical. Marrying someone you haven't seen in seventeen years . . . that's crazy."

"I need time."

"And I need tea. See you in the kitchen."

Catherine finished her third cup of black Chinese tea. "Well, that's about all there is. Now you know the life and times of Catherine Marie Goodwin. I trust I haven't wasted your evening."

"My goodness, it's the most excitement I've had since the explosion in the Victoria Mine. And you put up with my paltry account of a lady doctor in the West."

"I feel better being able to talk to someone and the hot bath has made me feel human again. But I couldn't help comparing what you have accomplished and what I haven't. I feel like I've wasted my life away," Catherine sighed.

"I'm not sure I've accomplished all that much. But I like what I do. You asked me why I've never married. One reason is that I had certain goals for my life. College . . . medical school . . . my own practice. I was too stubborn to allow someone to divert me from those goals. So, here I am, over forty and single. And I've reached those goals. But I'm not sure they are worth the price. It's lonely in this big house. And there is no one to warm me up in the middle of a frigid night."

Catherine touched Patricia's arm. "You're not too old to marry."

"There isn't a likely candidate within fifty miles. I hope that is not being too judgmental on your Phillip. I just never viewed him as a potential husband."

"No offense," Catherine said. "At this point, I'd agree with that assessment."

"But I believe the Lord evaluates our deeds at the end of life, not in the middle. Perhaps both of us have our best work yet to come."

"I will need to find a teaching job."

"Please, not for a while. I selfishly want you here. Oh, I'll learn to manage that horse some day. But I will so enjoy a few more evening chats over a cup of tea. You are a blessing."

Catherine took another sip of dark, black tea and placed the hand-painted porcelain cup down on the saucer. "Patricia, you heard my story. You know of my depression over Catelynn and Marie's death . . . and the drama with Zane . . ."

"And the strong, handsome Texan."

"Ah yes, Race Hillyard. Well, lounging on that

bench today produced the most helpless feeling. I couldn't think, or talk or move. I didn't know what to do. I asked the Lord to lead me by the hand or take me home with Him because I was at the end of my . . . well, the end of everything. We all have dreams about the future and what we will do next. Imagine coming to the place in your mind and in your life, where all the dreams run out. No more left. No plans for next week. Nothing to look forward to for tomorrow. No ideas for the next ten minutes. Just one big black hole."

Doctor Dechert folded her hands. "Oh, my, that is gloomy."

"Then you drove back into town. It wasn't a giant revelation, just a tiny stream of hope. I remembered how good it felt to hitch up your team. How comfortable it was to know that I still had a few skills."

"I was surprised how easy it was for you."

"Compared to that big, black hole, tending your horse and driving you on your rounds seems like a wonderful adventure. You are my angel."

"Well, this land can soon bore you. Or, as it does for some women, drive you mad. But I love it here. The smell of the pines. The wood smoke coiling up to the heavens. The sweet taste of a good venison steak. And most of all, the look of trust and gratitude in the patients' eyes when someone cares enough to tend their wounds. This is my place, Catherine. The Lord has led me here. And he's led you here, for a time. Enjoy the peace and quiet."

"I will try. I need to really think through my commitment to Phillip."

"And with your Mr. Hillyard."

"Yes, he is in my thoughts. But I will never see him again. Patricia, what would you do if someone like Race suddenly appeared in your life?"

"You mean, a tall, square-shouldered, ruggedly handsome man walked through my door? One who is principled, moral and a man of faith? One who made me . . . what did you say . . . made my heart 'flutter like a butterfly in a jar'?"

"Yes, what would you do with such a man?"

"You mean after I knocked him out with ether, dragged him to the altar, and tossed him in my bed?" They both laughed. "Well, I would aim to make life so wonderful for him he wouldn't want to leave my sight."

She paused as Catherine blushed.

"That blunt kind of talk doesn't sound like an angel's advice, does it?"

"It sounds like wisdom from a woman who knows what she is missing."

"I have a feeling you know what you are missing, too, Catherine. And what you have to decide is whether your Phillip is the one to provide that or not."

• • •

Catherine slept one whole day in the big bed with clean sheets and soft pillows. After that, the September days fell into a pattern. She cooked breakfast for the doctor and herself, did the dishes, then hiked down to Champion's and drank coffee with Phillip as they sat on the front porch.

She steered the conversation to their youth in Virginia. He always discussed the Goodwin wealth and how it might be recovered.

The subject of an upcoming wedding was seldom brought up. When it was, Catherine used it as a signal to leave.

After she rigged up the buggy, she drove the doctor on her rounds. Each day headed in a different direction. Catherine admired the compassion, skill and generosity of the only doctor within fifty miles.

Catherine held the babies, comforted the mourning, revived the fainting, and bandaged wounds. Each day left the women tired, but content. When they returned to Paradise Springs, Doctor Dechert took care of local patients. Catherine rode the black horse bareback into the hills. If the weather allowed, the two ladies sat on the porch in the evening, sipping tea.

"A rough morning," Catherine related at one of the sessions. "I'm sorry I fled the house when the baby died. I offered no help weeping like that."

"That's okay. I weep too. They expect me to save their loved ones. It's like I have disappointed them when I don't."

"There is nothing you could do."

"I pray, Catherine. I pray about every patient. However, it's the Lord who makes the final decision. I learned in my first year of practice that I had to trust him. I can't always understand, but I can trust. It reminded you of your little Marie, didn't it?"

"Yes. I'm still in shock."

"Did you go back up today?" the doctor asked.

"Yes, it is my quiet place. I know it's strange to put two grave markers up on the mountainside, when they are buried somewhere in northern New Jersey. But it helps me to find some sanity."

The doctor set down her tea cup. "Do you still blame yourself?"

"If it was indeed an accident, I blame myself for leaving Catelynn that last time in an argument. But if she took her life on purpose . . . Oh, Patricia, I couldn't live with that."

"Can you trust God anyway?"

"I hope I can. These three weeks with you have given me rest for my mind."

"I know your body hasn't rested much. You've done so much for me."

"Every act has been a pleasure."

Patricia poured more tea in both of their cups.

"Rev. Whiteside will be arriving tomorrow afternoon. Have you decided what to tell him?"

"Yes. I've told Phillip for several weeks now that I will not marry him. He seems difficult to convince. He is sure I'll change my mind, just as he is sure I have some great wealth that will miraculously materialize."

"It's the prospector's curse. Every one of them think they are only a day or two away from striking it rich. They haven't found a decent gold claim around here in over ten years, but the hills are filled with men still looking. Everyone of them getting close. So it is with Phillip . . . tomorrow he thinks he will hit paydirt."

A leather-tanned man with black shaggy hair led two burros down the road towards Faraway Basin.

"Just like Tuley out there. He's going to be rich one day and move back home to Tupelo. It's that anticipation that keeps him going each day. Same with Phillip. Do you need any help from me? We can be gone on some 'emergency call' when the preacher arrives."

The tea was too hot to sip. Catherine enjoyed the warmth to steam her face. "No, I want to confront Phillip in front of the Reverend."

"Then I will stay home and make a cake," Patricia announced.

"What for? I said, no wedding."

"In celebration of Miss Catherine Marie Goodwin who looks forward to the next stage of her life."

"It will be a relief. No more awkward coffees on the front porch of the store."

"I will make an angel's food cake, to commemorate 'good news of great joy.' "

Catherine chuckled. "You make it sound prophetic."

Patricia winked. "Perhaps it will be."

Catherine had known slow days, when time stalled . . . in a college classroom . . . or a family reunion in Richmond . . . or on the riverboat down the Ohio. But this day dragged beyond comparison.

She fed the horse.

Washed, dried and put away the dishes.

Retrieved the laundry from Mrs. Chin.

Groomed the horse.

Swept the front porch.

Scrubbed the buggy.

Still the clock on the mantle had just struck 10:00 a.m.

Catherine glimpsed Dr. Dechert at her desk. "Anything you need, Patricia?"

"You are more nervous not getting married, than many who say yes."

Catherine strolled towards the desk. "I just want to get this day over with."

"What is your plan?"

"Since Rev. Whiteside drives right over to the church, I'll meet Phillip on the church steps and we'll clear everything up."

"When do you need to meet him?"

"At three o'clock or so. But that seems like a year away."

The doctor waved towards the door. "Go for a ride."

"I've got him fed and groomed for the day."

"He won't care." Patricia strolled around the desk. "Go on. You'll wear out my carpet pacing like that." She pushed Catherine out of the room.

The black horse pouted for a mile or two, then resigned himself to the ride. Aspen trees had turned yellow, sun rays warmed her as long as she stayed out of the shade. She tied the horse off to a six-foot aspen, then hiked over to the large and small crosses.

She straddled the log that she had rolled to the site weeks before. She gazed at the larger cross. "Do you remember that day that Father sent us to New England? We were so mad at him. We wanted to shoot Yankees, not live with them. He seemed to know, didn't he? Everything was changing. We thought it was only for a short while, but it was the turning point. That's the last day we saw Mother and Daddy. Our world had changed completely, but we didn't know it for a long time."

She wiped her eyes on her dress sleeve.

"Oh, Cate, you and the baby died. Again, my world had changed and I didn't know it. Like with Mother and Daddy, I didn't even get to tell you goodbye. I don't know if I will ever get over that . . . but I will trust the Lord through it all."

She plucked pine needles off the dirt and weaved them together. "But this time it is different. I know that today is a turning point. I will tell Phillip goodbye and it will end this saga. I wish you could have met Patricia. She's just like Penny Randolf. Always focused. Always consistent. Always doing the gracious thing. She is my gift, a present from the Lord to get through this transition."

She tossed the needles down.

"Sometimes I am amazed that I found her. What's more amazing is that I'm a grown woman and sitting here on a mountainside in California talking aloud to a deceased sister who is buried in New Jersey. Those Goodwin twins . . . always a little strange, weren't they? Honey, I'll carry those good memories forever, but if you don't mind, I need to forget the bad ones."

For several minutes she gazed at the trees and said nothing.

"It's fall here. There's a change in the air. And

I know there is a change in my life. For almost thirty years other people have done things that controlled my destiny. No more. Just me and the Lord. There are no limits. I don't know how often I'll get back up here, but I'll carry you and Marie in my heart."

She stood and tugged her sleeves down.

"Race is wrong. I still have my heart."

Catherine moseyed back down the mountain. She saw Phillip on the steps of the church, but didn't hurry while brushing down the black gelding.

Patricia had a patient in her office, so Catherine cleaned up in the kitchen, then took one last look in the mirror.

If this were my wedding day, I look quite ragged. But it's not. This afternoon, I find direction for my life, and tonight . . . there is angel food cake. Lord, you've brought some wonderful angels into my life lately. Race . . . and Francine . . . and now Patricia. I need a lot of upkeep, don't I?

She strolled to the church. Phillip stood, hat in hand. He looked scrubbed clean, with a fresh shirt and tie. What little hair he had lay plastered to his head. He clutched a small bouquet of wild sunflowers. His gold tooth reflected like a beacon on some rocky coast.

"I was afraid you weren't coming," he muttered.

"I promised I'd be here."

"I got all dressed up, in case you changed your mind."

"You look very nice, Phillip."

"Mr. Champion lets me buy these shirts for one half the price."

"That's generous." She climbed up the stairs and sat down on the top one. "Phillip, I came over to be with you to explain the change in plans to Rev. Whiteside. I wanted you and him to understand I'm not going to marry you today."

"We could postpone it a few weeks, if you'd like."

"We've been through that. Not today. Not ever."

"He ain't here yet." He pointed at the empty road from the south. "There's still time for a miracle. You believe in miracles, don't you?"

"Yes, I do."

"That's what I pray for. I asked the good Lord to let me and you get married and that you will be restored to your rightful Virginia inheritance."

She looked down at the worn steps. "That would take a miracle."

Phillip talked non-stop for the next hour about gold mines he almost discovered, fast horses that he came close to buying, and famous people that he just about met.

Catherine never took her eye off the road from the west.

Two riders.

Three men on foot.

A freighter rattled by. None stopped in Paradise Springs.

Finally, a black panel wagon pulled by a wide mule broke out of the trees and rolled to the edge of town.

Phillip jumped to his feet. "That's him. That's the Reverend."

Catherine stood and brushed down her skirt.

He handed her the now wilted sunflowers.

"No, you hold them. I wouldn't want the Rev. Whiteside to get the wrong impression."

"You ain't been hit by a miracle yet, have ya?"

"No, not yet."

The gray-haired man with leathered face and wide-brimmed black hat tied the lead lines to the hand brake and scooted out of the wagon.

"Here is the happy couple," he beamed. "You must be Catherine Goodwin?"

"Yes. I need to talk to you, Rev. Whiteside."

"And I need to talk to you."

Catherine tilted her head and narrowed her eyes. "You do?"

"And I need a miracle, two of them," Phillip mumbled.

The Reverend pulled off his hat. "Don't we all, son?"

"Reverend, let me say this right away. I am not marrying Phillip Draper. Not now, not in the future."

Phillip rocked back on his heels. "I don't think she loves me anymore."

"That's a very fine reason for not getting married. You must be convinced that the other person is one that the Lord has created for you to share love, laughter and faith for a lifetime."

"You make it sound so serious," Phillip said.

"Reverend, I was told by a friend that I gave my heart away too easy. He warned me that I would not have any of my true heart left to give when the right man came along. My heart has been wounded at times. And I didn't treat it with the respect it deserves. But I am not going to give it away out of convenience or hope in some miracle."

"Well said." The Reverend nodded.

"So, you won't be havin' a wedding tonight," Phillip added.

"Unless, as you mentioned, there is a miracle." The Reverend grinned. "Now, Miss Goodwin, there is a friend of yours in the back of my wagon."

"A friend?" Catherine dashed to the back and flung open the door.

A familiar saddle perched on top of the luggage.

"Mr. Walker! How nice of you to come for a visit."

"The gentleman who sent it said to give you the saddle and say, 'Mr. Walker missed you.' "

She reached over and hauled the saddle out of the wagon. "Oh, Mr. Walker, I missed you very much, too."

Phillip watched her tote it up the stairs. "Don't that beat all. I lost my girl to a dadgum saddle."

A deep voice boomed from the other side of the wagon. "Yeah, the same thing happened to me, kid."

Her chin sagged. Her breath stopped. Her hands clenched. Then she spied him as he sauntered up to her.

"Oh, Race . . ." Tears streamed down her face. "You came."

"I couldn't stay away. I hopped off the wagon before we reached the church. I needed to know how you felt, before I butted in on your wedding day."

"Did you hear what I said?"

"I heard it all. I need to tell you something."

She threw her arms around him.

He pushed her back. "If we get to kissin' and all, I'll forget this speech. I've been workin' on it for a week now. So, just stand there and listen."

She glanced over at a beaming Rev. Whiteside and Phillip, who looked like a twelve-year-old that lost his only baseball.

"They can stay. I don't mind who hears this. I spent a couple days riding the foothills around Stockton lookin' for a man who isn't there. While I was doing that, I kept asking the Lord to send someone into my life that I could trust my heart to. I prayed and I prayed, but the Lord refused to answer. Finally, last week, He told me to quit that prayer."

"He did?"

"Yep. He said He already sent the most perfect woman in the world for me, and I let her walk away. He said He had more important things to do than line up more women for me. From now on, I'd be on my own." Race looked straight into her eyes. "Catherine, if you'd like to throw away that sweet heart of yours one more time, I'd like the opportunity to catch it."

"What?"

"Will you marry me?"

She threw her arms around his neck. "Of course I will."

To call it a kiss would be a misnomer. To Catherine it felt like two strong-willed people melting into one person. There was love, excitement, passion and surrender.

You just made my one to five scale obsolete, Race Hillyard.

When he finally pulled back, Rev. Whiteside spoke. "Could it be that I have a wedding tonight after all?"

"Yes, you do," Catherine grinned. "It will take place one hour from now. Open the church and get the papers filled out. I need to go home and change into my other dress. Patricia will be the maid-of-honor. Phillip, you can be the best man. We'll have the reception at the doctor's office. The cake is already baked. Phillip, you go invite Mrs. Chin and anyone else left in town."

Race rubbed the back of his neck. "You figured this all out while we were kissing?"

"Honey, I figured this all out when I was nine. Now you must find a wedding ring. I can't imagine anyone having one in . . ."

Race reached in his pocket and pulled out a gold band. "Happen to have one right here. Bought it in Sacramento."

"You brought a ring with you?"

"Phillip isn't the only one who believes in miracles. But I don't have a better suit. You'll have to take me like I am. What other things will you need me to do?"

"Figure out our honeymoon."

"Got it planned."

"You planned our honeymoon during that kiss?"

"Yep."

She kissed his cheek. "Where are we going?"

The wrinkles in the corners of his eyes melted away. "I hear it's springtime in Argentina."